I0658972

Do It

to

My Mind

a novel

N. Wood LANE

Copyright © 2013 by N. Wood Lane

The quote used on the cover of this book appeared in the September 2011 Midwest Book Review for Warped Intentions.

ISBN-10: 1937705196
ISBN-13: 978-1-9377051-9-0
Also available in E-Book
ISBN-13: 978-1-9377051-8-3
Library of Congress Control Number: 2013935427
Printed in the United States of America

𝓂

MavLit Publishing, LLC
www.maverick-books.com

P. O. Box 1103
Irmo, S.C. 29063
Cover Design: Maverick Literary

Do

It

to

My Mind

a novel

N. Wood LANE

Author's Note

I've wasted all these years in my life before I finally sat down and did it. Yes, I wrote a book! It's better to write when I have something to say than to just put anything out there for reading consumption.

This was a plot that I've been toying around with since I left my previous profession. Once I began putting those thoughts onto a computer screen, I must say that it became an enjoyable experience. It's really amazing how these things come together. First, the characters, plot, and story line. Then the book cover and its description. Finally, the promotional stuff and now you're reading my actual work.

Now, why write about a married couple that is having problems in the bedroom?

Well, let's see . . . how do I say this? Marital problems usually center around three issues: money, sex (the lack thereof and the quality thereof), and poor communication. All three issues are seemingly interrelated or separate, so this is something very realistic to put into fiction.

I'm aware of a passage that notes those who overcome shall inherit all things. I hope in some way when reading about the lives of Trent and Sonia Buckner that you might be encour-

aged to overcome obstacles in your life so that you might inherit all the good things that are stored up for you. Also, the
quality of life, including any and all relationships, is what you
make of it.

N. Wood Lane
nwoodlane@hotmail.com
2013

Do It

to

My Mind

a novel

N. Wood LANE

Introduction

'Can You Hurry Up, Please?'

Sonia often chided Trent about his lack of understanding that a woman's mind was the pathway to her experiencing orgasms.

"Baby, I'm tired of faking it with you. How long have we've been married?"

He began to form seven with his lips, but he was interrupted.

"Better yet, how long have we known each other?"

He paused. "I don't know. Twelve, thirteen years—"

"Fifteen," she corrected him.

"Okay—"

"How many times have I told you, you start off with the little things and they build up to bigger things? Maybe even something that's pleasurable for both of us."

Whenever Trent heard Sonia mention "the little things," he'd tune out on her and think about what might have been with Teale McFadden.

Ah, yes. Teale. Had it not been for the night he was unable to get inside her apartment complex that hot summer night in Atlanta back in 1997, and had it not been because he was unable to explain his side of what really happened, life might have taken a much different course.

Not that the former Sonia Chandler was a horrible consolation, but she was not Teale. In Trent Buckner's mind, Teale was a real woman. She knew how to be a lady in the streets and a freak beneath the sheets. She had no inhibitions.

Their relationship, although off and on, was kinetic and they had great chemistry. There was even reason to believe they were destined to be as one some day.

"Are you listening to me?" Sonia asked, cutting a mean glare at Trent.

He rolled his eyes. "Yeah, I'm listening. Do I need to tell you exactly what you just told me?"

Sonia could not hide her disgust. Sighing, she retorted, "So, it's gonna be like that?" She placed her hands on her waist, eager to light further into him.

Trent knew he was a bad response away from another stay in the Dog House Inn where the rates were always in the peak season, and there's never any sympathy for being sentenced.

Remember, it's the little things, a still, small voice spoke to him. But then another still, small voice had its say: *There are never any little things with women. They're always BIG things to them.*

"What's wrong?" Sonia bantered with him. "You can talk about anything else, but you become mute when it comes to a conversation of substance with me?"

Faced with a moment of demarcation, Trent remained silent and mulled his options. He could try holding his ground and risk a stay at the Dog House Inn. Or he could relent and risk another lengthy lecture.

His pride said risk it; however, the testosterone within him said to relent. He had already gone all week without any bedroom activity with Sonia.

"Sonia, baby. How long are we going to go on like this? It's like one day everything is all right. Then the next week or two weeks I can't even touch you."

"Let me try to explain it to you this way. You want to have sex with me, right?" Sonia said, appearing rather matter-of-factly with him. She then walked toward their king-size bed.

Trent's heart rate increased. This was not quite the right time for him to be aroused.

"Am I right?" she repeated.

Sighing, Trent responded, "Yeah, I would like to have some."

Sonia sat down on the mattress and folded her arms. "Okay, then tell me what have you done to get me in the mood; because right now, I don't feel like doing anything."

Remember those little things....

"See, I was ready for you this time. What about that text message I sent to you early this morning?" He had now joined her on the bed; he leaned back on his left elbow.

"Humph! A text message that said, 'What's up, sexy?' You call that setting a mood? Love making takes place long before the bedroom—"

"Wait a minute, I'm not finished. I called about taking you to lunch. But you never answered."

"Trent, in case you're having temporary amnesia, although I would strongly question it being permanent, I told you yesterday that I would be busy all day today. And it would be pretty hard catching me. It kind of goes with the territory working in contract services at United Care Plan."

"Okay, but I thought you still might have some time for me. But then what about the card that I surprised you with this evening?"

Sonia was moved to chortling. "My husband . . ." She then shook her head. "You gave me a card similar to that, like, three months ago, the last time you and I had a discussion like this."

She got up from the bed, kicked off her shoes, and removed her off-white business skirt and black blouse, leaving on her black French-cut panties and low-cut bra. Trent's eyes widened and he had a silly grin. After all these years, including the birth of their son, Taylor, at thirty-nine, she still maintained a shapely figure on her five-foot-five frame. He felt a rush of blood flowing downward.

"Don't get any ideas. I need to take a shower," she said, catching a glimpse of him from the corner of her eye.

"Well, let me join you." He stood up and began walking in her direction.

"No!" she snapped back at him, causing him to stop in midstep.

"Aw, come on. We used to take showers together all the time."

"No. Not tonight!" She proceeded at a saunter past him to the bathroom, knowing all along that she had her husband's family jewels right in her grasp. "Maybe while I'm in the shower you might want to think about how you could get me in the mood."

Wow, such torture. And to think there were actually much simpler times; Trent knew he had no choice in the matter.

Oh, well!

Sonia was never one for taking long showers. Five minutes was an eternity.

So, Trent rushed out to his work office of their four-bedroom home in Chapin, South Carolina—a fast-growing community just beyond Columbia—and brought a CD he recently burned full of R&B ballads and Quiet Storm music. He turned off the bedroom lights, leaving only a wall light on.

Then he rushed to the kitchen and returned with two wine glasses and a bottle of red Moscato in anticipation of her reappearing.

As soon as Sonia opened the bathroom door, Trent pressed the PLAY button, greeting her with Peabo Bryson's "Feel the Fire." Next, he walked over to his wife who was clad in only a terry cloth robe; she held up her hand.

"Aren't we going to have some God time tonight? You know we missed having it yesterday."

Trent held his breath. So much also for his arousal.

"I see. So that's where your priorities really are, hmmm?" Sonia was quick to surmise.

"I love God as much as you," he countered. "But even I think God wouldn't have a problem with us doing something that He ordained."

"That may be right. But don't you realize that there's something attractive about things being done in a godly, decent and orderly manner?" She walked past him, stopping at the dresser. She looked into the mirror back at him. "So, did you choose something that could do us both some good?"

"You sure know how to kill a mood, don't you?" Trent mumbled to himself.

"What did you just say?"

"Does it matter who we listen to?"

"No, it doesn't. I just think we could use some God time together."

While Sonia removed the rest of her makeup, Trent was less than enthusiastic about searching the Internet for any online ministry podcasts.

"How about Creflo Dollar?" he asked.

"No, I'm not feeling him these days."

"What about Charles Stanley?"

"He's starting to sound old, and I'm talking about him being, what, eighty-one years old?"

"Okay, how about Joel Osteen? You know I used to attend Lakewood before Lakewood became what it is today."

Sonia stopped and looked over her shoulder, nodding in approval. "Yes, I think something from Joel would be nice. What is he talking about today?"

"I don't know. You figure he'll be talking about the same old thing. He worked in the back and had no aspirations of preaching . . . When he met Victoria who was working in a jewelry store . . . God loves you and we love you . . . Maybe a story about how they moved into their new place. If not that, the favor of God can take you places that man cannot—"

"Well, I wouldn't mind hearing whatever he has to say. And to be honest, you're the head of this household. You should be looking out for us in that area, anyway."

It took all of him not to react angrily and lash out at Sonia for goading him. Eventually, he decided upon an Osteen podcast message that encouraged listeners God was in control of the storms in their lives. Then he went ahead with taking his shower.

Upon his return, Sonia, still wearing the bathrobe, sat in the bed eating from a bowl of fruit salad she bought from Bi-Lo supermarket. "Come on, baby," she said, shimmying her shoulders excitedly, "let's have that God time that we were just talking about."

Trent tuned out right after Osteen's opening monologue and faith proclamation. He sat with his head arched back against the headboard, arms folded, and his eyes closed during Osteen's message. Meanwhile, Sonia figured so long as his head wasn't hanging and he was snoring, why make any issue of it?

"What did you think of the message?" Sonia queried Trent.

He glared to his right without commenting.

She queried again. "Well, what did you think of it?"

After inhaling deeply through his nostrils, Trent was slow to speak. "I guess it was a timely message."

"You really think so?" she reacted with raised eyebrows.

"Yeah."

She gestured with a head nod for him to continue.

"I suppose God knows exactly what to do in this storm I've been going through. Hopefully, if He's in control of the direction of these winds, that means He'll be changing your attitude about us having sex."

"That's not what I got from his message. But if you want to take jabs at me, remember this: It's your responsibility to create the right environment." She then cut a conceited stare back at him. "You certainly had no problem making every effort when you were chasing me."

"Well, when I was 'chasing' you, you weren't holding things up for any God time. The only time I heard any mentioning of God was when my name was in the same sentence, your legs were wrapped around my waist, you were clawing my back, and—"

"We're married now. And it takes more to keep the fire burning."

"Uh-hmmm. Yeah. . . ."

Sonia sat up in bed; it allowed for exposure of her cleavage. "I see where this conversation is heading. Just remember that your prayers are hindered because of the way you treat your wife. Humph!"

Yeah, the little things . . . I better not say what's really on my mind, Trent mulled.

Once again, Trent allowed his thoughts to digress back to Teale. With her, he never had things held up because of God moments and potshots taken at him. Both of them had an uncanny sense of awareness whenever either one was in the mood or need.

"How many times are you going to beat me over the head with that verse?" he complained. "Don't you think you're taking it out of context? It does say you shouldn't be adding to it or taking away. And if you do, there's a curse."

Sonia inched closer to Trent. She was always drawn to his handsome features: a strong, angular face and square jaw; intense, dark brown eyes and a smile that reminded her of a couple of her favorite male actors. It also did not hurt, too, that he still maintained much of his former world-class track sprinter's physique.

"Baby, sharing God's word helps relax me, and I feel like it draws us closer."

She kissed him on the cheek. Next, she shed her robe, exposing her entire French vanilla flesh to him. She then turned onto her stomach, provoking him to freeze in thought and movement. "Aren't you going to give me a massage?"

This was beyond excruciating; he was at her mercy.

"Y-yeah. I guess so," he was reluctant to say.

"Good, I can sure use one."

Sonia had long since developed an affinity for Trent's large hands manipulating and kneading her body. On many occasions, the mere thought of him touching her was more than enough to place her in the mood for intimacy. An orgasm was merely a formality as it took minutes, maybe moments, before she felt all her body pores opening and a tingling sensation that followed; the most intense of them began from the deepest depths of her being.

It's not as if Sonia had taken those occasions for granted. She was happy that Trent was attentive enough and willing to do something as simple as a massage. But the moments had also become rather perfunctory and predictable. Eventually, Trent would begin rubbing himself upon her. His attention to her body would shift to satisfying his libido. And within minutes, his body would go limp within her embrace.

"Trent, when was the last time you told me you loved me?" she asked just as he placed his hands on her shoulders.

He paused.

"Don't stop. Can't you talk and give me a massage at the same time?"

"Of course I can."

Yes, those three words had been expressed fewer and fewer times in recent months, Trent acknowledged to himself. But even he didn't understand why.

"Anyway, Trent, when was the last time you said you loved me?" She moaned in approval as she felt the tension subsiding in her neck and shoulders.

"I can tell you when. But when can you tell me the last time you outright told me that you wanted to have sex?"

"I asked first."

"Let's see . . ."

"And I'm not talking about when you're about to release inside of me, either."

Trent continued working downward along her back. The mere sight of his wife's body was always a turn-on, especially the view from behind. His favorite was whenever she wiggled her hips.

"I'm waiting for an answer—"

"How about right now? I love you, Sonia."

She jerked her body in defiance. "That doesn't count!"

"Sure it does. You asked me when was the last time I said I loved you. So I just updated by saying it."

"When was the last time before now?"

He was slow to respond.

"Ah-hah! You can't even remember the last time you said it. And you expect for me to be in the mood whenever you want to have sex?"

"Look, it's kind of hard to say you love someone when she can't even say she wants you."

"Trent, it all goes hand-in-hand," she tried explaining to him. "I'm like a plant. You provide water to it with the things you say and do to me."

"Hey, aside from what I've done earlier today, I've shared some God time with you and I'm giving you a massage. Quite frankly, I think I've done enough today."

Sonia turned over and faced him. "You really think you've done something, huh?"

"Yeah, I do."

"Really?"

"Really."

"Okay, come on. Let's get this over with. January is a busy month. We have our highest call volume, and I need to be as rested as I can to deal with those crazy people when they call in yelling at my phone reps.

"Oh, and don't forget to pull out. I don't want to have to get up at all odd hours of the night tonight."

Trent hated the fact that this was just another get-me-off occasion, but something was better than nothing at all. He attempted to kiss his way upward starting from her inner thighs, but she shooed him away.

"Just get on top, please—"

Within moments of mounting Sonia, Trent noticed he was not making any significant progress. Her body tensed as soon as his rested atop of hers. But he was determined to follow through.

"If you really want to get this over with, you might want to get some lubrication," she suggested.

"I think you're right."

While Trent was in the bathroom, he found himself reminiscing about Teale. The lack of arousal was never an issue whenever they were together. They never had arguments over whether he loved her, liked her, or anything else in between. Teale was even multi-orgasmic, so there was no doubt she was going to get hers no matter what the mood was prior to the bedroom.

"Okay, do you want me to apply it on me, or on you?" he asked just as he left the bathroom.

"Yeah, use it on yourself. I just needed a little bit of help tonight. I hope you can understand that."

This time, Trent was able to find some kind of a rhythm. However, it was clearly evident that Sonia was going through the motions.

She went as far as to mention, "Oh, by the way. Taylor needs to be picked up tomorrow after practice. He'll also need fifty dollars by Friday for his athletic fees."

He paused in mid-stroke. "Why are you mentioning that now?"

"Because it was on my mind."

He resumed with Sonia. He hoped the mere sensation of his body working inside and upon her might incite some interest on her part. He reminded himself it actually worked one Thursday morning about six months ago.

"Baby, can you hurry up, please?"

So much for that ...

"Okay, I'm trying."

"Well, you need to try harder."

"Can you at least help me out?"

Ten minutes later, Trent was returning from the bathroom having washed off. Sonia had already rushed to visit the other bathroom and done the same thing before returning to bed. She was turned over on her right side with her back facing his side of the bed. He merely eased under the sheets and cover, turned over to his left and sighed.

There were no words exchanged, not even a good-night kiss. He wondered to himself how different a moment like this would have been with Teale.

Chapter 1

'We Need to Talk'

It must have been that time again, although Sonia hardly slept at all last night. She was awakened by the shifting of items in the bedroom. Next, there was Trent tapping her on the shoulder.

"Sonia, I can't find the belt I just bought last week. Do you know where it is?"

"Which belt?"

"You know, the brown one I got at the mall. You wanted to get it for my birthday, but I decided to get it."

She stretched and yawned. "Oh, that one. Have you looked in any of your drawers?"

"Yes, I have. It wasn't in there."

She got up and browsed the couple's other walk-in closet.

"Oh, that's right. I bought a belt rack for you; I put it in this closet. All of your belts are over here." She returned with the belt that he'd requested.

"Is this the one you're asking about?"

"And you're just now telling me?"

"I thought you already knew. At least you should have noticed something different."

"Not until this morning."

"Uh, Trent, while I'm at it, about last night—"

He came over and sat near the edge of the bed. "Yeah, what about last night?"

Trent often exuded arrogance once he had sex. Nothing had really changed this morning other than him not nudging up on her before getting out of bed.

"We need to talk about it."

"What is there to talk about?" he responded. "You gave me a long, drawn out speech about how I didn't really set the mood for you yesterday. Okay. I get it." He stood up, adjusting his belt.

"You think so?"

"I know so."

She sat up in bed. "Trent, the only thing you got last night was yours. Did it ever occur to you it's been almost a year since I've experienced anything, and before that maybe another two or three months?

"You're a smart man. Do the math."

Trent had already stopped by the closet and was about to retrieve on his gray Calvin Klein suit jacket. "I don't believe you. You're going to tell me it's been that long?" His mind went into scramble mode.

"I told you last night that I was tired of faking it with you. Apparently, you weren't listening."

"I was listening to you!"

"No you weren't. Did you not realize that I just went through the motions again with you? After all these years, you should understand some things about me."

"Sonia, darling, I've got to get on to work. But, yes, we do need to talk about this. We really do."

"I hope you will bring more to the table than just accusations and blowing up at me. Might I even suggest when you have some free time today to look up something on the subject on how to please your wife—"

Now, that was a dagger into Trent's ego. "What do you mean accusations? All I hear from you is how I've failed to do this, and how I haven't done that. Now you're saying I need to read up on how to please my wife in the bedroom?"

"Look, Trent, all I'm saying is neither of us know everything. And you certainly haven't learned everything about me just as much as I don't know everything about you. Doesn't it tell husbands to dwell with their wives with knowledge?"

"So, now you're also going to preach to me before I leave for work. You just want me having a guilty conscience, don't you?"

Sonia got out of the bed and nuzzled up to her husband. She did her best to gaze at him with admiration in her eyes.

"All I want for us is to get it right. All I want is to be able to enjoy sex with my husband all of the time and not just some of the time—and lately it's not even be some of the time. It's been virtually none of the time."

"I've got to go. But we'll talk about it."

"I pray that you do. Try to have a good day."

"Humph. Yeah."

She followed Trent out of the bedroom and watched him out the door and into his black Ford Taurus. She sighed deeply as he backed out and drove off. Then she closed her eyes and offered up a short prayer asking for the eyes of his heart to be opened.

Today was a late day at work for Sonia, anyway. That meant she would soon be making sure that Taylor was on the school bus—the stop was all of three houses away at the end of their cul-de-sac.

Once he's off, and with an empty house for the next hour or so, it would be an ideal opportunity for her to get in some uninterrupted praying time; there were a lot of cares she wanted to cast toward heaven.

"Tay . . . lor . . . time to get up!" she said, knocking on his bedroom door.

She knocked again; there was no response. "Come on, Taylor, time to get up!"

As much as her thirteen-year-old son was her pride and joy, he was one big frustration in the mornings. It was a work in progress to get him up in time for school.

Taylor grumbled and tossed and turned. "Mom, I'm sleeping . . . Can't I have just five more minutes?"

"No. It's time for you to get up. Now, get up!"

"Come on, five more minutes. I promise I'll get up."

Sonia pulled the sheets and covers off him. Immediately, he turned over and was wide eyed. "I could have gotten up in a few more minutes and still be ready!"

"And I was just two seconds away from putting something on you to get up. Now which would you have preferred?"

"Okay, okay. I'm getting up! Can you at least turn on the television for me?"

"You get up and turn it on yourself. And you need to clean up this room. I'm not going to do it for you."

Grudgingly, Taylor got up. Looking at him shuffling around reminded Sonia just how much he was his father's spitting image physically, but he was very much his mother's child when it came to his personality. She could only smile and nod her head because she used to do the same thing when she was in the eighth grade like him. The difference was the distance was much farther to board school buses back in the late 1980s and early 1990s.

"Make sure that you have a belt for your pants and you have all that you need for school, because I'm not going to leave work and bring anything to school for you," she said. "I did that three times last week. It's time that you become a little more responsible since you don't want me to call you 'baby' any more."

"Okay, I will," he shouted back from the bathroom. "Now can I get ready for school?"

Children!

"And turn down that iPad with that music!"

"Mom, it's my favorite song. It's fabulous. It helps me get ready!"

While Taylor was in the bathroom, Sonia stopped in Trent's work office and browsed the Internet for material on improving marriages and relationships both romantically and in general.

The first noteworthy Web site was one that challenged husbands to listen to their wives. A statistic that stood out with Sonia was men tend to process language with only half of their brain.

That might explain part of the problem with Trent! she remarked to herself.

She glanced down at the time on her computer. It was 7:33. The bus was scheduled to stop at 7:38. "Taylor, are you ready?

It's time to be out there for the bus! Come on, I'm not going to give you a ride if you miss the bus!"

A loud pounding of feet resonated from a one hundred and fifteen-pound boy in back of Sonia. "Okay, Mom, I'm leaving. Are you happy?" he said, stopping at the doorway of Trent's office.

She stood up and gave Taylor a quick look-over. "Hmmm, I'm impressed. You're actually ready."

"Mom—"

"I know. You have to be at the bus stop. Do you have your school ID and lunch money? Do you have your homework? Do you have all of your books? And I see you have a jacket . . ."

"Yes, yes, yes . . . and yes. Bye, I gotta go!"

"You forgot something," she said just as Taylor reached for the front door handle.

He turned slowly, looking side-eyed at his mother. "What now?"

"Aren't you going to give your mother a kiss goodbye?"

"Mom, I'm in a hurry. Next time. Bye!"

"Bye, boy!"

Whew!

Once Sonia heard the school bus's warning siren and the air brake releasing, she felt much more at ease returning to the Web page on husbands listening to their wives. She was equally intrigued that its content enabled her to realize she wasn't the only woman experiencing similar frustrations with her husband. More so, she was impressed the material was provided by a man, not a woman.

Is my marriage better today than it was yesterday? she asked herself just as on the Web page.

Sighing, she shook her head and read further.

Just as the Web site described, Sonia had always felt it was important to know that she's been the center of Trent's attention and universe and that she's respected, valued, and cherished just as she was once told when he was in pursuit of marrying her.

She recognized that she'd gone as far as trying to arrest Trent's attention by mentioning other positive male examples in the way they've regarded the woman in their lives.

Humph. All that did was enrage Trent, so she stopped mentioning the likes of Gen. Colin Powell and the way he's regarded publicly by his wife, Alma.

From that disappointing result, she realized she'd become turned off by any thought of intimacy with Trent. There were times when she hinted at him exactly how she felt, but then there were times like this morning when she didn't hold back with her displeasure.

Although her dissatisfaction had not reached a boiling point, she identified Trent's errant thinking that everything's been fine with one of the blog posts: It described how unfortunate it was the only time a husband might recognize he has a major problem with his wife is when it's too late.

"By then, the wife may have reached a point of detachment to the extent that she's already considered leaving the relationship. Then the husband's reduced to asking, 'Why didn't you tell me?'

"Her response: 'You never listened to me!' "

"I know that's right," she exclaimed. "This is exactly what Trent needs to read along with me!"

Encouraged, Sonia saved the page among her favorites and retreated to the bedroom where she spent the rest of her free time in prayer.

I thank you for letting me see that I'm not alone in this, and You're watching out for me. You know that I have no desire to cheat on my husband. All I want is for things to get better. I want to enjoy those moments with my husband as much as he seems to enjoy himself when he's inside of me. . . .

Please help me with having wisdom and patience to share this information with him. Please do a work within Trent as I know You will do a work within me. . . .

Amen!

Chapter 2

'Oh … My … god!'

Lord, help her, Sonia mumbled as she began reading through the e-mail from her boss Phyllis Blake, director of UCP's contract services department.

Somewhat amused by Phyllis' latest proclamation, Sonia left her cubicle and visited with Vicki Lawson, who like Sonia was among eight team supervisors.

"Hey, don't you ever think they need to fix the problem and not just put another Band-Aid on everything around here?" Sonia whispered into Vicki's cubicle.

Vicki swung to her left. "I know what you're saying. But you know it is what it is around here." She smirked and shook her head. "All I'm trying to do is last another six months, and then I'm looking for the first train out of here."

Sonia merely smiled.

"I stopped reading after the subject line that said, 'Meeting, New Hires'," Vicki continued. What else did it say?"

"Other than the fact we're meeting at eleven, you know

Phyllis must have gotten the OK to hire more people," Sonia answered before letting out a muted hiss. "You know once they lift this hiring freeze they're going to be right back in the same ditch—"

In recent years, contract services has had the dubious reputation as the Iraq of United Care Plan. It's had the highest casualty, uh, turnover rate out of all UCP departments. There's no secret, as conveyed by UCP's upper management in its typical downward communication, the department's one hundred-plus phone representatives were the insurance carrier's infantry personnel positioned at the front lines.

The bullets, missiles, grenades, and bombs fired at them— an average of more than eleven thousand phone calls each business day—came from medical providers and UCP policy holders who inquired about benefits, claims, and other related information.

"We're the ones who hear it from the reps how they're not prepared once they come out of training. You think they would try to fix that problem so that they might have a chance of hanging around long enough," Vicki said.

"I know," Sonia chimed in to say. "And then we have to spend half of our time teaching these people things they should have been taught during training. Remember how it was for you when you came out of claims training?"

"I don't remember."

That's because Vicki, then just two months shy of her thirty-fourth birthday, transferred into contract services from UCP's federal benefits subsidiary after a 2009 downsizing.

Whereas, Sonia began as a contract services phone representative in 2006 and worked her way up into UCP's lower management structure in 2010 after a two-year stint as a work leader.

Because of the company's micromanaging culture, Sonia

was well aware that unit supervisors were also subject to the same measured scrutiny as the phone representatives. "I better get back to my desk. You never know who's monitoring you for whatever report du jour they feel like generating," she confided in Vicki. "Just remember, eleven o'clock."

"I hear you."

No sooner that Sonia returned to her cubicle her phone intercom had gone off. She recognized the extension.

"Yes, Phyllis—"

"Hey, Sonia, would you check on Waqueenah's not-ready minutes, please?"

Dutifully, Sonia changed over to a screen that confirmed Phyllis' observation. "Okay, will do." Humph. She'd long since formed the opinion that Phyllis was one of the most insincere and power hungriest people in the building.

"And while you're at it," Phyllis added, "you might want to have a sit-down with Carlee's call-time average. Thank you."

Thank you, Sonia shook her head from side to side while mimicking Phyllis' voice. She was also quick to write herself a stick 'em note to handle the latter chore after returning from lunch.

A low-volume buzz of conversation and the pecking of keyboards mixed with sporadic bursts of sighing in exasperation had increased since the ten o'clock hour, a sign the department had reached one of its two peak calling periods.

"Oh my god, please! Learn some English!" Tanya Fuller reacted after she punched the call-control mouse.

A couple of representatives and Sonia rubber necked to witness Tanya's notorious histrionics in action. She was one of the department's longest tenured phone representatives, having worked in contract services since 2007.

"Ms. Sonia, I swear, one of these times I'm not going to be

as courteous and professional as you people want me to be—"

"Just make sure when you're not as courteous and professional that you're not on company time, okay? I don't need Phyllis or anyone above her coming down on me for failing to monitor my staff."

Tanya's rural South Carolina dialect was unmistakable during her frequent rants, and it often provided moments of comic relief.

One would think she was a woman considerable height stature because of the loud tone of her voice; she stood all of about four feet, ten inches.

"I'm sorry, Ms. Sonia. But these people from India, ugh, are just plain ignorant. There's no other way of describing it.

"Why don't you talk to Shabu a few times and get back with me!"

Sonia had already lowered her head and began accessing reports on the two employees from Phyllis' hit list—for the moment.

"Uh, if I were you, I suggest that get back on that call. You've let your caller marinate long enough."

"Yeah, yeah, Ms. Sonia," Tanya retorted. She then released the call-control mouse, continuing the call at an agitated pitch. "Okay, so let me get this correct . . ."

The eleven o'clock meeting could not have come at a better time. One by one, Sonia and her fellow team supervisors entered the meeting room looking to vent their frustration.

Already, she had Tanya's outburst and four phone representatives approach her for assistance with difficult callers about medical claims, and she generated three daily reports as required and requested by Phyllis—all within her first two hours of the work day.

"Hey, Sonia. It's a shame we work in the same department,

in the same room, and I can't even remember the last time seeing you," said Charlotte Dillingham, who supervised incoming appeals; her team also answered phone calls on an as-needed basis.

Sonia could not resist but stare at Charlotte before she responded. In Charlotte's eighteen months in contract services, she quickly built a reputation for dressing appropriately yet provocatively, and this morning was no different. She proudly wore a salt-and-pepper Cardigan sweater, tight-fitting grey skirt, and black knee-length boots.

"It's like that sometimes around here," Sonia finally replied. "Are you looking forward to this meeting, hmmm?"

"It depends. I hear they're talking about hiring as many as twelve temps as permanent." A mischievous grin emerged as she paused. "Maybe I might get lucky this time."

Sonia shook her head. "I don't know what you mean about getting lucky. All I hope to do is manage the hand that I'm dealt. So far, that's the only way I've maintained my sanity around here."

At that moment, Phyllis entered the meeting room, taking the end seat nearest the door. She thanked everyone for their dedicated work and proceeded to explain the department's staffing situation.

All the work teams would receive at least one new hire, but Sonia's and Vicki's team would receive three each since they had the highest call volumes and workloads per phone representative.

"Vicki, you will be interviewing Robert Jeffries, Jade Stahl, and Dorean Rice," Phyllis said. "And Sonia, you will be interviewing Kai Long, Hannah Freeman, and Lance Miles—"

Almost simultaneously, Vicki and Charlotte slowly turned their heads and stared at Sonia. Both were surprised that Sonia offered no reaction other than a shrugging of her shoulders.

"If the people we've identified complete the hiring process, we hope to have them over to your teams, hopefully, in about four to six weeks," Phyllis continued.

"Then of course, they'll all have to go through claims training, and then that's when the rubber will meet the road once again. Are there any questions?"

There was no response.

And with that, Phyllis thanked the supervisors for attending the meeting, stood up, and left the room.

Vicki and Charlotte refused to let Sonia leave so inconspicuously after the meeting.

"Uh-uh," Charlotte said, shaking her head. "Do you not realize who you'll be interviewing?" She was quick to fold the packet that was handed out during the meeting and fan herself with it.

Sonia returned a semi-blank stare, prompting Vicki to wave her hand in Sonia's face.

"Did you not hear the woman to your left?" Vicki reacted.

"Obviously, I have no clue as to what you ladies are talking about."

Charlotte rushed to sit in the seat across the table so that she had direct eye contact with Sonia. "Dear Ms. Leader, Phyllis, said you will be interviewing Lance Miles. I know we're here at United Care Plan, but that man . . . oh . . . my . . . god!"

"Sonia, I might have to visit the ladies' room after this," Vicki added. "Humph, I usually have to go there after I've passed by where he's sitting. Talking about male eye candy—"

Sonia hunched her shoulders. "Apparently, I've been too busy to pay attention to who works here other than the people I'm directly responsible for."

"Well, that's all fine and dandy. But maybe you need to go

over by the row directly across from Regina Talbert's office and check out . . . oh . . . my . . . god!" Charlotte had to fan herself again. "Vicki, I might have to sit in the stall next to you, because I think you know what I'll be doing in there."

After Charlotte rushed out of the meeting room, Vicki stood up, which hinted at Sonia it was okay to leave. But she was determined to convey her point to Sonia.

"I want you to follow me," she whispered to Sonia. "Please!"

Sonia retorted, "I hope you don't make a fool out of yourself."

She looked back at Sonia. "I've got this under control. Just make sure you don't make a fool out of yourself."

Sonia and Vicki had walked past Phyllis's office and two others before Vicki froze in mid-step just as a tall, extremely handsome and composed male employee in a lavender long-sleeve shirt and brown slacks turned in front of them. She almost bumped into Vicki because of her sudden stopping.

Meanwhile, Vicki tried saving face by apologizing for not recognizing Lance Miles after he walked past work leader Amanda Sawyer's cubicle.

She said, "With so much going on around here, I should have been paying attention where I was walking."

He smiled back at her. "No, I'm sorry. I should have been watching where I was going."

"Excuse me, Vicki," Sonia interrupted them; she then acknowledged Lance as she walked past Vicki. "Hello. Better yet, good afternoon."

Chapter 3

'I Was Seeking Da Lawd's Face...'

Cortez Anderson came strolling into the branch like he was a dignitary awaiting a band to play, which marked his arrival. And he had a cell phone up to his ear talking pompously until his conversation ended.

Dressed to enviable perfection, Cortez was a talented loan officer whose own success helped bolstered Trent's career as manager of one of regional bank Palmetto Fidelity's most profitable branches.

"Well, if it isn't Bishop Moneymaker, having decided to grace us with his presence," Trent greeted Cortez in the employee's room. "Shall I break out with the spikenard and use a beach towel to anoint thine feet?"

Cortez held up his hand and peered over his nose. "It is better to give than to receive, my brother. Peace, and so forth, to you—"

Both Cortez and Trent started as tellers in the late 1990s, an era when male tellers were still rare in banking. They pursued different career paths, but they were paired again nearly a decade later in the St. Andrews location.

"So, what you've got going on this week?" Trent asked.

"Nothing yet. But you know I'm always working on something."

Trent bumped fists with Cortez. "I just want to let you know that we'll probably have some people over from corporate in any day. They want to show us off again."

Cortez looked around and marveled. To him, he found it rather amusing that of all places, the St. Andrews branch had earned the same prestige as branches in more affluent areas of Richland and Lexington counties.

"Hey, we'll do what we have to do, right?" he answered; he then nodded back in the direction of the bank teller windows.

"Hey, what's up with Ms. Wanda today? She looks like she's riding her broom again."

Trent frowned at Cortez. "Watch what you're saying. I know you're around me. But one day that's going to get you in a lot of trouble."

"Okay, okay." Cortez held his hand up in submission. "What's going on with Ms. Wanda? I'm concerned about her."

"Probably the usual. She's had a lot going on lately. But who doesn't these days?"

Cortez snapped his finger, revealing also a mischievous grin. "I've got something to show you." He began scrolling through his cell phone screens.

Trent rolled his eyes. "Have I seen her before?" He also looked behind them in both directions before he turned his attention back to Cortez.

"Ah, amen, brother—"

He held a woman's nude picture in front of Trent. She appeared to be sitting in front of a mirror pleasuring herself.

"Mmmph! You are the man."

"I know," he reacted, full of arrogance. "That's one of the reasons why I'm still single."

"At least you're smart enough to realize that." Trent could not resist the temptation to peer over at Cortez's phone for another look. "I take it that she's a part of your harem?"

"Let's just say that she's on the bishop's staff of nurses." He chortled at his own comment. "She sent it to me this morning right after she'd gotten out of the shower." He then pointed casually at Trent. "She also text me a short video."

"I'm not mad at you a single iota."

"Thank you, deacon. And now shall I commence to my ministry of fiscal and fiduciary reconciliation?"

"Absolutely."

While he tried going through the previous day's statements and balances, Trent found himself thinking about his marriage.

There was once a time when he might not have been so easily swayed into viewing Cortez's latest cell phone pictorial. When his sex life with Sonia was more fruitful, they would tease each other with suggestive text messages or even pictures during the course of their work day.

Whether it might be judged as mischief or compromise, Trent was well aware that one thing could lead to something else. Then he might be the one pulling Cortez off to the side showing nude pictures of other women.

He reminded himself about Sonia wanting to have a meaningful discussion about what happened the night before. He tapped his pen on the desk and retrieved his cell phone.

> Darling, I was thinking about you right now. Hope your day is going well. Did Taylor get to school on time?

About twenty-five minutes later, Trent noticed his cell phone buzzing nearby. It had a message icon showing.

> Yes, Taylor got on the school bus. That is YOUR son. No question about it.

Trent chortled at the message. He sent a quick reply.

> Remember, I was the one who went to church seeking da Lawd's face. You were there seeking flesh, not da Lawd.

Another message showed up on his phone.

> Have a good day!

Perhaps this was the start to something better. And for another moment, Trent mused about his last exchange with Sonia, because that was the basis of how Taylor was conceived.

They had been dating off and on for two years. They'd gotten into an argument over him accusing her of being a hothead after she reacted angrily to him gawking at another woman while they were in a Walmart parking lot.

Yes, he was guilty. But he tried defending himself by claiming that he happened to have turned his head just as a woman with wide hips and a rather shapely backside was bent over putting items in the trunk of her car.

Sonia and Trent did not speak to each other for the next three weeks.

Feeling rather discouraged about his relationship and the way other things were going in his life, he decided to attend a Wednesday night service at Bethesda Fellowship. What he did not expect when he arrived was Sonia sitting in one of the front pews.

There was something about the way she appeared to him that night. They spoke to each other after service, expressing surprise that they would see each other. Trent then offered her to meet him at the Chili's restaurant on Two Notch Road just beyond the Columbia Mall. She accepted.

While at Chili's, both recognized that they missed each other dearly. They agreed to take their conversation back to his apartment. The night became one of reconciliation and conception in his living room. Taylor Jordan Buckner was born a little more than nine months later.

Chapter 4

❧

'I Hope ... I Don't Get There'

By 5:15 in the afternoon, Trent had come crashing back down to reality. So much for nostalgic thoughts about him and Sonia.

He figured it would be easier to tell her that he had a busier than usual day at the bank, hiding behind the excuse that he had visitors from Palmetto Fidelity's upper management.

It was more desirable, though, to tell her he was not interested in looking up p-whipped suggestions on how he could enhance their sex life.

So, Trent did what he thought was the next best thing. On his way home, he stopped by the Columbiana Mall. There, he picked up flowers and bought Hypnotic Poison perfume from Belk's department store—something he'd overheard Sonia telling her sister Shonna about recently.

"Thanks. This just might keep me out of the dog house," he quipped to the Belk's sales consultant.

"Really? You're in that much trouble with her?"

Trent tipped his head downward, responding, "You know

how you women can be with us—"

"It depends," she answered. "You men usually deserve it."

"I guess I'll find out in a while, hmmm?"

"Good luck—I hope."

Trent had about an hour or so before Sonia would be home from work. He figured he might be able to ring up a few extra points with her by stopping off at the grocery store and starting dinner for the family.

"Dad, is that you?" Taylor yelled from his room upon hearing the front door being closed. He rushed to greet his father in the foyer.

"Yeah, how was school today?"

"Horrible as usual."

Trent gave Taylor a suspicious look. "Why does school have to be horrible every day?" He motioned for Taylor to follow him into the kitchen.

"School's horrible because it's horrible. I hate my teachers and I don't like most of the people I go to school with."

"But you play sports; you're good at them. Aren't you popular?" He stared briefly at Taylor. He reminded himself he was not popular until his eleventh grade year; that was when he won the 100-meter state title back home in Louisiana.

Meanwhile, Taylor went along with helping him put up the rest of the groceries.

"Depends on who you are."

"Don't worry about that. Hey, have you started on your homework?"

"Yes, I have," Taylor grumbled. "Between you and Mom, I don't know who's worse getting on me about my homework."

Trent leaned against the kitchen counter and folded his arms. "Let me just remind you that I'm not raising any lazy son around here—"

"I know, I know . . . Your mother told you the same thing

when you were growing up, and if I don't like it I can let the front door hit me where the good Lord split me, right?

Both father and son stared each other. Moments later, Taylor started laughing.

"I couldn't help it. Dad, sometimes you sound like one of those commercials when they keep repeating the same old thing."

"Well, since it's gonna be like that. . . ."

"Dad, chill out. I'm going back to my room and finish my homework." Taylor stopped first in the dining room. "Oh, by the way, I got a ninety-three on my history test."

"Okay. Good job!"

Sonia walked into the living room around 7:30. She glanced at the mail that was left on the coffee table and plopped on the sofa. There, she kicked off her shoes, closed her eyes, and began rubbing the back of her neck. The relative silence in the house was welcomed.

Having collected her thoughts, she yelled, "Trent, I'm glad you didn't wait for me to start dinner because I sure wasn't in the mood to do it!"

Sonia's sudden conversation startled Trent, prompting him to come out from his work office.

"How long have you been home?" he inquired.

She stood up and walked over to offer him a hug. "I guess a few minutes. Thanks for starting dinner."

"It should be ready shortly. How was your day?"

"You would ask, wouldn't you?"

"Why not? It is what married people do—"

"Perhaps they do." She followed him into the kitchen. "Is Taylor doing his homework?"

"Yeah, we've already had that discussion."

She nodded. They sat down at the kitchen table. "You asked about work?" She took a deep breath and leaned back in her chair. "Work was . . . absolutely . . . work today. We got word that we'll be hiring for some permanent positions. Other than that, it was the usual insanity with upper management and those callers.

"And how about your day today? Did you have any time to look up anything that might help us out you know where?"

Trent did not immediately answer Sonia. Instead, he excused himself and checked on the potatoes and corn.

"You're not going to answer me?" Sonia asked.

He stopped by the refrigerator. "I'm going to answer you." He turned around holding a flower vase.

Sonia returned a surprised look. "Is this one of the things they said you should do?" She accepted the half-dozen red roses with a smile .

Should I tell her or not?

"I've got something else for you." He disappeared from the kitchen for several moments, returning with a small box.

"This goes with it—"

"For me?"

"For you."

Sonia nodded while she peeked inside the box. "Wow, I am impressed. Perfume. Dinner. Roses." Then she stopped in mid-sentence, brooding. "What, no card?"

"Not after last night."

"Okay, I'll let you slide on that one." She stood up and held her arms out for him. "Thank you for being such a wonderful husband. Having said that, did you really look up some material for us to go over?"

They sat back down at the table.

"Sonia, I don't need a book to tell me what I need to do for my wife. I did this on my own for you."

"We'll talk about this later. I don't need Taylor getting an earful of our business."

* * *

Trent knew as he joined Sonia in the bedroom later that evening his moment of truth was nearing. This time, he was determined to hold his ground with her.

Ah, but he thought he might have seen a reprieve since he saw Sonia already turned on her side apparently sleeping. He eased into bed next to her without saying anything. Immediately, however, she turned over.

"I waited to find out if you would actually make an effort at adding to our conversation," she said. "It's obvious you have nothing to say."

She turned back over.

"If you think that I did all that with hopes of asking you for any sex tonight, you're sadly mistaken," he countered; he then sat up in bed with his arms folded. "I, uh, nothing—"

"Nothing, what?"

"Nothing."

She also sat up in the bed. Bits of what she read earlier had also returned to her.

"Let me explain something to you, Trent. The reason why I keep bringing this up to you is because I don't want to reach the point where I no longer care about our marriage or you.

"Can you understand that?"

Trent closed his eyes, bunched his lips and nodded in thought, mulling exactly how he would respond to Sonia.

"You remind me of my track career. I was fast, but I realized at some point my best wasn't ever going to be good enough to beat the very best. My best times were like a bad race for them," he said. "Humph, it's obvious my best may never be good enough for you. But I'm okay with that—"

"Is bringing up something about your track career your way

of dealing with it?" Sonia interrupted him. "One has nothing to do with the other. What we're talking about here is you being a husband. I appreciate many of the things you've done, don't get me wrong—"

"Here we go again . . ." Trent remarked, rolling his eyes.

Sonia cut an angry glare at him. "Yes, I'm about to go there. Apparently, you don't understand when trust is broken, when you've caused pain upon someone, especially the person you're supposed to be closest to, you've got to do more to show that you want to make it right with that person."

Hissing, Trent countered, "How long? Sonia, it's been at least five years and counting [that] I've been trying to make things right with you. Five years! And what makes it so bad, half of it is over trivial stuff."

"What is trivial about you admitting to maintaining phone contact with another woman, a single woman at that, and you said it was only business every time I confronted you about it? Then I happen to see a picture of her sitting on your lap on an employee's phone at my job—I still don't believe you claiming that you never had anything sexually to do with that . . . I better stop before I begin cursing!"

The incident with Annette Sloan occurred two years into their marriage. Although Trent had been truthful that he was never sexually involved with Annette, it was apparent in the way he acted that he'd become too friendly with her.

Sonia's initial complaint was about the phone calls he began receiving in the evening from Annette. It got so bad that he would leave their home once he'd take the call and return after a lengthy period.

"Look, I told you that I was wrong for having anything to do with Annette Sl—"

"Don't ever mention that woman's name!" she snapped back at him. "Trent, I can't tell you how embarrassed I was to see that picture on some stranger's phone. That really hurt me. I can't begin to tell you how much I prayed that I wouldn't hear anything else about it. Did you think that you could have gone on any longer doing things like that? Did you really think so?"

I might not have, but she sure felt and smelled good sitting on my lap. Maybe I should have done more with her. At least I could have said I'd really gotten something out of it.

Trent held his breath again and commenced to counting backwards from ten. The Annette incident was just one of several convenient pieces in Sonia's arsenal she used against him.

"And you know what makes it so bad? She looked slutty," she continued. "There was no hint of decency about her. None. Zilch. Nada."

Stung by Sonia's machete hacks at him, Trent felt he had no choice. "Uh-huh, so all this talk about setting moods, and dare I say God time, really has to do with what happened in the past. So you're going to keep living your life back there?" he retorted. "I'm sure you would not want somebody bringing up your dirty secrets and skeletons."

Sonia bolted out of bed and stormed off to the bathroom, fuming. She returned the same way moments later.

Pointing sharply at him, she said, "Trent, you begged and pleaded with me after that incident not to leave you. You begged and pleaded with me!

"You said that you would do everything in your ability to make it right with me."

"I did say that. And I have tried. But it's obvious, more than I care to acknowledge it, that my best isn't enough."

She climbed back in bed with Trent. "I have forgiven you. And I have done my best to forget. But it's obvious you don't realize how unresolved issues can hinder a woman emotionally."

"There's a saying out there," Trent said, pausing to suck his teeth. "It's called guilt tripping someone."

"Trent, you have to do your part to help with the healing. My suggesting that you find material on marriage might also help you make things better. It's not all about me."

"Are you sure about that?"

Any sense of bonding between them this night was undoubtedly broken, Trent thought. It was as if he and Sonia were separated by a large body of water while lying in the same bed. Experience had long since taught him don't attempt touching her, no matter how generic or innocuous it might be.

"Don't ever say that I've not tried telling you about the things that are hindering me from enjoying sex with you," Sonia warned. "Like I said, there may come a time and day when I will not care any more. I hope for your sake I don't get there."

Trent merely shook his head. Then he turned onto his side and drifted off in thought. He knew his room at the Dog House Inn was already prepared for him. A king-size bed, non-smoking preference. He also knew it was not easy to check out any time that he'd like.

Silently, he prayed, " . . . *Is this Your idea of showing me, yes, You forgive us and maybe You forget about it from the east to the west. But there are still consequences for our actions? Isn't there a statute of limitations on them?*

Oh, but I know this goes deeper. . . ."

Chapter 5

'It's Okay ... No, It's Not Okay'

A t least Trent knew where he stood with Sonia. A stay in the Dog House Inn could last hours, days, and even weeks.

Usually, there's no way of camouflaging it when they're in public. They hardly minced words with each other. They tend not to walk together. When they're in the car together, Sonia had a way of angling her body away from him to avoid looking at him.

"One of these days before it's too late, you just might get it right," she told him in passing. "Hopefully, it's before you're eighty-six."

Humph, maybe you'll be long gone by then.

"What if I'm eighty-five and I finally get it?" he countered. Sonia could not resist relating a portion of her now-favorite Web site to him.

"Well, if you don't, it might be your last words because you never listened to me."

"And what do you mean by that? My hearing's great."

"That's your problem. You just don't listen."

Trent smirked at Sonia. "And you're such a open and willing vessel, huh?" He walked over toward her as she came out of their walk-in closet. "Your problem is that if nobody goes along with what you say, they're judged severely. They're cast away from thine righteous presence."

Sonia had now walked into the kitchen with Trent following closely behind.

"All I'm going to say is I read where a man's last words before he died was an apology to his wife for not listening to her."

She went on to describe the man had been married for more than thirty years and he was in the latter stages of prostate cancer. His wife told him not to get out of bed before she went to a store located about ten minutes away from their home. The man did not heed his wife and he tried going to the bathroom. He slipped and fell, hitting his head on the bathroom sink. Somehow, he made it back to the bedroom; there was a bloody trail that marked his painful, final trip.

"When she returned, the first thing she did was remind him he should not have gotten out of bed," Sonia continued. "Before he slipped into a coma and died, he said, 'You were right . . . I should have listened.'"

Trent was more than tempted to mimic Sonia by playing a violin.

"Okay, so you're saying that when I finally 'get it' that I might as well be dead?"

"I didn't say that."

"Well, that's what you're inferring."

"Trent, I was simply making a point. The reason why we've not been speaking to each other lately is because you're like most men."

"And you're like most women. *Nag, nag, nag, nag, nag!*"

Sonia leaned forward at the table and pointed at Trent. "Do you know the reason why women nag?"

"Yeah. Women nag because it's in them to nag. It's a part of the curse after you women disobeyed God and we took the blame for it." Trent then leaned back in his chair, puffing out his chest.

"And you wonder why I try to get us to have some God time. It's obvious how much time you spend with Him."

Refusing to be denied her say, Sonia impressed upon Trent a woman's nagging was because there's something wrong and she's trying to get her husband's attention. "So, you're saying that you have more than just a personal problem you've yet to share with me?" Trent quipped.

Sonia stood up, shaking her head in dismay. "Some things . . . only the power of prayer can help."

"Yeah, you do that. Pray for me, sister! Pray for me!"

She went ahead with preparing dinner. Meanwhile, Trent walked off to his work office down the hallway.

* * *

Trent knew staying at the Dog House Inn did not exempt him from Valentine's Day, which, in his opinion, was one of five mandatory dates on the calendar that a husband was obligated to do something for his wife. The other dates were Christmas, Mother's Day (as applicable), their wedding anniversary, and her birthday.

This year, he had no intention of doing anything that might be perceived as romantic. Thus, he did not plan on sending her flowers to her job as he had done on a couple of occasions. Nor did he consider serving her breakfast in bed.

"I tell you what we'll do today after work," he proposed to

Sonia that morning. "I'll take you to that restaurant that you like nearby the mall, and we'll go over to the mall and I'll even walk with you the entire time as you go shopping. I'm sure there's a dress, shoes, and a handbag that you've been thinking about getting lately. And that's going to be my Valentine's gift to you this year."

Sonia merely stared at him, wondering if this was the same man who had essentially ignored her the past three weeks—as if she had not been guilty herself ignoring him.

"Valentine's Day is a day in which you're supposed to show me that you love me." She then sighed. "But I'll take it. I guess your willingness to walk with me no matter how long it takes to find something that I like is your way of showing me that you do love me—"

"Come here."

"Why?"

Trent was reduced to tugging at Sonia by the hand so that he could draw her closer and hug her.

He whispered, "Why do you have to be so difficult?"

"No, why do you have to be so difficult?"

He squeezed her backside. "I still love you." She shooed his hands away.

"Yes, hubby, I love you, too, even though I didn't think of anything for you today."

So, Trent confirmed again with Sonia that she was leaving work at 5:30. Then they were to meet at home around 6:30 and proceed with what he planned for her. Neither would be in any rush because Taylor would be spending the night at one of his classmate's home in the neighborhood.

Sonia decided to start a conversation with Trent as they left home for the mall. When they first dated fifteen years ago, this might have been a part of the discovery process. Now it seemed outright awkward.

"Did you think about me at all today?"

Do I have to answer that question? he first mumbled to himself.

"Yeah, I thought about us being together this evening."

As if it went against her better thinking—and mere emotions—Sonia reminded Trent about their first meeting each other occurred close to Valentine's Day.

She went into Palmetto Fidelity's Decker Road location near the Columbia Mall to cash a check for her grandmother, Esther. She also happened to have been waited on by Trent.

"You would have to come to my window," Trent said, chortling at the memory. "But I'm not complaining at all."

"Are you sure about that?"

Sonia's grandmother was waiting for her in an old white Ford Escort. She brought her grandmother's ID, a driver's license, but Trent told Sonia that she would need to come back with her grandmother to cash it.

Sonia protested that her grandmother was not able to stand up for long periods. Several minutes later, she returned with an elderly lady. She held Esther's hand while she took slow, short steps.

"I told you so." Her voice was just as defiant as it was fifteen years ago.

"Yeah, you keep forgetting I was new there and I didn't want any trouble with anyone." Trent found work at Palmetto Fidelity after he decided on giving up track and field for a living. "You never know when they have their own people coming through as fake customers."

"You know I could not have cared less about that. All I wanted to do was to cash a check for my grandmother." She also remembered her grandmother promised to give her some extra money if she would drive her around to handle several other transactions.

In the aftermath, Trent felt so bad about it that he mailed an apology letter to Sonia.

"You're the only customer I ever did anything like that." His voice hinted some bashfulness about his gesture of kindness.

"It was thoughtful of you," she replied, teasingly. "In fact, it was rather sweet. My grandmother, God rest her soul, said she was impressed. She was the one who told me that I should go by there and thank you personally."

She closed her eyes recalling how she made sure he might recognize her by wearing a low-cut turquoise dress that clung to her body. Moved by the thought, she placed her hand on his thigh, stroking it lightly. The warmth and softness of her touch hinted at he might be given a reprieve out of the Dog House Inn.

"I could tell from your eyes and the way you smiled that you were attracted to me," he said. "That was when I had to find out if there was any chance with you."

"Mmm-humph," she reacted, rolling her eyes at him. "You had that look as if you were trying to get your swag on, any-way—"

"Hey, I already had it going on. It was pretty cool on my part that I passed a note to you with my phone number asking you out on a date, hmmm?" He leaned back in his seat.

Sonia squirmed. "Don't let all of that go to your head." She darted her eyes downward then eye-to-eye with him.

"You've been saying that for the past fifteen years."

They both shared a laugh, marking their first time that month.

The mere fact that Trent was with Sonia while she browsed the stores in the Columbiana Mall selecting her Valentine's Day gifts was an encouraging sign, she thought, and it also helped that he acted as though he was genuinely interested what was important to her at that moment.

She wanted to share with Trent it was a moment like this that had the makings of setting the right mood. While they were in New York & Company, for example, Sonia went as far as rubbing up against Trent while she tried on several color block sleeveless sheath dresses.

"Care to follow me over to one of the dressing rooms?" she bantered with Trent.

Initially, Trent seemed caught off guard by Sonia's sudden, sultry transformation. She cast an alluring glare at him, teasing, "What's wrong, scared?"

"Me? Scared? Whatcha gonna do once we're over there?" he responded.

"That's for you to find out—"

Sonia decided on a sheath dress to go with the handbag and shoes. "I've got one more place I want to check out, if you don't mind. It's on our way out."

At Bare Minerals, Trent waited near the entrance while Sonia sampled some of the foundation and makeup she planned on getting next time she came to the mall.

It had already been a long day, and Trent's attention span was on the wane. There was only so much of a mall experience a man could bear. He checked his watch, noting that it was about 8:45; the mall would be closing in fifteen minutes.

As soon as he lifted his head, his eyes locked in on a younger, statuesque woman whose hair that trailed down the middle of her back. She took long, graceful strides; there was more than an ounce to her bounce. He raised his eyebrows and shook his head in wonderment. Then he brought his hand up to his mouth and smiled to himself.

Bad decision.

"So while I'm trying out different makeup, you spend your time checking out other women?"

Trent jerked to Sonia's voice snapping him out of his trance.

"Would you rather that I'm checking out a guy walking past me than a woman?" he reacted.

"Both would be wrong, bottom line." She began walking ahead of him.

He caught up with her just as they reached the exit. "Next time that I'm seen in public with you, I'll make sure that I'm wearing a Sonia Buckner-approved blindfold and I'm using a walking cane. Maybe then you won't be as paranoid!"

"Who you're calling paranoid?"

"You!"

"Trent, I almost needed a forklift to place your tongue back inside your mouth. You sure know how to ruin a nice evening."

He jerked his head in her direction. "I haven't ruined anything. And I was not looking at another woman!" Mindlessly, he clicked the car doors open.

"I'm not going to argue with you. I saw you, Trent," she yelled once the doors were shut. "You looked as if you were going to drop my bags and follow her . . . Lust of the eyes, pride of life—"

"There you go again!"

Sonia returned to angling her body away from him and she peered angrily out of the window while Trent rushed to start the car and drive off.

Both were as if they'd given off like charges, and they seemed mutually repulsed and repelling from each other. It was not until Trent reached I-26 exit No. 91 before the silence was broken.

"It's time that you listen to me, and listen to me good," Trent said, looking straight ahead. "I am not a child. I have a mother. She did a good job raising me. And I will not—I repeat I will not—go around as if I need to consult with a censorship board before I think or do anything involving you.

"And I refuse to go around like some other men I've seen before talking to themselves like they belong in a mental ward because of a woman!"

Sonia reared back, turned and stared at Trent. Her eyes were narrowed as if they'd become lasers that locked in on a target.

"Let me get one thing straight with you," she said, rolling her neck. "The only reason why I've continued to be married to you is because of our son. I want him to have both parents growing up like I did!"

They happened to be at a red light when Trent turned his head slowly and glared at Sonia. He then looked straight ahead as the light changed.

"Oh, now you're taking shots at my background again?" he said calmly. "Obviously, I wasn't bad enough for you. Humph, your credit was bent worse than a fender after an accident. I had my act together—"

"That's debatable."

"No, that's not debatable! I could handle my business. I had to in order to get the job that I've had handling money."

Trent stuck out his chest knowing that his comment insulted Sonia. Early in their relationship, many of the major transactions they made together were on the strength of his credit. Admittedly, she made mistakes like many young people with access to credit cards. It took her nearly five years to repair her credit—with his help.

He did not bother to brace himself for the imminent counter attack.

"I know you're not trying to say I was one of those 'ratchet' women when you met me. Because if you are—"

"You know it's true!"

"Trent, I'm asking you, with the love of God in me. . . ."

"Asking me what? My mistake was that I should have checked it out before I really got caught up being involved with you."

"Trent, I strongly advise you to stop while you still have rope to grab on to," she snarled at him.

He smirked at her. "And happy Valentine's Day to you!"

Later that night, Trent joined Sonia in bed. It was customary that he slept in the nude. In fact, it was one of Sonia's preferences. She was clad in only a silk pajama top.

Neither still had said a word to each other since arriving home. Suddenly, Sonia turned onto her left side. She reached over and began to clutch onto Trent's chest. She then nuzzled up to him. It was as if she had done it out of habit.

Eventually, Trent reached back and placed his hand on her hip. She turned over again and he began caressing her body. Next, it was as if they began a dance under the sheets as they rubbed their bodies together. Neither seemingly gave thought to whether they were initiating any reconciliation. Nor did it seem as if this was an aberration of some kind, either. Maybe this was a new form of sex à la sleep walking style.

Without saying a word, Trent now positioned himself by lying on his back, and Sonia had removed her pajama shirt and mounted him in the cowgirl position. She began giving him a passionate ride, to say the least.

When they changed positions, Sonia seemed instinctive to get on all fours and allow Trent to offer her long, deep strokes doggy style. Sonia bit her bottom lip and closed her eyes tightly.

Trent finally broke the silence between them. "Why can't you ever admit to being in the need?" Why is it you have to make it seem as if I'm the only one—"

"Just keep on, please!" She beckoned him to work it harder

by the loud smacking of her flesh against his.

It was more than tempting to ask Sonia if something was happening. Usually, she'd give him hints whenever she was close, or something had occurred.

"I'm almost there, baby," she whispered. "But I don't think it's going to happen tonight."

His breathing was beginning to increase. "It can, if you want it to—"

"I'm sorry, baby. Just go ahead and get yours. It's okay."

"No, it's not okay."

Trent decided at that moment to withdraw from Sonia.

She did not protest, either. Rather, she eased back under the sheets and resumed lying on her side; he turned his back to her and stared at the ceiling until he fell asleep.

Chapter 6

'Can I Be a Fly on the Wall?'

Vicki had already spotted Sonia walking down the hallway. She waved furiously for Sonia to stop and join her in a carved-out area that housed a drink machine, refrigerator, sink, and a coffee maker.

"When you pass by my rows, please don't laugh, okay?" Vicki implored Sonia.

"Why should I not laugh?"

Vicki looked over her shoulder and surveyed the immediate area. The coast was clear. She shook her head before she proceeded to divulge.

"What is the world coming to when a man is wearing Mary Kay pink colored slacks to work?" She then placed her hands on her hips.

Sonia returned a confused look. It took a few moments before it processed with her; she didn't bother to ask who it was. "That doesn't even sound right."

"I know. And it doesn't even look right."

Alvantrae Benson was of a medium height and build, but he would hardly be mistaken for a ladies' man. His subtle effeminate mannerisms were the subject of many other jokes about keeping it on the down-low.

"And guess what, Sonia?" Vicki added. "His pants fit tighter on his booty than any pair of jeans that I wear!"

Sonia returned a side-eyed stare. "Come on, now. It isn't that against company policy?"

"I should send him home, but I think what he's wearing is considered appropriate for the workplace."

"Then I guess there's nothing else to say."

Vicki hissed. She could not get past the fact Alvantrae's nails and shoulder-length hair—it was usually combed to the back—was better kept than most of the women in contract services, including hers. Adding more to the envy was when her team had a recent Friday potluck for lunch. Alvantrae put many to shame with his homemade potato salad and chili.

"Humph, I told him last time if it weren't for the fact that I was already married, I'd propose to him."

"Do you think he would accept?" Sonia queried.

Vicki looked herself over. Slightly taller than Sonia, she was on the brink of giving up on her resolution to lose fifteen pounds by the beginning of March.

"Well, I guess it would be a question of whether he could handle all of this; I also would have to get used to being the aggressor and being on top all of the time."

They both shared a laugh. Then they began a slow saunter into the workplace.

There were two phone representatives already standing near Vicki's cubicle awaiting her return. Sonia had indicated that she would chat with her later, but Vicki insisted that she take a seat.

A native of Gaffney, a South Carolina city famous for its large peach-shaped water tower next to the I-85 freeway, Vicki was a country girl at heart. She was known for her hospitality, and she was the de facto candy store owner because she always kept two large jars well stocked, making her desk one of the most visited.

"Janine [Townsend], I monitored one of your calls yesterday. You couldn't talk for all that candy in your mouth!" she chided her phone rep. "I might have to restrict the number of times you can come up here."

"Aw, Ms. Vicki. It wasn't that bad." Janine shifted the weight from her left foot to the right. "That call came in before I could finish."

There was no doubt Janine had a playful demeanor. She was in her early twenties, but she could have easily been mistaken for being a teenager in high school. Her high-pitched soft voice did not make it any easier.

"A member calls in, and what they hear is you crunching candy in their ear," Vicki said. "Would you want that happening to you?"

Janine hunched her shoulders. "As long as they're not yelling at me, I guess I'm cool with it."

"Are you in not ready?" Vicki asked; she now searched a screen that gave real-time updates. "You better get back to your desk. The last thing I need is Phyllis calling me."

"Yes, Ms. Vicki."

Vicki then turned to the other phone representative—Alvantrae.

"And what do you need?"

After sighing, he began explaining the difficulty he was having utilizing the correct call-up code on UCP's system. A doctor had given him only a check number, and she wanted to know what policy holder or person was associated with it.

"Have you referred to your resource directory?"

Alvantrae sucked his teeth, hissed, and walked off.

Meanwhile, Vicki smirked and turned her attention to Sonia. "I know that kills them. But I'm not going to spend all my time with stuff they can research on their own."

Humph, they end up coming over to my desk instead when you're not around, Sonia said to herself. And then I hear their complaints about you being so lazy.

Hence, Vicki always had time for gossip. She gave Sonia a nod that evinced mischief.

"Okay, I see what you were telling me outside," Sonia said, smiling. "They did seem too tight for comfort."

Sonia then glanced over Vicki's shoulder. She noticed it was 8:58. Her shift began in two minutes. She apprised Vicki that she would be interviewing her candidates starting around mid-morning.

Vicki's eyes widened.

"Does that mean you'll be sitting face-to-face with . . . oh . . . my . . . god! I wish I were a fly on that wall."

"As if you aren't already one around here."

* * *

Shortly before lunch, Sonia walked over to the rows of temps and signaled for Hannah Freeman to log off after her next call. She was more than eager to get off the phone. They walked side-by-side until they reached the end of the second floor corridor where the meeting room was located.

Sonia did not bother preparing herself for interviewing any of the employees. There were already mandatory questions the supervisors were required to ask; all each candidate had to do was not make a fool of themselves.

"How have you liked working here so far?" Sonia asked as

they sat down.

Hannah, who was in her late forties, had been a victim of the economy as many have come to know since 2008. She owned and operated her own business, a graphics design shop in nearby West Columbia, for nearly a decade but had to close it

"It beats sitting at home sulking and hoping to find work," she said.

"I understand," Sonia replied. "I do want to tell you that we think you've done quite well so far with us. That's why we've set up this interview with you."

"Thank you."

She appeared resigned to her new reality, although she tried putting on her best face. The job paid probably a fraction of the money she made owning her own business.

A quick perusal of her performance thus far suggested that she had caught on fast to understanding UCP's system. But Sonia was more than aware how it all seemed easy while working as a temp. All a temp phone representative had to do was answer questions about benefits from an insurance contract. Also, they did not have to learn nor did they have access to as many call-up commands and screens on UCP's system.

"So, Hannah, tell me what do you think is the most important thing about customer service?" Sonia read from her list of required questions.

Hannah straightened up in the chair. "Having owned my own business it's often the difference between having repeat business or not having repeat business, gaining referrals or not gaining referrals."

"I see. But how do you think it applies in this job, contract services?"

She acknowledged the question with a nod. "I see. Well, here, the last thing a company wants is a bad reputation for not giving good service." She seemed uncomfortable answering the question, but it was acceptable to Sonia.

"If you're hired permanent, there are times you'd have to work on Saturdays. Also, you have to work most weeks a minimum of three hours' overtime. Would you have any problems or anticipate any difficulties with maintaining that kind of schedule?"

"I reckon not. I'm here to do my best."

"Great. Well, the next step in the process is if you're chosen by us, you'll be contacted by our human resources department.

Once you're on board permanently, you'll move to the other side of the office and you'll be official."

One down, two to go.

After lunch, Sonia made the same gesture to Kai Long, indicating that she could log off her phone. Immediately, Kai looked herself over in her pocket mirror, which was something she often did during her shift.

Kai, in her early twenties, was a recent college graduate. She attended school in North Carolina, where she earned a degree in marketing, but moved back home to be with her parents. An avid reader, she browsed through a fashion magazine or paperback book whenever she wasn't preoccupied with her average-at-best beauty.

"Tell me, Kai, what have you found most satisfying so far about contract services?" Sonia asked.

She repeated, "What I like most about contract services?"

Sonia shifted her weight in the chair. "Yes, that's right. What have you found most satisfying about contract services.?"

Looking first off to her right—a view of the parking awaited her—Kai chose to think through her response thoroughly. Then she made eye contact with Sonia.

"Honestly, it is nice to help someone who really seems to appreciate it." Her voice was on the lower, sultry range—a true telephone voice. Sonia mused to herself a voice like Kai's might go a long way when dealing with a disgruntled male caller.

"Anything else to add?"

"No, nothing else."

Phyllis had made Kai a priority hire because she proved her worth a little more than a month earlier when it snowed nearly a foot in the Columbia area. She was one of four phone representatives who showed up for work. Only three members of management also showed up: Sonia, Phyllis, and George Faley, a team supervisor of liaisons who answered calls and visited medical providers at their place of business.

"Last question, Kai."

"Sure."

"A lot of the work other than answering phones requires meeting deadlines. What do you think is most important when meeting deadlines?"

She sat back and studied Kai's composure and response. Kai's eyes shifted from left to right and stopped.

"I'm sure being organized has a lot to do with it. I know it helped me get through college."

And with that, Sonia thanked Kai for her time and apprised her of the same hiring information as Hannah.

One to go.

Vicki was more than eager for Sonia to return to her cubicle. She gave Sonia a knowing nod and a stare after taking the chair to the left her.

"You must have some more gossip, don't you?" Sonia reacted.

"Does it always have to be gossip?"

"With you, nine times out of ten, it is."

Vicki crossed her leg under the desk and leaned forward. It was quite common for their conversations to be barely above a whisper.

"You know I want to be that fly on the wall since a certain department manager did not assign a certain male employee on my team—" She then leaned back in her chair.

"You and Charlotte are just beside yourselves, aren't you?"

Sonia responded. "You two are acting like he's the only man in Columbia."

"No, he's just the only man worth looking at in this department. And how many of those come along through here?"

Perhaps Vicki had a point. Women comprised more than ninety percent of the permanent employees in contract services. There were only nine men, of which four were gay. Two were considered physically unattractive. Two were, well, average at best.

Sonia shook her head. "I don't know why you're making such a big deal. You're married."

"Uh, that's on a need-to-know basis," Vicki corrected Sonia; she then wiggled her hips as if to make a statement.

Occasionally, Vicki would divulge bits of information about her current husband, Jermichael. Sonia knew that Jermichael worked as a mechanic at a car dealership near Lugoff, which was about thirty miles away from where they worked along the I-20 freeway.

She divulged even less about her first husband. "Fooled me once, shame on you; I never gave him the chance for it to be shame on me—"

Sonia placed her hand on her thigh, rolling her neck at her. "Since it's on a need-to-know basis, just remember that interviews are confidential. They are protected by privacy laws, thank you."

"Well, I'll talk to you later." Vicki then looked over her shoulder as she left Sonia's cubicle. "Just don't swat me if you happen to see something flying in there."

About 3:15 p.m., Sonia made her final trip over to rows where the temps were assigned. She found it a bit surprising that her heart began beating faster. She tried dismissing it, but it seemed to beat even faster as she approached desk No. 164 on the department's seating chart.

"Thank you for calling," Lance said before he typed in his last paragraph of notes; he then looked up and noticed Sonia standing about two steps away from his desk area.

"Hi, you're scheduled to interview with me right about now," she said. "You can log off and follow me once you're finished."

"Okay, I'll be right there."

Sonia's could not believe what was happening. Her mouth became dry, and she was consumed with fear that Charlotte and Vicki would see them waking over to the meeting room.

Once she reached the conference door, she looked up, took a deep breath, and offered Lance a seat. His moves were fluid. Not bad for someone who bore features similar to Rick Fox, former professional basketball player and actress Vanessa L. Williams' ex-husband. He just did not stand six feet, seven inches; it was more like six-three, maybe six-four.

After taking another deep breath, Sonia said, "I'm sure it's already been a long day for you. Just imagine what it's like for us supervisors?"

"I can only imagine."

"Well, let's get started."

Sonia was unaware that Lance, who was in his late twenties, graded out with the highest cumulative score from his training class of nine employees. The current statistics that were kept on him also had him at or near the top in several categories. He was possibly the best candidate to have come her way.

"Lance, if hired, what do you think would be your best quality or attribute you'd bring to contract services?"

He seemed just as engaged with Sonia's question as he was on the phone. "The ability to learn fast and adapt."

She nodded.

"Tell me, what are your thoughts about dealing with criticism? Constructive criticism, that is—"

"Criticism can be helpful or harmful. I'm sure that a supervisor will only bring something to an employee's attention if it will help him or her improve, not regress."

She nodded again and scribbled down a couple of notes. She was conscious to avoid eye contact with him—the last thing she felt she needed was her nipples becoming erect through her beige blouse while interviewing him.

Leaning back in her chair, she asked, "Tell me a little more about yourself?"

He smiled. "I'm originally from Washington, D.C. I went to school there. Then I met someone who was from South Carolina, and I guess you could say that I was looking for love; it turned out to be in the wrong place.

"I wouldn't say that I was stranded. But since I sort of liked it here, anyway, I'm trying to rebuild my life, one day at a time."

"That's interesting. Had you ever done any work involving the insurance industry or customer service before working here as a temp?"

"No."

"Working here can be rewarding depending on what path you take. If you're chosen, we will try to do all we can to help you in whatever path you eventually choose."

Sonia thanked Lance for his time and apprised him of the same hiring information as her other two candidates. Once again, she opened the door for him. This time she walked slowly behind him as he strode back to his desk. She even dared to inhale his cologne that wafted in his wake.

Chapter 7

'Is This for Business or Pleasure?'

One of the tellers casually greeted the female customer as she entered the St. Andrews branch. Instinctively, Trent looked up. The view was quite appealing.

Since it was slow at that time of the morning, Trent got up from his desk, went out into the lobby and greeted her as well.

"Is there anything we can help you with this morning?" he asked.

She glanced at her watch. "I'm supposed to meet with Mr. Anderson in a couple of minutes. I guess I am a little early." She spoke in broken English, but it was intelligible.

"Sure, Mr. Anderson will be with you shortly." Trent then gestured with his head. "We're severely short-handed this morning and he's working the drive-thru teller. But I'll let him know you're here for him."

Trent took a step toward his office, but then looked back at her. "And your name is?"

"Ah, yes. Alcione de Oliveria."

"I'll let him know." He held his hand out offering that she could help herself to the coffee at the table a few steps away from where they stood.

"No thank you. I will just wait here."

"His office is the one directly behind us. You can wait there, if you'd like."

"I'm fine. I will sit here."

At the counter, Trent whispered to Wanda Odom, the branch's lead teller, that Cortez had a customer waiting for him. He did not bother attempting to repeat her name.

On his way back, he stopped by again. Selfishly, he had to look at her. There was something exotic about her slender face, but smooth skin; her olive complexion; her long, thick, dark curly hair that came down past her shoulders, and her smile.

"Cortez will be with you shortly, Ms. Al . . . ci . . ."

She smiled. "Alcione de Oliveria." She pronounced the "de" in her name like the letter "J" as it's done in Portuguese.

Trent could not resist letting out a weak grunt in admiration of the woman on his way back to his office. A few moments later, Cortez had come over to the sofas in the bank lobby. He held out his hand as she stood up.

"Mr. Anderson, it's good to see you again," she said. "How are you?"

"I'm doing great." Cortez began swelling with pride. "It's good seeing you. How can I help you today?"

I should have known, Trent mumbled to himself. It had become commonplace that many of Cortez's customers were women. In fact, there was often a steady flow of them that came to see him. But Trent never made any issue of it because it always added to the branch's numbers each month.

Meanwhile, she followed Cortez's lead over to his office. Once inside, he closed the door behind them. Trent watched the entire interaction, shaking his head.

"Is this for business or pleasure?" Cortez asked, as he waited for her to take a seat.

She placed her purse down on the carpet next to the chair. "How about both?"

Cortez grinned, as did she. Fresh on their memory was an encounter of passionate, erotic, freaky sex they enjoyed from the night before in her Lexington County residence.

Leaning back in his office chair, Cortez remarked, "I've seen a few videos featuring Brazilian women lately, and I've always been intrigued. But there's nothing like the real thing."

"I told you we are passionate, fun-loving people," she said, crossing her legs; her voice had a mellow, soothing attraction like the place she called home—a land of samba, bossa nova, sun-drenched beaches, Carnival, and great weather. "And when we're with someone we like, we like to have lots of fun."

They both stared at each other. Cortez eventually broke the silence between them.

He said, "You've never told me that you had some business you actually wanted to consider with me."

"Yes, I do." She searched her purse and pulled out a couple of sheets she printed from the Internet.

Alcione's family owned a string of Brazilian steak house restaurants in Texas, North Carolina, Florida, New York, and South Carolina. Usually, she spent the spring months in the Columbia area, the summer in Florida, and the fall and winter months back in Brazil.

The restaurant in the Columbia area was well frequented, but it consistently received mixed reviews. Her family's advisors felt it was still in their best interests to keep the location open because of the growth of Brazilian businesses in the

Carolinas.

Never one to forget an attractive woman, Cortez recalled meeting her for the first time a year ago while he dined at her family's restaurant. He broached a conversation with her three weeks ago during a recent visit. They've since been on a whirlwind of a fling.

"I want to secure a car loan. I've done my research about your bank, and I feel comfortable about wanting to do business with Palmetto Fidelity," she said. "And it helps knowing someone like you already."

"As a businessman, I'm flattered. As a man, I think you've arrived at a great decision. How much of a loan were you thinking of, and what car did you have in mind?"

"I've been looking at the Audi cars. Not anything too fancy. Probably an A6."

"I'll have to complete an application—"

"I thought you already have my information," she joked with him. "I think you have become quite familiar with it."

"Oh, yes. I do . . . Uh, I mean, I have." He paused and returned suggestive stare at her. "But we're talking about financial information."

She sat back in her chair, pushing out her chest. "I am sure everything is in order." Then she cast an alluring stare at him, to which he glanced down at her blouse.

"I'm quite sure that it is." Then he looked upward, making eye contact. "Absolutely, in fact." He turned the computer screen toward him and began with the application. Within fifteen minutes, Cortez obtained approval for a loan for the Audi she was looking to purchase; he also secured the bank's best interest rate available. He explained to her all she had to do was stop by the bank with her proof of insurance.

He would also look at the car physically, completing the bank's lending requirement.

"Let me know if there is anything else that I can do to help you." He then tipped head toward her. "Next time, I won't nibble. I'll just bite."

Alcione's eyes lit up. "You remember, don't you?"

"That's not all I remember."

She laughed. "Thank you for taking care of this for me."

The moment seemed rather awkward for Cortez and Alcione. It was as if both wanted to do more than just shake hands. Their moves would have been for all to see, anyway, because of the see-through glass that served as partitions.

"Before you leave, may I introduce you to my bank manager?" Cortez said as he followed Alcione into the lobby.

"Of course you can."

He led her over to Trent's office; there were no customers with him at the moment.

"Hey, got a minute?"

Trent turned slowly to his right. "Yeah, what you got?"

"Just want to introduce you to our newest customer, Ms. Alcione."

Along those lines, Trent knew that meant Cortez had made it full circle cultivating of both business and pleasure—one way or another—with another female customer.

Trent followed Cortez out into the lobby. Alcione offered him a warm smile. "Yes, we talked earlier." Their eyes locked in on each other.

"We did, didn't we?" she answered.

Cortez interrupted the exchange. "Ms. Alcione will be financing her next car with us. We're just waiting to complete everything later today."

Trent extended his hand to her. He sensed the same kind of feeling as when their eyes met. "Thank you for the chance to earn your business."

The feeling was mutual.

"Thank you," she said. "I will be seeing you this afternoon."

Within moments after Alcione left the bank, Cortez strode into Trent's office with a look of exaltation. He sat in the chair across from Trent, leaned back, and placed his left foot on his right thigh; a victory cigar was the only thing missing.

"So, what was that all about?" Trent inquired.

Cortez folded his arms. "Remember that picture I showed you a while back?"

"Which one?" Trent said, smirking.

"You know which one, but I'll just refresh your memory."

He reached into his pocket and scrolled through his cell phone screens. A big grin had now appeared as he placed the phone on Trent's desk. He pointed at it enthusiastically.

"That one!"

Trent froze. He remembered the olive complexion and the long, thick, dark curly hair. He shook his head slowly at Cortez.

"No, you didn't—"

Cocking his head back, Cortez gloated. Big time, in fact. "I certainly did. This woman is w-i-l-d! And she's got more where that came from." He nodded his head for emphasis.

Trent held his hand up in concession. "I don't know what you say to them. And I really don't care what you actually do with them. But you are the man. Shall I now toss money at your feet, Bishop Moneymaker?" He now held that same hand out toward Cortez.

"You can," he answered, stroking his chin. "But I think this month's bonus check will be a lot more than what you can offer, thank you."

Chapter 8

'We'll See ... Who Can Relate'

Trent attempted to be proactive with Sonia after help-ing Taylor with his homework. To avoid her nagging about God time, he was the one who suggested they listen to a David Jeremiah podcast.

"Wow," Sonia remarked, "I'm proud of you!"

"Every now and then, a dog learns a new trick."

"I hope this is one of them."

He even suggested that they do something different. They would remove each other's clothing and lie in bed naked while listening.

While cuddling up to Trent, Sonia added, "This might be exciting. The two of us like we are . . . I can't imagine many people I know doing anything like this."

So it seemed that Trent was on to something, he thought. He went ahead with playing the pastor's message about the world seeming increasingly crazier to everyone.

According to Pastor Jeremiah, the problem many have is

trying to fit God with their own ideas about the world. He reminded his audience that many miss the most obvious because it might be surrounded by the least important. Everyone must remember what is most important, although what's important may be an elusive target.

Periodically, Trent sneaked glances at Sonia to gain a sense of how she was taking in the message. More importantly, it seemed that she enjoyed being in her husband's company, and she showed it by stroking various parts of his body.

Toward the end of the podcast, the pastor noted nothing has ever escaped God. It never had, and it never will. And there were certainties in life: death for all, judgment; and despite all that, life goes on.

"I like that," Sonia said, sitting up bed; she then looked over at Trent. "What did you get out of that message?"

Here we go … Cross-examination time, Trent scoffed to himself. But since both were naked and it seemed Sonia was in a good mood, it took all of him to come up with a sincere and coherent response.

"Wait a minute." Sonia wiggled around under the sheets and covers until she had found a more comfortable position nuzzled up against Trent. "Okay, go ahead—"

"Are you sure?"

"Yes."

"What I got out of it, the world's craziness may seem to goad everyone into wondering how to deal with it," Trent said. "And the pastor says the only certainty of dealing with the world's craziness is not leaning on our own understanding. That's when we're better able to realize and recognize what is most important."

Sonia closed her eyes and began rocking herself within Trent's embrace. The lengthy silence that accompanied her rocking made it seem that she'd gone off into meditation.

The rocking stopped when Trent altered the way he leaned against the headboard. Sonia then looked over her shoulder at him.

"How do you think not leaning on your own understanding helps you in our marriage?" she asked.

Trent replied, "It depends."

"On what?"

"On what direction you're trying to steer this conversation," he answered, sighing. "In some life situations, all the teaching in the world is not going to help you when it gets bad. You're stuck with having to fend for yourself just like when you're out in the streets."

Sonia repeated closing her eyes and rocking herself along with another lengthy pause in silence.

"You know, I was thinking about something I read online before going into work this morning." She stopped long enough to sit up in bed, continuing, "And a wife had complained about being married to her husband for over twenty years; she'd forgotten the last time they had a meaningful conversation."

"Okay, what does that have to do with what we just listened to?"

"Nothing."

Trent was on the brink of losing it. Slowly, he inhaled deeply through his nostrils and held his breath.

"Can I ask you something?" Sonia queried him.

He darted his eyes at her. "It's obvious you want to talk about something else. What is it?"

"Do you still remember what my favorite food is?" She did not divulge to Trent the same woman complained about her husband not knowing anything about her after all those years of marriage.

"Everything," he answered.

"Come on, answer the question!" she pleaded with him. She even offered him an enticing stare.

"Let's see . . . you like baked chicken. Remember I showed you about adding oregano as a spice when baking chicken?"

She rolled her eyes. "Yeah. Okay. You got that one correct. I've got a couple of more to ask you.

"What is my favorite color?"

"I don't know. You've got a lot of clothes stuffed in both our closets."

"Trent, stop playing. What color do you see more than any other color?"

He scratched his head. "Black?"

"And . . ."

"I don't know."

She sucked her teeth. "Black and gold."

"I missed that, right?"

"Yes you did."

She turned onto her side facing him. "What is my favorite TV show?"

"That should be easy. Lifetime channel."

"That's not funny. Come on, be serious."

Trent chortled. "I am."

"Last question. What's my favorite flower?"

There was a lengthy pause. Again, it took all of Trent not to blow the moment, especially when she had offered him an unobstructed view of her body.

"Roses. Red roses."

"Yes," she said, smiling broadly. "So you have been paying some attention to me."

Looking down at her, Trent stroked her thigh and hip. "Why were all those questions important?"

Initially, Sonia wanted to explain to him that husbands must also regard a wife's input into their marriage. When a husband refuses to do so, it hinders the communication process. It also hinders her willingness to open up to him.

Sensing his impatience, she answered, "It was something important for me to know, okay?"

"I guess. So what about me? Let me ask you those same questions."

Sonia now sat up next to him, and she placed her hands on the bed covers.

"What is my favorite color?" He then puffed out his chest.

"Money."

He rolled his eyes.

"What is my favorite food?"

"Me."

He shrugged his shoulders.

"TV show?"

"*Night Court*."

Sonia could not resist making further retaliation against him. "And favorite position? Any."

"Close," he retorted.

The interaction seemed to invigorate Sonia, so she tried bringing up another topic for discussion. She mentioned, "Did you know that most communication is non-verbal?"

"Okay—"

Trent then entertained a mischievous thought. *Does giving somebody the finger count as being non-verbal communication?* He then chuckled to himself.

"What's so funny?" Sonia inquired.

He shook his head. "Nothing."

Sonia turned over onto her side again facing Trent. "You know, if that is true, how do you know when I'm actually in a good mood?"

"You might have to refresh my memory."

"Why?

"Do I have to answer that one?"

Sonia dismissed Trent's response. "Moving right along, what about when I'm in a bad mood?"

"That's easy." He savored that gift of a question. His face became exceptionally animated, and he began making hand gestures and waving his arms. "The wind blows so hard the trees in the neighbors' yards bend, and the lights begin to blink in here."

She socked him on the shoulder.

"Hey!" he reacted, smarting her stinging punch below the ball of his shoulder.

"You deserved it!"

She turned onto her back. Trent placed his hand on her stomach and stroked it—with her assisting him. Then she led him into her next question, smiling.

"Okay, what about when I'm in the mood?" She shimmied her shoulders and wiggled her hips. Her smile lasted for several moments.

Meanwhile, Trent smirked at another mischievous thought he'd just entertained; there was no doubt he wanted to milk this one for all it was worth. He looked around the room, whistled, and stared at the ceiling. Then he whistled again.

Sonia grew impatient with him. "They're holding tryouts this coming Thursday afternoon at the comedy club. Make sure you're in line!"

"All right, all right," he said, sighing; he turned on to his side and looked at her. "You like to rub up against me, and you like to give me silly, wide-eyed looks. Sometimes you'll text me a sexy picture or message."

"That's pretty good, but you missed one."

He returned a surprised look. "I did?"

She stroked his forearm. "I'd already told you that I was in the mood." She then gave him a light kiss on his chest.

"Huh?"

Sitting up in the bed, Sonia explained, "That just proves my point. How can I allow myself to enjoy anything with you and there's no security in knowing you're really into me?

"I mean, it's a secure feeling when a woman knows her husband's really in tune with her. She knows then that she is the apple of his eye—aren't I?"

Trent was tempted to roll his eyes, but he remained stoic with her.

"Sex becomes an extended form of communication," she continued. "It becomes an expression that is unmistakable."

This was about all that Trent could stand. They had been "talking" for more than ninety minutes, and he felt they'd gotten nowhere.

"What's wrong with for once, you just show up, naked, and tell me that you want us to get it on?" he ranted. "That's unmistakable, too."

"More times than not, a woman would like some romance to go with it."

He began inching away from her. "You want romance? Remind me to stop by a bookstore on the way home, and I'll find you one of those cheesy Harlequin novels you women like reading!" His voice was just short of yelling at her.

Sonia got out of the bed and searched for some bed clothes to wear. From the closet, she said, "Trent, I'm not wasting my time any more with you, because that's all I've been doing."

"Hah! And I have to go through all these hoops just to have the slightest chance at a sniff between your thighs? My name ain't Gumby, damn it. And I shouldn't have to do it!"

Sonia matched Trent's loud tone. "Don't worry about it, Trent. Just keep on doing what you've been doing. Your game's tight. Just like when you had that," she paused and hissed. " . . . that disrespectful, skank of a whore you had sitting on your lap in that picture!"

Trent's lips bunched and his eyebrows moved closer. He also jumped out of bed, yelling, "Why do you keep bringing that up?"

"Because why would you, a married man, take a picture with her in the first place? You've never answered that question." She rolled her neck, establishing her ground with him.

"Then you have the nerve to be gawking at some horse-butt skank in the mall . . . I didn't know you had a thing for those kinds of women—"

Trent was now enraged. Their conversation could be heard in Taylor's room.

"I know how to connect with a woman—"

"Apparently so. Horse butts and skanks!" she interrupted him, now placing her fist at her waist.

"And," he continued, "I emphasize the word 'woman'. I don't relate well with petty children who are always whining and complaining because they don't get their way in a conversation."

She pointed at him. "You better listen good at this: No woman will put up with the mess that I've put up with you. I've been disappointed so many times that I've become numb, Trent. And then you wonder why I don't experience any pleasure with you?

"I've become numb to you disrespecting me. But I tell you this, too: If I can ever prove that you were sleeping around on me, it . . . is . . . over! I'll be at Lexington County courthouse the next morning. And we'll see then who can relate!"

Suddenly, Trent and Sonia were interrupted by Taylor's knocking on their bedroom door.

"Dad, Mom, what's wrong?"

The moment was hardly comparable to in better times when Sonia and Trent would joke about Taylor being B.C., which stood for birth control, because he would interrupt them in the midst of good moment.

"Nothing, Taylor," Sonia yelled back at him. "We had a disagreement and we're about finished. Just go to your room."

Trent assured him as well. "That's right. We're about finished. Everything's all right."

"Okay, I hope so." He made a slow procession back to his room still wondering about his parents.

Trent turned his attention back to Sonia. "I hear there's a man who makes life-size dolls. You can name it anything you want; you can talk to it any way you want; you can do anything you want to and with it; and it can listen to any preacher you want it to listen to. You might want place an order for one."

Sonia laughed with derision. "It just might be the answer to me finally experiencing some pleasure in bed. At least I know it wouldn't disappoint me, which is more than I can say about you!"

"Whatever!"

Waving Sonia off, Trent slipped on some pajamas and stormed off into his work office. He clicked on his computer and began browsing the social networks. He figured that maybe a better connection was out there destined for him.

Chapter 9

'Dinner or Happy Hour?'

UCP's human resources department confirmed that Lance had accepted the position he interviewed for nearly a month ago.

Sonia sent a copy of the e-mail from H.R. to Phyllis. Then she sent an e-mail to Lance welcoming him. She also wrote:

> When you get a chance, stop by my desk and I will introduce you to your new work teammates. Thanks!

About five minutes later, Lance stopped by Sonia's desk. His sudden presence startled her. "I wasn't expecting you so soon."

"I came over here as soon as I could," he said, catching his breath.

She stood up, extended her hand out to him, and welcomed him again to her team.

"Since you're here, I might as well introduce you to every

one. Follow me."

Most of the teams were organized in two rows of six work spaces. Each work space consisted of an office suite desk with file cabinets, a computer, and an overhead storage area; Sonia's team fit within that configuration.

First, she showed him the work space he was assigned—third one on the right. Then she began introducing him to other representatives starting with Tanya, whose desk would be across from his.

"Lance, the person you just heard blow a gasket for the two millionth time is Tanya. She's my most seasoned rep—and most volatile. But I still love her." Sonia winked at Tanya and laughed.

"Ms. Sonia, you didn't tell me that we were getting new people!"

She had a wide-eyed reaction as if she'd just seen her favorite television star paying her a visit. Then sat up in her seat, offering a look as if she was blameless.

"Don't believe ninety percent of what she just said about me. I am a peaceful, loving person who comes here, does her job, and goes back to her home in Swansea. And that's the story I'm sticking to." She blinked her eyes several times for emphasis.

"Lance, she tells that to everyone," Sonia chimed in to say.

"You'll find out soon enough."

"That's right, Lance. You'll find out soon enough just how crazy it is over here. Just wait until you start working claims."

He took Tanya's personality and the warning in stride—what else was he to do?

"I'm sure I'll be asking you a bunch of questions real soon about claims and all the other stuff. Nice meeting you." He extended his hand out to Tanya.

"Yes, nice meeting you, too." She appeared awkward in the

way she shook and released Lance's hand.

Sonia made her way down the aisle introducing Lance to the other representatives. Then they returned to her cubicle. They were in there no more than a half-minute before someone else had interrupted their conversation.

"Excuse me, Sonia . . . Oh, hello there—"

It took all of Sonia not to scold Charlotte for her blatant ploy for attention.

"Charlotte, this is Lance. He's the first of three new permanent hires I have coming on board with us."

"Pleased to meet you," she said, offering a pleasant smile.

Lance's eyes were trained on Charlotte's sensual lips and other attributes. "Yeah, pleased to meet you, too." He adjusted himself in the chair across from Sonia.

Charlotte, who wore a loose fitting dress that allowed much room for the imagination, proceeded to hand Sonia an intracompany mail folder. She took a step backward, enabling her to keep both of them in her range of vision. She also sneaked a peek at his left hand. He wasn't wearing any rings.

"You asked me to drop this off to you today. These are copies of the revised explanation of benefits statements your rep will need to send to that doctor's office up in Rock Hill."

It was 4:25 p.m.; Charlotte was not scheduled to leave until 5:30.

"Thank you, Charlotte." Sonia replied, expecting that she would pick up on the tone of her voice.

She promptly left, but not without a display of at least forty ounces of bounce in her walk. Lance happened to catch a view of it in the reflection of the Plexiglas that enclosed all team supervisors' cubicles.

Not surprisingly, Lance found himself half-listening to Sonia while she went ahead detailing to him about his actual shift and a brief checklist of administrative tasks to be completed.

* * *

It was common practice that supervisors, upper management, and other designated individuals eavesdropped on the calls that came through contract services for evaluation and training purposes.

Periodically, Sonia entertained herself by listening to some of Lance's calls even when she was not required to do so. She found herself mesmerized by his smooth tenor and his ease of getting along with people.

"*I thank you for the compliment*," a female from a medical billing office said; her voice was firm with him. "*But I've got work to do and money to account for. So you better be on your 'A' game today.*"

"*Yes, Ms. Margaret. I can tell in your voice you're on a mission today. But may I still ask how are you doing?*"

"*Lance, how long have you been working there?*" she asked.

"*Oh, about two months since I've been working over here and it's been almost six months all together.*"

"*I wouldn't say this unless I mean it. You're becoming one of my favorite reps to work with.*" It was quite apparent to Sonia that Lance's caller was being charmed out of her wits. It was enough to make Sonia almost erupt into laughter, but it also increased her curiosity about him.

"*Thank you. And you're one of my favorite callers I talk with on a regular basis.*"

Very subtly, Sonia walked over to Lance's work space and suggested that he logged off at his earliest opportunity. "I've got some material I need to go over with you."

Lance joined her at her cubicle moments later. He let out a loud sigh of relief after she invited him to sit down. "Actually, I'm glad to get away from those phone calls today." He described to her how vicious some of the callers were with him.

"It's all in how you handle it most of the time," she explained. "When they sense a phone rep is new and not as confident, they'll exploit it."

Sonia had already warned Lance that it might take him as many as six months after he completed claims training before he'd have a clue about what he was doing. Until then his calls might take twice, even three times longer than when he was a temp.

"Even then," she added, "it might be another two or three months before you really begin meeting all of the department's goals for phone reps on a consistent basis."

"I'll take your word for it." He shook his head in amazement. "And you say that you started out here doing exactly what I'm doing?"

"I sure did. I answered phones at a desk like yours for nearly two years, and there were many days I felt the same way you're feeling." She then maintained eye contact with him as if to test him.

The leopard print dress she wore did not reveal any cleavage, but her fullness was more than enough that he tried visualizing what she possessed beneath it. She ignored his wandering eyes between responses.

"There's a long, steep learning curve for your position," she said. "But you're doing fine—about as well as we might expect of you at this point."

The closeness of interaction gave Sonia another lasting mental, visual, and audio image of him. And since things at home with Trent had soured in recent months, those images of Lance were fast filling a fantasy void. Nor did she really care knowing her most private thoughts were consumed over somebody who was about twelve years younger than she. About forty-five minutes later, Lance found himself having difficulty with another claims call. His was first inclined to visit Sonia's cubicle, and perhaps for another mild thrill. But two people were ahead of him waiting to speak with her.

One of the phone reps, Staci Longwell, suggested that he go over to Vicki's cubicle. There was someone already there, and that individual, Alvantrae, had been there a while.

Lance was now in scramble mode, but he caught a break. "Do you need any help?" a female's voice asked from behind him.

He looked over his shoulder. Charlotte happened to be walking toward him. The smile that appeared on his face was one of great relief.

"I sure do."

He explained a doctor had filed an appeal and she wanted an update. He had searched two screens that he was familiar with, but there appeared to be no additional information available.

"Follow me," she said; the view from behind was much to his liking.

At her desk, she went through screens with blinding speed compared to how he'd been operating. She told him what call-up commands he needed to use.

"You might want to check back with your caller first before I'm finished here with you," she suggested; she also reminded him of UCP's stated goal of not leaving callers on hold for longer than three minutes without checking back with them.

"Sure."

He was quick with his return. "I really appreciate your help."

"As long as I'm available, stop by," she replied before she continued with showing him exactly what to look for on the screens she accessed for him.

He thanked her again.

Sensing this was as good an opportunity as any, Charlotte

grabbed a stack of sticker note sheets and wrote the words "CALL ME" on it along with her cell phone number. She then pushed the sheet off to the side and stared at him.

Lance coolly acknowledged her with a nod, picked up the sheet, and returned to his caller. After the call, he text messaged Charlotte to establish his name with the number.

He then sent another message.

Dinner or happy hour?

She responded just as fast.

Both :)

A few more exchanges of text messages confirmed that they would meet at 6 p.m. at the bar and restaurant inside the Double Tree hotel, which was across the I-20 freeway from where they worked.

During their exchange of messages, she found out that he was twenty-seven, single, with no children and he had been checking her out from a distance ever since he was assigned to Sonia's team.

He found out that she was thirty-one and she had broken up with her boyfriend about three weeks ago; she had no children. She did not divulge in any of her text messages that she had been checking him out, but he began piecing together moments that suggested she might have been all along.

Lance was far from giddy about going out with Charlotte, yet it was better than going back to his apartment in West Columbia. He mused to himself how he worked in a building with hundreds, maybe even a couple of thousand people, and he had never bothered to socialize with anybody until now.

Then again, he wondered how many others had Charlotte approached. But he convinced himself that all he had to do was look around. The answer was quite simple.

* * *

"Yay for happy hour!" Charlotte exalted while she waited for Lance to park his silver Hyundai Sonata next to her jade Toyota Corolla.

They paired up and walked at a brisk pace over to the hotel. The last of spring time still clung uncharacteristically onto the Columbia area, although it was now early June.

"This is the first time I've gone out with anybody since I've been in Columbia," he told Charlotte.

"I don't believe you!"

"It's true. Working in that building can be very tiring mentally.

I can't tell you how many times I've crashed in my bed once I got home."

"That job will do it to you, but you didn't answer my question about this being the first time you've gone out—"

Lance opened the door for Charlotte and they went directly to the hotel's bar. "What would you have to drink? It's on me." He cut a quick glace at her.

"Since you're buying, I'll go easy on you and have a glass of white wine."

They sat down at one of the tables instead of the bar. There, Lance figured he would take in as much of a view of Charlotte as he could. After some small talk, he went over to the bar and brought back their drinks.

"Thank you," she said, clicking her glass to his shot glass of Jack 'n Coke.

"No, thank you for agreeing to meet me here."

Charlotte shared with Lance that she was originally from Durham, North Carolina, and she came to the Columbia area to attend college. She did not finish her degree in computer science, but she decided to stay rather than return home.

"So that explains why you have such a knack for that system at work," Lance observed. "Have you considered a job in their IT department?"

She shrugged her shoulders. "Of course I have, but I need that piece of paper before they'll consider me."

"Have you thought about going back to school and finishing?"

"I have, but I also like making money." She took a sip from her glass and crossed her legs. "And what about you? What brought you to Columbia; you don't sound like you're from around here—"

He sat back in his chair and straightened out his legs. "I'm trying to start all over again." He offered a nonchalant expression.

"Because?"

"It's not a long story, but I'm from Washington, D.C.; born, raised, and went to school there. After graduating, I met a woman who was from South Carolina, and I followed her here. She was from Charleston."

"Did you get married?"

He shook his head. "I got stranded, somewhat."

"How does someone like you," she said, looking him over with admiration, "get stranded?"

"I get here, I began looking for work, but she already had plans. It turned out her plans were with another man, a childhood sweetheart of hers. I had to move out and start all over again."

"Oh, so you got played?"

"Yeah, I guess you can say that." He sucked down the last of his drink. "I've liked it here in this state despite what happened. I managed to string together some temporary jobs after moving to Columbia. And now I've got this permanent gig. I guess somebody's been looking out for me."

"So tell me, you say you've not been out with anyone since you've been here in Columbia?" she asked again. "And how long that's been?"

"Almost eight months."

She licked her lips and smiled. She shifted crossing her legs again. "I still don't believe you."

"What would you rather me say?" he reacted.

"Does it really matter?"

"I guess not."

Lance recognized he'd better move on to another topic—fast. He sat up and leaned forward upon his forearms.

"That was a pretty cool move you made today at work," he said, casting an alluring stare at her. "I might have to try that myself."

She chortled. "That is not an original, but timing is everything."

"Just like all those times you've come down our aisle standing right next to me while you chatted with Tanya? Or when I've been at Ms. Sonia's desk, you've had something for her?"

She sipped the last of the glass of wine she'd been nursing now for more than a half-hour. "I won't confirm or deny anything you've said."

"I thought so."

"Don't go around assuming anything—"

"No, I won't. You've made sure that I've seen plenty of it already." He lurched over to the side, looking past her.

Charlotte was moved to laughter. "I have what I have. And I've never had any complaints so far."

"And you won't with me." He returned the same gesture of

smiling and licking his lips. "Would you like to continue this conversation somewhere else?"

"Where did you have in mind?"

He rocked his head slowly, contemplating a few places. "Well, since I'm not entirely familiar with Columbia, we can go somewhere for dinner, or maybe even—"

"What, where?"

He sensed the attraction between them was growing stronger. Her eyes told him so, and so did her other mannerisms. He was more than certain that he'd transmitted similar messages to her.

"We'll see after dinner, okay?"

After dinner at Outback in the Harbison area, they agreed to get a room at a Hampton Inn just farther down the road on Harbison Boulevard.

"Yes, I want to see how far this goes," Charlotte told him.

"I like how it's gone so far, too. Come on, let's make that move."

They stopped at her car where he gave her a hug and a peck on her cheek. Then he confided in her that he had sex on a first date only on a couple of occasions; that included the woman who stranded him in Charleston.

"As it stands, I'm fifty-fifty. One turned out to be a nice relationship; the other turned out to be a disaster," he said. "I'm at your mercy."

She traced a light trail of his bottom lip and chin with her index finger.

"I'm just like the insurance commercial. I'm on your side—good, that is."

Once inside the room, Lance led Charlotte by the hand over to the bed. He guided her to sit down on his lap. She wrapped her arms around his neck; they indulged in a long, searching tongue kiss.

Lance closed his eyes and savored the definitive ice breaker. He opened them and led her into the next kiss along with a tight embrace.

Upon separating, he queried, "Are you concerned that somebody at work might find out about us?"

She sucked her teeth. "Humph, I've been there five years and I've not gone out with another male employee until today. So I can assure you that I'm not one for broadcasting my business."

"You don't have to worry about me. You're the only person in that building I've shared much of anything about myself."

"For some reason, I believe you."

"You should." He explained that he'd already learned, one way or another, it's much easier to be forthright with the truth when it comes to women. "At least then that's one less thing a woman would have to dislike about me."

She returned a side-eyed stare at him while removing her bra and panties, revealing a well-proportioned body. "All right now, don't get strange on me."

He laughed. "Freaky, yes. Kinky, maybe. Strange, I don't think so." He then stood up and began removing his slacks, Polo shirt, and bikini briefs.

Charlotte was incredulous. She nestled her head onto his chest and began kissing and nibbling at his nipples. He stroked and caressed her everywhere he could.

"Come on, let's take a shower."

"I didn't bring anything."

"Neither did I, remember?"

"You do have a point there," she commented. "Well, in that case, why not?"

Both took turns soaping each other down. Between washing each other's backs, they nuzzled up under the flow of shower water and exchanged several passionate kisses.

She was the first to come up for air. "Your body feels so good against mine." She then turned around and bent over against the shower wall for him. "How about right here?"

They both moaned as their bodies entered into a lustful dance in the shower. Desiring for more, Lance suggested that they continued in the bed. They did not even bother to towel each other dry. Rather, they placed the towels beneath them.

"As you can tell, I believe in letting a man know if I like him and want him," Charlotte whispered to Lance as he mounted her. "That's my way of sharing truth with him."

"I never would have imagined ending my day in bed with you. But it's all good. Definitely all good." His pathway inside her was met by maximum arousal and minimum resistance to his strokes.

"Mmmm, yesssss." She worked her hips to meet his steady, rhythmic thrusts. "So good that I can't hold back any longer!"

"Already?"

"Uh-huh," she replied, gasping. "Already. Oh, god! Hold me, baby. Hold me—"

She bit into his chest as her body tingled and tensed. Lance felt invigorated and emboldened by her sweet moment of release. He even encouraged her to bite his chest again if she felt like doing it.

"I didn't want you to think I'm a wild woman," she said, looking up at him; her face still reflected the afterglow of her moment.

"It's all right with me," he assured her. "A woman's bite mark is a signature of the passion she expresses to a man."

"Well, if that's the case, you'll be leaving here black and blue tonight."

"Do your thing, baby. Do your thing!"

* * *

Lance and Charlotte left the Hampton Inn around eleven o'clock. Both appeared giddy beyond description, and they were reluctant to depart from each other's company. So they chatted on their cell phones until they reached their respective apartments.

"Have you already thought about how you might react when seeing me in the morning?" she asked.

"I have an idea," he answered. "I just hope I'm sitting down when I do see you."

They both laughed. Then they gave each other a kiss into their phones before hanging up.

Chapter 10

'It's Nobody's Business'

Now that it happened, showing up the next day wearing dark shades and avoiding each other would not make any sense.

Lance and Charlotte agreed while chatting on their cell phones driving to work that they would simply be themselves, although it would be tempting to find out if anybody might notice anything different about them.

"It's nobody's business who I'm screwing," she said. "Humph, and quite frankly, I don't really care what any of them would think if they found out."

Lance added, "Hey, no disagreement from me. Stuff like this happens all the time, right?"

"That's right."

Even so, Charlotte knew that management never hung out or even ate lunch with the phone reps—at least not in the workplace—and very few friendships were known to exist between management and the phone reps.

She also knew that UCP was not the kind of place where

many secrets were kept. This was a place that encouraged a culture of backstabbing and turning people in for the most frivolous of workplace offenses.

"Lance, if I were to suggest anything to you from this point forward, watch your back," she warned him. "There are a lot of snakes and piranhas off in that building."

He was not surprised by that comment. "An uncle once told me a wise man is the one who keeps his mouth shut. That's because nobody knows what he's thinking."

"Sounds good to me." Charlotte then announced that she had just turned into the parking lot at work. "How far are you from here?"

"Not too far. I just got off the freeway at the Bush River Road exit."

She spoke in a sultry voice. "Okay, well, I'm sure I'll be seeing you at some point today—"

"I'm sure you will."

There was an afterglow still on Charlotte's face from the night before. She was determined not to allow anything or anyone diminish it.

Perhaps she may have over done it, though, because it caught Vicki's attention as they passed by each other.

"Are you all right?" Vicki inquired.

"I'm fine."

Vicki stopped, turned around, and followed Charlotte over to her cubicle.

"Are you sure?" she asked before taking another sip from her cup of coffee.

Charlotte began sorting through the stack of work that she left from the previous day. "Yes, Vicki. I'm fine. Is there anything wrong with you?" She gave her matter-of-fact stare.

Seemingly convinced, Vicki started walking off.

"Hey, come back here!" Charlotte whispered loudly to her.

Vicki walked cautiously back to Charlotte's cubicle. She was even more curious once Charlotte revealed a sneaky grin to her.

"I know that look," Vicki said, eager for the next bit of gossip.

Charlotte peeked out from her cubicle before she answered. "You should have seen how defensive Sonia was yesterday when I happened to have stopped by her desk."

"That doesn't sound like Sonia, but go ahead—"

"It might if you'd listen," Charlotte retorted; she now sat up in her office chair. "Lance was there, and . . ."

"He was?" Vicki rushed to take another sip from her coffee. Problem was that she almost choked on it. "Not Sonia. Uh-huh."

"Yes, Sonia. I had to drop off an envelope for her, and she rushed me off, saying, 'Thank you.'" Charlotte rolled her eyes and wiggled in her seat, as if to mimic Sonia. "I know when a woman's up to something, and she was. Sonia may be quiet and calculating, but she can't fool me."

Vicki contemplated Charlotte's criticism of Sonia, but then she turned dismissive of it. "I mean, I know he's fine and all. But I do know how to be discreet especially in a place like this."

"Hey, sometimes a woman can't help herself," Charlotte said. "And there's no telling why, right?"

"Well, to tell you the truth, I'd probably be the same way. I wouldn't want tricks like you trying to beat me to the punch, if I knew I had a chance."

Charlotte looked Vicki up and down before she responded. "Both of you are married, so I don't really understand that comment. I guess that means married women aren't any different."

"Eventually, the newness is going to wear off and you're going to say to yourself he's just another sexy, fine man in here." Vicki became incredulous at that thought, shaking her head.

"Mmmph! I'm sorry. If her situation is like mine, I guess I would have to find out something."

A flashback from the night before just occurred. Lance gazing into Charlotte's eyes, telling her that she was the sexiest and most passionate woman he'd ever met. Him with his head nestled between her thighs causing her to writhe and grasp at anything on the bed.

Instinctively, Charlotte made herself appear even busier at her desk as a way of hiding her own mischief.

Just be yourself, she reminded herself.

"I would not be surprised if he and Sonia already have something going on," she said while browsing through her e-mails.

"I'm telling you, the quiet ones are the most dangerous. And Sonia is one of those quiet ones. "

"Sonia, quiet? Humph, as much as I'd like to agree with you, Sonia can be loud when she wants; it just isn't often," Vicki argued. "Even if it is true, is it really any of our business?"

And with that, Vicki finished off her cup of coffee and tossed it in the trash container next to Charlotte's desk. There was no further exchange between them.

* * *

Charlotte did not think twice about what she would do next. She ventured over to Sonia's cubicle, inviting herself to sit in the other chair adjacent to her colleague.

Meanwhile, Sonia was in the midst of running reports from the previous day. The information was used toward evaluating the phone reps' daily performance. If left uninterrupted, it would take about a half-hour to complete.

"I'm almost finished, if you can wait," Sonia said. "I should have done this before I went to lunch."

"Not a problem." Charlotte leaned back in the seat and exhaled loudly.

Sonia mumbled silently about the rate her team was managing its unresolved phone inquiries might lead to them working a Saturday morning to catch up. That was not something she looked forward to doing, she added.

Then she turned to Charlotte. "Okay, finished with that. You must not be as busy as me?"

Charlotte rolled her eyes. "Oh, I'm busy. I just decided to get away from it for a couple of minutes. Besides, I had something I wanted to tell you."

She shifted her eyes to her left and right. Then she sneaked a glance out into the aisle where Lance worked. He appeared to be engaged in a phone call.

"And what might that be?" Sonia replied.

Charlotte attempted to show contrition. She lowered her voice to just above a whisper. "I wanted to apologize to you about yesterday."

"You're talking about the way you tried getting what's his face's attention?" Sonia had cut a menacing glare at her.

"Yes, I'm talking about that. I shouldn't have done it. I could have waited another half-hour to give you that envelope."

"I'm glad you recognized it."

Charlotte nodded, but inwardly she wanted to double over in laughter. She then shifted her weight in the chair. "It was on my mind, so I thought it was only right that I came by and shared it with you."

Sonia was matter-of-fact with her. "Apology accepted. Anything else?" She returned to completing her reports that she needed to e-mail individually to her reps before the end of the day.

"Humph, aren't we offended?"

Sonia never flinched at Charlotte's sarcasm. "Not in the least bit."

Just as Charlotte stood up, she spotted Lance striding up the aisle and rounding the corner for Sonia's cubicle. Their eyes met; she was frozen in time. He managed to cast a seductive, but subtle gaze at her. She blinked her eyes in acknowledgment. In that exchange, the tension between them was so strong that if it was gaseous, the explosion would have knocked Sonia out of her chair.

Chapter 11

〰️

'I Wasn't Expecting This'

T rent continued with his phone conversation once he recognized the woman who walked into his branch. He was deadpan with his thought.

Humph, another one in his harem.

Feeling obligated, he ended the conversation, arose from his desk and greeted her. He knew exactly what to say. "He's with some people right now. But is there anything I can help you with?"

"No, thank you. I'll wait."

It had been a little over a month since Deloria Lovett last appeared in the St. Andrews branch. Although she was brusque with Trent once again, he dismissed it as merely her way of keeping others out of her business; it was hardly effective.

Cortez had long since confided in Trent that she was a married woman who freely spent her husband's money. According to Cortez, her marriage with local businessman Primas Lovett, owner of a dozen long-term care facilities throughout the Carolinas, had evolved into one out of convenience.

She was in her late forties, well-kept in her appearance and stylish in the way she dressed. She was not gaudy with the jewelry she wore, and outside in the parking lot was a gold Lexus RX 350 luxury crossover with a personalized license plate, MZWOMAN.

Cortez happened to glance out of his office while his customers were signing off on the IRAs and annuities they had opened with the bank. He and Deloria acknowledged each other in their eye contact.

"Well, that should do it, Mr. and Mrs. Reilly. We certainly appreciate the opportunity to serve you," he said, flashing a wide grin; he also shook hands with them after they stood up in his office.

"Here is another of my cards. Please contact me if you have any additional questions. We are here for you."

After Cortez walked the Reillys to the front door, his expression changed from jovial to stone faced. He was rarely seen this way with any of the women who visited him.

"What is your problem?" He spoke loud enough that only she heard him.

Deloria glared at him. Not wanting to make a scene of things, Cortez gestured for her to follow him into his office; he left the door open.

"You know why I'm here," she said. "What I don't understand is why all of a sudden?"

Cortez leaned forward upon his desk, placing his weight on his forearm. "I told you last night that I've gone on, and you should understand that."

"So, you've fired me?" Her expression was of total disbelief.

He shook his head. "It's more like I resigned." He did not tell her he was now involved with another woman.

"You could have at least called me." She pulled her cell

phone out of her purse and put it in his face. "All I got was a text message in which you beat around the bush saying that you decided to move on."

The more Deloria talked the more Cortez realized just how bad of a risk he took involving himself with her. They met at a party in March 2011.

She pursued him the entire time until he finally agreed to accept her phone number. She did not hide from him that she was married. In fact, she boasted that she and her husband was a sexless couple and it had been that way for nearly eight years.

"Do you call it mature that you've come here on my job to complain about it?" he retorted.

"Cortez, I liked everything about you. A professional working man. A gentleman with me when we were together. Passionate and freaky in the bed . . . You seemed to have your act together, and you carried no drama."

"I thought all this time there was no drama with you," he countered. "Apparently, I was wrong."

She returned a vicious, hard glare at him.

"I really feel like a fool. I wasn't expecting this. I thought there was more to what we had together," she said. "I chose to be solely yours, and yours only—now look at me!"

Cortez remained silent. In fact, he stared beyond her out into the bank lobby hoping that somebody—anybody—would interrupt them.

What he did not tell Deloria was that he'd grown weary of their incompatibility. He realized each time she opened her mouth there was nothing that intrigued him. If he were to remove sex and the $10,000 personal loan she took out eight months ago, she would be doubly insignificant to him.

"Deloria, I don't appreciate you coming here with this," he said. "I wish that you would be mature about it and leave. I don't think you would appreciate if I came on your job with the same drama?"

Deloria nodded. "You're right. I wouldn't want that kind of drama at my job. But I don't work, and I don't have to work!"

"It really doesn't matter what you say." He leaned back in his chair and folded his arms. "I can't believe I allowed myself to get caught up in something like this. This was a complete waste of my time."

"Are you saying I was never worth your time?" Deloria reacted, leaning forward in her chair. She looked herself over, as if to inspect herself.

"You can take that any way you want."

"Are you saying I was never worth your time?" She repeated in a slow and deliberate tone, hoping that he realized the mistake he was making.

Peeved, he leaned forward and mocked her tone. "Yeah, I said it. A complete waste of my time." Then he stared at Deloria, daring her to respond.

She reached into her handbag and folded her arms while holding a 9 mm Glock pistol. Cortez did not panic; he tried reasoning with her—fast.

"Now, one of maybe three things is going to happen. You're going to shoot me with that," he said, eying the gun she hid under her left arm. "Somehow, I might take it from you and end up shooting you with it.

"Or, you're going to put that back in your handbag and quietly leave. And I promise you that I would never say anything ever about it."

She began rocking back and forth in the chair.

There was another option that he considered. He could trip the bank's silent alarm at his desk, and he'd hope the police would respond to it in a matter of minutes, if not seconds. The branch was in an area where both the Richland and Lexington county sheriff departments frequented.

He tried reasoning with her again. "Deloria, I apologize for not communicating to you in a way that would have avoided the way you're feeling today."

"Cortez, you messed with my emotions, and I warned you about that early on never to do that! I told you that my husband and I were no longer active together, and he doesn't care about me—"

With her non-trigger hand, she paused to brush her hair to the side. "And to think, I trusted you with my money and credit makes it even worse," she continued.

"Listen, I didn't do anything wrong. You told me you only wanted me for sex, and later we wound up doing business together," Cortez rebutted. "You could have done it with anyone."

"But I came to you." She was increasingly agitated with him. "That should have let you know how serious I was—I can't believe I was falling for you!"

Cortez felt he was running out of options. He was poised to trip the bank's alarm; he elected to reason with her a final time.

"Deloria, this doesn't have to happen. I think it will be in everyone's best interests if you would put that back in your purse," he said calmly. "Nothing happens to you, and nothing happens to me or possibly anyone in here."

She shook her head. "Apparently, we have a misunderstanding here. You failed to understand that you don't mess with a woman's emotions. I don't like being made a fool!" She spoke loud enough that it caught Trent's attention.

Curious, he made a casual pass by Trent's office. He also heard what she said next.

"You're lucky you didn't meet me ten years ago, or I would have already shot you with this gun—"

Quietly, Trent walked beyond Cortez's office and pulled the bank's security guard to the side. He whispered to him to go outside and contact Lexington County sheriff's department and direct customers away from coming inside.

Afterward, he tipped across the lobby to the tellers, pulling aside Ms. Wanda. He instructed her to direct the tellers quietly into the break room. There was a doorway to it behind the teller's counter. He told her he would be near the front door waiting for the police.

* * *

"Deloria, you know what?" Cortez posed. "I'm probably better off a dead man, anyway."

"You're right."

She aimed the gun at him, holding it with both hands. Cortez never flinched.

"Deloria, I'm asking you to put that down."

She shook her head. "I can't."

At that moment, a Lexington County officer entered the bank, with his gun drawn, and eased his way to alongside of Cortez's office.

Deloria was within aim. Once he caught a glimpse of the gun, the officer yelled, "Put the weapon down!"

Immediately, Cortez ducked to his right onto the floor. Deloria reacted nervously and squeezed the trigger; the bullet lodged into the wall behind his desk. The officer fired his gun. He did not miss. A bullet pierced her neck, and her body toppled over to the left.

"Stay down!" the back-up officer yelled to Cortez as he rushed inside the office.

The officer who fired the shot checked Deloria for any movement. Then he checked her pulse; it was quickly fading. Her eyes were partially open and a small trickle of blood trailed out her mouth. He looked at his partner and shook his head. He left the room and requested for an ambulance.

The other officer instructed for Cortez to slowly get up and leave his office. Things happened so fast that it did not dawn upon him until he was in the lobby that Deloria was probably dead.

"Aw man!" He buried his head into his hand and slowly sat down on one of the sofas. He was numb, stupefied. Yet he was right about one thing. This did not have to happen, he mouthed to himself.

Trent sprinted inside the bank. His next move was checking on his staff which had been in the break room nearly forty-five minutes.

"What happened out there?" Ms. Wanda asked nervously. "I heard a couple of gun shots."

"I was outside in the parking lot after the police came in," Trent explained. "But I do know the woman who came in to see Cortez had a gun and she threatened to shoot him in his office."

"Oh, my god!" one of the tellers yelled; she began shaking and sobbing.

"We all could have been shot. Who knows?" another teller reacted.

"I've never been in anything like this before," Trent said. "I'm just glad, as a branch manager, that none of my people were hurt or harmed."

Whew!

"Have you talked to Cortez?" Ms. Wanda asked.

"No, I haven't. I came straight over here. I better check on him. He didn't look too well."

Trent led his tellers out of the bank amid the police completing their follow-up work. Then he went back inside for Cortez, who was being questioned by a Lexington County officer; he was hunched over, sitting on his hands, and rocking back and forth.

"Do you have any idea why she came in here with a gun?" the officer asked.

Cortez looked up at the officer. "Humph, she was mad at me I ended an affair we had."

"You mean to tell me that she came up here to confront you about breaking up with her?"

He whispered, "Yeah." Then he rubbed his eyes. "I'm surprised I didn't panic. I tried talking to her, but she was dead set on shooting me."

Shaking his head, he added, "I was that close to being a dead man. That close. . . ."

Trent now joined Cortez on the sofa next to him. He leaned over and patted him on the shoulder.

"That was close, man," Cortez repeated himself.

"I know," Trent answered. "I knew something might be up when you left the door open because you never leave your door open when you have a woman you know inside your office."

"Is that right?" the officer asked.

Trent nodded. "She came here looking a bit annoyed and preoccupied asking for Cortez. I didn't think anything about it at first because she's come here many times like that. When she'd see Cortez, everything seemed to be fine. Apparently, it wasn't this time."

The officer asked, "Which one of you contacted us?"

"I had our security guard call once I realized what was happening," Trent explained.

"Do both of you realize that this could have been a lot worse? She could have used him as a hostage. There could have been a standoff in here. She could have shot him then herself. Anything—"

"We understand that," Trent answered. "Somebody was on our side today."

* * *

A pair of EMS workers walked past them with a gurney. Within minutes, they left the bank without any urgency with Deloria's covered body.

Trent and Cortez eventually went outside and they were besieged by their colleagues. Silently, they all huddled together. It was as if they all let out a collective sigh of relief.

"We're just glad you're okay, Cortez," one of the tellers said. I hope never to go through anything like that again!"

"I know what you're saying." He seemed contrite but also embarrassed.

"Yeah, we've seen all those women come inside for you, one by one," Ms. Wanda said; her voice had a maternal tone to it. "Hopefully, that will all change."

"I think it will."

"You think? How 'bout it better!"

He merely nodded in acknowledgement.

Unbeknownst to Trent's bank crew, two satellite dish-equipped television trucks turned into the parking lot. A reporter from the city's lone daily newspaper also arrived. The camera crews quickly set up for live remote broadcasts.

Meanwhile, reporters milled around asking questions with the police and others standing in the parking lot. Eventually, they made their way over to Trent and the rest of the bank crew.

"What was it like while all this occurred? Was there any panic or concern for your own lives?" asked Martine Day, who was from the NBC affiliate WCAE-TV.

Talise Knighton, who was from the CBS affiliate WMDL-

TV, also tried questioning them.

"Mr. Buckner, we understand that you were the one who called Lexington County sheriffs. What prompted you to make that decision?"

Trent finally spoke up. "A situation occurred here this morning, but we have no further comment. It's company policy that we refer all questions from the media to our local banking center's corporate communications department."

Chapter 12

'Reach Me from Within'

The decision was made to allow Trent's staff a couple of hours to regroup and collect themselves emotionally before the bank's re-opening at three o'clock.

All of the tellers except for Ms. Wanda elected to hang out together at the mall. She chose to visit her mother who was an assisted-living resident near the Harbison area.

Trent insisted that he spent time with Cortez, who did not refuse.

They agreed on driving to a Fatz restaurant in Irmo. It was less than five minutes from the Columbiana Mall and about ten minutes from the bank. They arrived there at the peak of the lunch rush.

"We go way back, don't we?" Trent said, while they waited for a server.

The young lady who informed them she was their server directed them to a row of booths next to the bar. They still had full view of the television just above them; neither was in any mood for it.

"You know from the beginning I would tell you about some of the women I'd be with," Cortez recalled.

Trent quipped, "That would be a lot of them."

"As if you're going to say you've not been with your share of women?" Cortez managed a weak laugh.

"Seriously," he continued, "I've always prided myself on being selective when it comes to women. I know it may not seem that way, but it helps once they do business with me. Then I get to see them for who they really are."

"I don't, and I will not, judge you for that."

Trent mentioned to the waitress he would have a basket of their poppy seed rolls, a steak and ribs combo platter and a Heineken. Cortez, who claimed he was not hungry, still ordered a margarita, grilled Calabash chicken platter with barbecue sauce, and double the fries.

"I do have a problem with I how I went along with you having that flow of women coming to see you at the bank," Trent continued with Cortez. "All I was willing to think about was how much money I saw coming. I figured that you would be able to handle your business."

Cortez took a sip from his margarita. "Well, look where it's gotten me?" He looked around, pondering the thought; he became terrified.

"There's no telling how this is going to turn out. Columbia is not a large place, you know . . . Have you already forgotten this woman was married?"

Mmmph!

Trent nodded. "You should have thought about that all along. Now we've got a potentially bigger situation on our hands." He pointed at Cortez as if to make a suggestion. "We may need to re-assign you to another branch— anywhere but Columbia."

"Now you see where I'm going with this!"

Cortez rambled about the police may have taken Deloria to the hospital where it was likely her death was confirmed. But someone also had to also identify her body.

"She had a couple of sons, too. I think both were adults, in their early twenties. But it's that husband I'm most concerned about." He put his hand up to his mouth as if he were strategizing his next move.

"I may have laughed a lot to myself when I thought about how I was the one doing his wife and she bragged about how good it was to her. But it's no longer a laughing matter. You just never know who knows who—"

Trent suggested that they hurried up eating. More importantly, he decided that Cortez would not to return to the bank for the remainder of the day.

"I'll need to speak with corporate when I get back. Yeah, that's exactly what I'll need to do."

"How am I going to get home today, man? I've got only one car, that Mustang GT," Cortez complained. "So you expect me to take a cab home?"

"I wouldn't do that to you. I'll drop you off at your place, and I'll bring the rest of your stuff home later this evening. I'll also put a sign in your car as if it's being put up for sale until tomorrow. We'll take care of it then, okay?"

Cortez went along with Trent's suggestion. He offered him a fist bump. "Thanks, man. How much more am I going to owe you after today?"

"I'll give you an invoice at the end of the week. How about that?"

On their way to Cortez's home in nearby Lexington, he confided in Trent that he often sought a woman's validation. He said while growing up on Lady's Island in the coastal city of Beaufort, South Carolina, he recognized that his mother never reinforced words like she loved him or that she was truly proud of him in any of his childhood activities.

"So it really meant a lot when a female would say she liked me, or she thought I was talented in the things that I did in high school like basketball and football," he said. "I'm now realizing I had to keep hearing things like that."

"They say a mother's love is important," Trent observed; he related about his childhood in Slidell, Louisiana.

"I'm so glad my mother was the type of woman that she was. She always told me that mama will always be your best friend, no matter what. I've never doubted that she loved me."

Trent became silent. He always cherished the closeness of the relationship he shared with Melinda Hightower especially after she divorced his father, Darrow Buckner, while he was in elementary school.

"Man, it just hit me how profound of a statement she always shared with me—"

"I wish I had that. My mother died after I finished college. We never were that close." Cortez spoke with much sobriety in his voice. "I would have been nice."

According to his observations, Cortez believed women liked men who paid special attention to them. "As a man, I noticed they're more willing to open up to a man when he does things like that. And at least for me, in doing so, they made me feel validated."

"Sounds a little twisted, but you've definitely had a way with women," Trent commented.

"No it isn't," Cortez argued; he then shifted in the passenger seat. "A woman likes feeling cherished and loved. That validates her. It may just be my opinion, and my opinion only, a man likes feeling respected and appreciated. That validates the man."

Trent joked with Cortez he sounded like his own counselor. "But you still have a problem on your hands. The question is how do you better deal with this 'validation' problem from this point onward?"

"I don't know."

They had just driven past Lake Murray along Highway 6 in Lexington. Cortez's neighborhood was a couple of stoplights away. Trent's curiosity got the best of him.

"What was so different about this woman?" he queried Cortez.

"Which woman?"

"Hey, we're only talking about one right now."

Cortez cleared his throat. "Oh, her? Oddly enough, nothing. Maybe it was because she pursued me the way she did. She refused to be denied. She said all the sexy, freaky things I also like hearing from a woman. It played in my mind, and it gave me a kind of validation that I've been telling you about."

Trent felt inclined to lecture more about the need to find some resolution with his hunger for a woman's validation in his life.

The boss in him, however, could not get past the reality a woman came into the place of his responsibility wanting to retaliate against one of his employees. Some of this could have been avoided.

"I don't know what happened while she was in there. I do know that a woman doesn't come on a man's job the way she did unless he's done her scandalously wrong, and she's looking to make a statement," he said.

Cortez pointed to his neighborhood. "Hey, go two houses down on your left. I'm at the one where the State College flag's hanging."

"As I was saying," Trent continued, "there has to be more to this."

He turned and faced Cortez, expecting an answer.

"I'm telling you, man. There's nothing more to it!" Cortez replied, sighing at the thought. "Maybe I went along with things longer than I should, but I didn't play any games with her. I really didn't."

Trent continued staring at Cortez.

"What is it you want me to say? That I promised her something I didn't keep?" He leaned against the passenger door, staring back at Trent. "I don't operate like that.

"The truth is that I realized she had nothing to offer or add to my life. I'm forty-one years old just like you. I still like being Bishop Moneymaker, as you call me. But you can't fault me for wanting a little more quality."

"Like the woman whose name I can't pronounce?" Even Trent recognized there was a marked difference in the two women's demeanors and mannerisms.

Cortez nodded in agreement. "Yeah, like that. Now that's a woman!" He was clearly emphatic about describing Alcione.

"All right, I've got to get back to the bank. But take care of yourself. Hopefully, we won't have to put you into any witness protection program."

* * *

Trent decided on popping in a Stephanie Mills CD. Fittingly enough, the song "Home" blared inside his car, and her strong voice and delivery took him on a mental journey to a place where he longed to be.

Now if only his home could be enhanced by a loving and sensitive interaction with Sonia. The coldness between them had gone too long.

He mused that at least he was living a life far more stable than Cortez despite his current extended stay in the Dog House Inn.

Things could be better, nonetheless.

Sonia should stop blaming him for her inability to experience orgasms. She should stop lecturing and preaching to him about his responsibilities in their marriage. Maybe, just maybe, she should be less insecure. Maybe she should even be a little more forgiving, and maybe she should stop hiding behind God about everything.

I'm not a bad person, he said to himself.

"I'm home, everyone!" Trent announced, entering the living room foyer.

Sonia walked casually from the kitchen. "Hey, I'm almost done with dinner. I fixed something that I know you'll like."

He gave her a hug and a pat on the backside.

"Is that the way you say hello to your wife, now?" She gave him a playful pelvic thrust.

He smiled back at her. "It certainly is."

"No problem. Actually, I kind of like it. At least I know you're still affectionate —"

Trent chased her playfully into the kitchen. There, he cornered her by the refrigerator. He gave her a bear hug, kiss, and he squeezed her backside again. Then he attempted fondling her breasts.

". . . Hey, watch it! I'm still cooking in here!" she reminded him.

"Okay, I see that." He went ahead with getting water from the refrigerator.

Sonia announced that she made pepper steak, baby potatoes, green beans, and yeast rolls. Then she sat down at the table, expecting him to join her.

"How was your day?" she queried him.

Trent removed his brown Perry Ellis suit jacket and unloosed his tie. He sat down in the chair to Sonia's right. For several moments, he simply stared at her.

He was right. He did have a stable home life but things could be better.

"I had a crazy day today. That's the best way I can describe it," he said. "Have you seen the news at all?"

"You know I don't look at any of that mess," she answered. "I'm sick of the media."

Trent leaned back in his chair. He yawned and stretched before he continued. "Well, late this morning, we had a woman coming in to see Cortez."

The mentioning of his name prompted Sonia to roll her eyes.

"Yeah, it was like that, and more," Trent continued. "I happened to hear the conversation she was having with him, and she threatened to shoot him in his office. That was all I needed to hear."

"So what happened after that?" Sonia leaned forward with anticipation.

He described to her how he told the security guard to contact the sheriff's department, and he had the tellers to leave the floor and wait in the employee's break room until the conflict ended.

"I just had this strange feeling that this was not going to be civil," he said. "And I was right. The police came there. I heard two gun shots. I went inside. Cortez was talking to one police officer. The other officer was calling for an ambulance; he'd shot and killed the woman who had threatened Cortez."

Sonia brought her hand up to her mouth. The story was too incredible to fathom.

"The television stations even showed up after the fact," he added. "I'm just glad to be home."

"Is that all that happened?"

He shrugged his shoulders. "Pretty much."

"Trent, you know there was more to what happened. And you say this was on TV today?"

He nodded.

"The woman happened to be married. So you can pretty much put a few things together," he said.

"Like what?"

"Knowing Cortez the way you do, you know it's like a revolving door for all the women he's had come inside that bank. But he says she confronted because she didn't like that he dumped her."

Sonia simply stared at Trent as if there had to be a punch line coming.

"I just pray that you had nothing to do with any of this except for what you've just told me," she said. "Because there was a time when you two were like Tweedledum and Tweedledee, remember?"

Trent sat up in the chair, maintaining eye-to-eye contact with her.

"Hold that thought, will you?" Sonia darted over to the stove and turned off the vegetables. "Dinner's ready when you want it."

"Thanks."

"Okay. Now what were we talking about?" she said.

He breathed through his nostrils before responding, "Sonia, a woman is dead because of something that probably went deeper than either of us know what really happened. Cortez and I talked for a while afterward; he's got a lot of stuff he's got to sort out and reconcile to himself."

He paused to stress the seriousness of what occurred.

"For once, can't you put things aside—no, better yet, behind you—and stop bringing up the past?"

"Trent, I'm willing to do that. But there are just too many things that reminds me of what used to be," she said. "You were not the most faithful man before we were married and shortly after we were married.

"A lot of that was because of your close friendship with Cortez, in case you've forgotten. Stuff like that just doesn't go away."

For the first time in a while, Trent paid closer attention to Sonia. He recognized the pain and frustration in her face re-minding him of his past behavior.

"With the exception of a couple of incidents that I care not to mention, can you not admit that I have tried to win back your trust? Can you not admit that I am not the same man that I was years ago?" he argued. "If I that were the old man, that could have been me instead of Cortez."

His eyes remained riveted on Sonia. He was determined to make some kind of headway in this two-month impasse. Sonia offered no response. Rather, she sighed and resumed staring at him. He leaned forward and reached out for her. Literally.

"Hey, I'm not the same man that I was a few years ago," he said. "I'm not perfect by any means."

He grasped her hand tighter. "The least you can do is try embracing me for where I'm trying to be as a man and a hus-band." He did not say another word.

After several moments, Sonia broke the silence by shifting in her seat. She then withdrew her hand from him, but only to move her chair closer. She offered a smile.

"What you've just said means a lot. I'm willing to move on, but I can't go back to the same old, same old, okay?"

They hugged and kissed, but the moment didn't last long They heard Taylor coming down the hallway, causing them to separate prematurely.

"That's your son." Trent tipped his head at Sonia.

She pointed back at him. "No, that's your son!"

* * *

Later that evening, Trent and Sonia attempted to recapture the better times they once enjoyed in the bedroom.

Their moment together seemed fluid and passionate. For that matter, Sonia had not been as willing of a participant with Trent since before the holiday season. She initiated many of the positions and copulations they indulged.

"Baby, I miss this so much," Trent whispered between kisses to her.

"I do, too. I miss being with my husband."

When Trent reassumed mounting Sonia, she urged him on by stroking his back and alternately holding her legs apart for him.

In a sultry voice, she cooed, "Please, baby. Take me there. I want to get there tonight. Help me make it happen—"

He reached beneath her and commenced to delivering strokes inside her that she hadn't felt in recent memory. But she still desired more from him.

"Baby, come on. Reach me from within. Come on, you can do it for me, baby," she moaned. "I need for you to do that for me."

"Sonia, I've wanted nobody else but you," he responded.

"I'm here for you, baby. I'm right here—"

She bit her bottom lip and closed her eyes. She felt as if she would finally break through. The momentum was slow but steady; it began from her inner depths. All Trent had to do was wait for her.

She began matching him stroke-for-stroke. "I feel it, baby . . . I feel . . . I feel it . . . Help me get there!"

"Let's do it together," he whispered back to her. "Let's take this to another level—"

Suddenly, the feeling disappeared. A moment that was on the cusp of fruition had become just another perfunctory occasion.

Minutes later while she was nestled up to him, she felt obligated to share the outcome with him.

"I'm sorry, baby."

"Sorry about what?"

The tone in Sonia's voice did not resonate well with him. A feeling of numbness began circulating.

"I didn't want to spoil it, so I faked it," she said. "I'm sorry I'm just not there yet."

Mission not accomplished.

Rage began welling up. Trent entertained letting out a tirade of profanity.

Prior to this night, Sonia's complaints had been about the past; they had resolved it. They had been about the lack of meaningful dialogue prior to the bedroom; there was plenty of it despite its source for the dialogue. She'd also complained about him failing to make a mental and emotional connection with her; he felt he made a sincere effort at reaching her where she was.

"Sonia," he said, sighing. "I'm not giving up on us. But it takes two, baby. It takes two."

Sensing the frustration in Trent's voice, she replied, "I know, baby." But her voice was void of emotion.

Eventually, Trent and Sonia turned onto their respective sides of the bed. Both stared silently and aimlessly at the ceiling; neither were aware nor seemed to care about what the other one was thinking.

Chapter 13

'You're Not in My Bedroom with Me'

S onia had asked God to do something for her this day. Something that would let her know that He was listening to her. Something that would let her know that He cared for her.

After returning from lunch, she received a text message from Shonna inviting—no, make that insisting that she accompanied—her to dinner. This was not her idea of answered prayer.

> I know it's been a while since we last talked. Let's meet at this place I know of in Cayce. I've got some things I want to talk to you about. OK?

Sonia ignored the message and deleted it. In fact, she retuned to closing out unresolved phone inquiries for her representatives.

Her team, as well as Vicki's, faced having to close out as many as three hundred and fifty-seven, by the end of the workweek to avoid working Saturday overtime.

About twenty minutes later, she got another text message from Shonna.

> Listen, trick. Answer this text message or I do I need to come over where you are and handle you like when we were kids?

Sonia rolled her eyes. Again, she deleted it without replying. It was quite common for Sonia to treat Shonna the way she had. Shonna was four years older than Sonia; their birthdays were five days apart. Despite their age difference, there was no doubt that Sonia and Shonna were sisters among strangers with their indistinguishable features, although they had distinctive tastes.

While growing up in the shadows of Columbia's downtown area near Farrow Road, the two sisters consistently argued and fought.

Both were seen as daddy's girls. Both clamored for Tillman Chandler's attention and received it. But Sonia always felt Shonna was favored more—there were countless of times their mother Prentiss found herself umpiring their skirmishes by separating the parties with hopes of keeping the peace.

Sonia also wanted badly to be Shonna's equal and not be overlooked. That was because Shonna was the popular one. In high school, she was an honor student and a cheerleader. She was the first in her family to attend college and graduate. Teachers who remembered Shonna easily recognized Sonia, and they often compared Sonia to Shonna. Some of Sonia's classmates whose own siblings were Shonna's classmates referred to her as merely Shonna's sister.

It took Sonia being well into her twenties before she emerged from Shonna's shadow as her own woman. More importantly, she learned how to accept herself.

Another messaged buzzed on Sonia's phone. This time, Sonia decided to at least consider Shonna's message.

> Sis, I'm asking you to meet me for dinner. There's this out-of-sight place in Cayce. Stop being so stubborn. I love you, too!

Sonia smiled. She figured that she'd engaged in enough mischief with her sister—a playful reminder of their childhood years.

> I love you, too. What time are you talking about? I get off work at 5:30 today.

> Can you meet me there about 6?

> Where?

> The Groovy Soul. On Knox Abbott Drive. It's in the shopping center with the Bi-Lo.

> OK. I'll see you then.

* * *

Sonia knew that six o'clock meant probably as late as 6:30 with Shonna—punctuality was one thing that truly distinguished the Chandler sisters. She arrived there right shortly before six o'clock and waited for Shonna's burgundy GMC Acadia SUV. After ten minutes, she decided to go ahead inside the strip mall restaurant; she had not eaten anything all day.

"Good evening, and who do I have the pleasure of welcoming to our restaurant?" a casually dressed man in his early fifties greeted her.

"I'm fine, thank you."

He smiled. "I certainly wouldn't argue with you about that . . . How many will be in your party this evening?"

"Two."

"Our policy is we won't seat anyone until all members of their party have arrived," he said, "but I'll make an exception for you—"

"I'll just wait."

Sonia knew that Shonna was well connected when it came to hot spots in many cities. She previously worked twelve years in Atlanta in various capacities in the media before she returned to Columbia two years ago, accepting a job as general manager of WNPW-FM, the area's most popular station for urban radio.

The Groovy Soul, which boasted of serving buffet home cooked and southern style meals, opened for business less than eight months ago. The restaurant's growing clientele consisted of working professionals, politicians, college students and employees from the major university—all coming from the other side of the Broad River bridge—in addition to residents in the immediate area.

Minutes later, the same man who greeted Sonia returned. "Would you like to browse through our menu while you wait?" he asked.

Sonia glanced at her watch, then outside the window, before she responded. "I think I'll continue waiting, thank you."

He was quick to turn his attention to a group of people that just entered.

"Good evening, thank you for visiting us. This will be for a party of how many?"

Finally, Shonna showed up as late as Sonia had predicted, parking next to her silver Infiniti M35. She walked at a fast cadence from the parking lot. Sonia stood up and awaited her with a scowl on her face.

"Remind me next time that I should never take you serious when you set a time for anything," she said.

"Please do that."

They smiled at each other and embraced.

"How are you doing?" they both said to each other simultaneously.

Sonia broke their embrace first. "What is so special about this place?"

"I hear that this place is it," Shonna answered. "You'll give up cooking at home and just eat here all the time."

"You don't say?" Sonia thought about The Groovy Soul being in the opposite direction of home, and she rarely came to this side of the Columbia area.

Shonna went on to tell Sonia about WNPW having a remote broadcast next Saturday at The Groovy Soul. She decided to visit the place personally since she'd heard so much about it.

It was not long before the man returned to the cashier's counter and greeted the Chandler sisters. His face lit up knowing now that he had double his visual pleasure.

"I really must have been a good little boy!" He turned his attention to Sonia. "And so this lovely lady completes the party of two you were telling me about?"

"Yes it does," Shonna interrupted.

"Ladies, follow me, please."

He seated them at a table somewhere in the middle of the restaurant. And Shonna's eyes followed the man back to the cashier's counter—she took note of his still well-defined physique and smooth, but rugged features.

Mmmph!

"What was that mmmph'ing all about?" Sonia looked up to say. She had been text messaging Taylor and Trent where she would be for the next hour or so.

"Nothing," Shonna replied, waving Sonia off. "I'll go first and get myself a plate."

She looked off to her right hoping to make eye contact with the man who greeted them. Apparently, he had made himself busy by checking on the other patrons. The place was already two-thirds full.

When she returned, Sonia walked over to the buffet. She was unaware the man who seated them coolly made his way back over to the cashier's counter, enjoying her view from behind. He returned his attention to the restaurant's patrons once she sat back down with Shonna.

After praying over their food, Sonia was quick to inquire about her being asked to join her sister for dinner.

"I'll have you to know that I'm now dating someone who is twenty-seven," Shonna announced.

The food on Sonia's fork fell back onto her plate. "You said what?"

"I'm involved with a man who is sixteen years younger than me."

Sonia shook her head slowly. All she could think of was Shonna the perpetually single woman who'd never kept a man for any significant duration—this being the woman who bragged of having little or no patience with men. And if they made a mistake it was one-and-done; she was gone.

"Why?" Sonia asked.

A silly smile appeared on Shonna's face. "I don't know. But stranger things have happened. He reminds me of that fella who keeps checking us out." She darted her eyes over at the cashier's counter.

Sonia cut a quick glance to her left, but returned her attention back to Shonna.

"Can you imagine how our mother would react if you told her you're involved with a man sixteen years younger than you?"

"Actually, I really don't care," Shonna answered. "I'm forty-three years old. Our mother's lived her life, and so has our father. You need to meet him before you start judging me. I didn't go into this like some desperate, horny woman."

Sonia chortled. "It sounds like both to me. Desperate and horny, the both of you."

"Ha, ha!" Shonna accompanied her response with mocking head gesture. She took a sip from her iced tea and resumed her conversation.

The first thing she wanted to make clear she was not joking with Sonia.

"I just had to tell someone, and I felt the person I trusted most was my sister," she said. "I might not have said anything if he were ten years older than he is now, or even if he were ten years older than me."

Sonia shrugged her shoulders. "Hey, it's your life. I hope you're happy with whatever you decide. I just know how I'd be if Taylor came to me about him dating a woman sixteen years older than him." She cringed at the thought. "So, what does your boy toy do?"

Shonna returned a menacing glare at her sister. "Oh, so you think that he's just lying up in my place while I'm out running the station?"

"I never said that."

"Well, for your information, he works."

"Where?"

"That's none of your business. Just know he works and

he has his own place, car, and he's single with NO children, thank you."

"You still sound a bit secretive there. Do you care to at least tell me his name?"

Sighing, Shonna sat back in her chair and crossed her legs. Then she rolled her eyes. "His name is Kirk; it's short for Kirkland."

Before Sonia could respond with the sarcastic thought she entertained, the man who seated them stopped by their table. He first looked at Shonna, but settled his attention on Sonia.

"How is everything?" he asked.

"This is wonderful. I've heard a lot about this place. Now I'm convinced," Shonna said. "I never had turnip greens without the meat tasting as good as this."

The man appeared extremely pleased and proud of Shonna's raving of the food. "And how about you?" he asked Sonia.

She looked down at her plate of smothered chicken steak and rice then looked up at him. His eyes were riveted on her, to say the least.

"Tell whoever the cook is back there that they can really do it up good. I'm really impressed."

He tipped his head, grinning. "We certainly appreciate you dining here." Then he looked toward the cashier's counter. "We have a drawing every week for a free lunch or dinner. We would love for you to leave us with your business card, if you have one."

"We'll keep that in mind," Sonia said.

He thanked them again. He noticed another dinner party coming in. Shonna's eyes followed him back to the waiting area.

"Hey, didn't you just say you were dating someone who's almost young enough to be your son?" Sonia teased Shonna. Immediately, Shonna turned her attention back to Sonia.

"I certainly did. But there's nothing wrong with admiring a handsome man."

She contemplated her comment. Then she added, "I forgot you're married. You don't know about those things."

"Maybe you're right." Sonia resumed tearing into her smothered chicken steak. After a few bites, she could not resist tearing into her sister.

"Hey, you're involved with a younger man whom you'll have to teach him certain things. Why trouble yourself?"

Shonna sucked her teeth after a long sip from her tea. "I'll have you to know I've not had to teach him a single thing so far. He's a lot more mature than you're imagining him not being."

"You know what? There's a guy on my job who's probably about the same age as your little boy toy—"

"That's Kirk."

"Okay, Boy Toy Kirk."

"Whatever."

"And he seems to be mature and all. But if I were single, I would not give him the time of day, no matter what."

Shonna tipped her head toward Sonia, maintaining eye contact with her. "That's the difference between you and me. I don't limit myself. You always have."

"Me, limit myself?" Sonia straightened up in her seat.

"Yes, I said that. You're about as boring and straight-laced as any prude that I know."

Sonia's eyes widened. "Boring? Prude? You're not in my bedroom with me!"

"I don't have to be," Shonna retorted, placing her hand on her hip. "Remember, you and I shared bedrooms for a number of years. Remember when I first told you about sucking a boy's you-know-what? Remember how I tried teaching you how it should be done? I bet you still have problems with doing that."

Sonia did not respond. Apparently, it was evident with her that Shonna was stuck in another era. Things do change, although she would never confide those things in her.

"I have a man. A husband at that. And I don't have to find myself one, if you know what I mean—"

"I love you, sis. That's the reason why I asked you to meet me for dinner. I can always depend on you keeping me grounded—by your insults."

"Yeah, somebody has to pray for you because nobody else will."

On their way out, Sonia and Shonna were stopped by the man who greeted them.

"Ladies, before you leave, here is a five-dollar coupon for both of you."

"I'm sorry. I can't accept this," Shonna said.

"I don't understand?" He appeared disappointed.

"I absolutely enjoyed the food, but I can't accept it because our station will be coming here very soon," Shonna explained.

"Oh, you're from—"

"Yes, WNPW. I'm the general manager there. But I'll be sure to pass the word on to our announcers and have them tell our listeners just how good the food really is. You'll be hearing it tomorrow."

His eyes lit up, and he extended his hand out to her. "I'm Wharton Milner. I'm the owner. This is truly an honor."

"I'm Shonna Chandler." She accepted his handshake then looked to her right. "This is my sister, Sonia."

He was more than happy to shake Sonia's hand. "Hello, Ms. Sonia. Thank you for visiting us."

"Thank you. You have a very nice place here." She was slow with releasing his handshake.

He cocked his head back, folding his arms. "Oh, by the way. The lead cook back there is my sister. She loves overseeing the dinner menu." Then he lowered his voice. "I also get back there and help during lunch."

"I'm impressed," Sonia replied. "So, this is a family business?"

"Yes it is. My niece also works here. You'll see her doing exactly what I'm doing if you come during lunch. And those coupons are good any time."

Milner offered to walk Sonia and Shonna to their vehicles, but they declined. They indicated their vehicles were parked directly in front of The Groovy Soul; there were no other cars in the immediate area surrounding them.

Out in the parking lot, Sonia and Shonna hugged and then waved goodbye to each other. Meanwhile, Milner watched the entire interaction from his vantage point back inside the restaurant.

He paid particular attention to Sonia, nodding his head in thought. He was confident his instincts had not deceived him.

Chapter 14

'I Thought This Was Over'

Within a couple of days, the sensational nature of Deloria Lovett's death went viral on the social media networks describing her chaotic affair with Cortez.

"You're not going to believe what I just saw on my time-line!" Paula Freese exclaimed to her Palmetto Fidelity colleague Tondy Pratt.

"Hold on. Let me log on and see what you're talking about."

Paula spoke with more urgency. "This is funny. Absolutely crazy!"

"Wait a minute. I'm trying to log on!" Tondy now sighed in relief. "Okay. I typed in the wrong password. Now I'm on—"

"Now scroll down and click the one from noseyrosie.com . . . Come on, hurry up!"

There was only a slight delay before Tondy also shrieked inside her apartment. "This is crazy. But you know what? I'm not surprised at all."

Popular columnist Nosey Rose featured the shooting inside Palmetto Fidelity by critiquing just how careless Cortez apparently was managing his fling with Deloria.

The article said there were three things people should always keep in mind when having an affair with a married person: a) Don't expect anything in return; b) Limit times of communication; c) Keep everything low-key.

Tondy could not hold back laughing. "Well, I see why Nosey Rose had Cortez in mind because he definitely flunked on two points for sure. The only one I might give him a pass on was not expecting anything in return."

"What do you mean not expecting anything in return?"

Paula reacted. "Any woman who walked into the bank and saw Cortez on a regular basis, he was expecting something.

"Okay?"

Paula admitted that she might not have seen things the same way as Nosey Rose. A divorcée herself, she was the wronged party in her nine-year marriage.

"I'm going to tell you this. Once I found out that Randall cheated on me, I didn't bother asking any questions," she said. "I packed his stuff and threw them out in the parking lot at his job. The next time he heard from me, I was collecting alimony and child support!"

"I never knew that," Tondy commented. "Then again, I've never bothered to ask you why you were divorced. I figured that was none of my business."

Tondy had been working at the St. Andrews branch since 2010. Paula was hired and placed there in 2012; she was shadowed by Tondy during her training and probationary period.

"Read the advice given about keeping things low keyed, which was something we know Cortez was very slack about," Paula suggested.

According to the article, Nosey Rose contended it went almost without saying the cheating parties should never be seen at places where it's likely they would run into people they know.

Both laughed about how Cortez may have forgotten about the people on his job. And if anyone really wanted, they could have found out exactly who any of the women were.

"Yeah, like that foreign woman who last came into the bank," Tondy said.

"You're not going to believe this," Paula interrupted. "If you really search this, there's at least two whole search pages full of results on Cortez and that woman—"

"Now that's crazy!"

"And just think, he comes strutting in there all the time like he's royalty."

"Wouldn't you?"

"I don't know."

"One thing I do know I always had a creepy feeling about Cortez."

"I hate to admit this, so have I."

"Check out this article!" Paula blurted out. "This one is from discreetnews.com. Are you familiar with that one?"

"No. There's so many of them out there. But what does it say?" There was much intrigue in Tondy's voice.

"According to this gossip piece, it says Cortez was the third wheel in a threesome that went wrong," Paula said. "The husband was sixty-four years old."

"What?"

"Go to www.discreetnews.com and read it for yourself!"

"All right, hold on . . ." Tondy erupted into laughter after she read the first two paragraphs. "I would have never believed that about Cortez. Never in a thousand years him being the third wheel in a threesome, and anything to do with another man!" She burst into laughter again, and so did Paula.

"They say what's done in the dark will be brought to light, and this just about does it," Paula said between laughs. "I'm not sure if I'll ever look at Cortez Anderson again with a straight face."

"Yeah. And if he's been a third wheel in something like that, ain't nothing straight about him."

Tondy mentioned that Cortez was still single. "Isn't he, like, forty, he doesn't have any children, and he's never been married?"

"That's what I hear."

"How many men you know who are single, forty years old, never been married, and have no children?"

"Not many," Paula said. "And if they still are, they're weird and ugly, or they're bisexual or gay."

"Well, I can't say that he's my type. So I guess that leaves us with one other choice. Maybe even sterile."

They both laughed again.

* * *

Cortez more than shocked by what he saw parked outside his house, and it shocked him even more as the cameraman and woman with a microphone approached him while he tried getting inside his car.

She identified herself as Chantal Frye, a reporter for the *Brown Onion*; it was a reality and gossip-based television show based out of New York City. The cameraman, who was burly and stood about six-five, was out of breath trying to catch up with her.

"Mr. Anderson, we'd like to know your side of what really happened at the bank the day that Deloria Lovett was shot?" Frye asked.

"I have nothing to say."

She persisted with him. "Is it true that you had promised to marry Deloria Lovett once she divorced her husband?"

Cortez stared at Frye, flabbergasted. He contemplated responding to her, but he decided against it. This was not his idea of being intruded upon.

"Mr. Anderson, we understand you have a playboy's reputation. Can you even begin to explain why a married woman would come to any man's job and threaten to shoot him?" she asked.

Having heard enough, he brushed aside the woman and cameraman, got inside his car, and drove off to work. The cameraman continued filming him until he reached the end of his neighborhood.

I thought this was over, Cortez said, hissing at the thought of being approached by media. Miffed, he contacted Trent.

"Man, I can't believe what just happened to me," he said.

"Where are you?" Trent responded.

"I'm close to the dam on Highway 6. Humph, a television crew from I don't know where was filming me while I was in my driveway."

"Really?"

"Yeah. Even asked me a bunch of stupid questions about that incident inside the bank!"

Trent did not immediately respond. Rather, he mused to himself talk about something getting more than its fifteen minutes of fame?

"I hope you didn't answer any of their questions."

"No way. How do you respond to a stranger wanting to know my side of the story? Then they asked if it was true whether I promised to marry her once she was divorced—"

"Well, did you?"

"Come on, man. I told you. I never promised her anything. We never talked about her wanting to leave her husband,"

Cortez answered. "She made it known there was no way she'd give up any of the financial security she enjoyed. I was fine with it."

Cortez had now reached the other side of the Lake Murray dam and turned right onto Bush River Road. He was less than ten minutes away from work. Meanwhile, Trent had reached Irmo on I-26 eastbound; it was about the same distance away.

"There's no telling what is out there about you and that woman," Trent said. "Have you bothered to look?"

The thought repulsed Cortez. "No, why should I?" He ranted about appearing on television was one of the reasons why he never considered politics because everything he'd say or do would be scrutinized, analyzed, debated, and regurgitated several times daily.

Just the night before, he added, a couple of people pointed him out at the Walmart near his house in Lexington. It was as if they wanted to approach him but were not sure if it was a good idea.

"I can understand this making the news because it happened, but isn't enough is enough?" he wondered aloud. "I really would rather be left alone."

"Wouldn't we all? I just hope it doesn't become a distraction," Trent said. "If it does, then that's another problem on top of a bigger problem that already exists."

Trent said he'd just passed the Zaxby's to his left on St. Andrews Road. That meant he was a little less than two miles away from the bank.

Cortez indicated he was nearing the railroad tracks from the opposite direction on St. Andrews Road; the bank was within sight on his left. "I hope this will just go away. I really do."

Until the office bullet hole could be patched, Cortez worked out of the third office space inside the branch—it was not designed for full service being that it was smaller.

Around mid-morning, Cortez noticed a woman who appeared to be in her late sixties or early seventies standing in the lobby. Trent got up and greeted her.

"How may I help you?" he inquired.

"I'd like to speak with Cortez Anderson, if I can." The woman appeared drained of emotion and her voice was troubled.

Trent had already instructed the tellers to say Cortez was out of the office for training if anyone asked for him. He was not about to stray from script. Meanwhile, Cortez remained quiet and closed the door.

"Is there anything I can help you with?" Trent asked.

The woman, who stood no more than maybe five-three, looked up at Trent. His patience was already wearing thin. The last thing he wanted was another Deloria-like incident.

"I would like to speak with Mr. Anderson. The lady who was killed in here was my niece. I just want to speak to him. That's all."

"I'm sorry, but there's nothing we can do here to help you. I can recommend that you go to the Lexington County sheriff's department and maybe get a police report," Trent said. "Or you can contact our corporate office and speak with our director of security. His name is Ralph Triton."

He offered her his business card and wrote Triton's phone number on it.

"And you're Trent Buckner?" she asked, associating his face with his name on the card.

"Yes, I am."

Trent glanced over at John Tinsley, the security guard on duty. He understood that meant be ready to escort the woman out, if anything got out of hand.

"She was my oldest niece," the woman said. "I had a bad feeling that something was wrong. I didn't know who I needed to pray for. Then it was too late."

"Well, ma'am, I'm going to have to ask you to leave the bank," Trent said. "Or I'll have to have you escorted out of here."

"That won't be necessary."

After the lady left on her own volition, Trent stopped by Cortez's temporary exile. He was visibly annoyed by the visitor.

He looked back into the lobby. "I don't know how much of this we're going to be able to handle before we call in the calvary for help." He told Cortez the woman claimed to have been a relative of Deloria's.

Cortez scratched his forehead before burying it in his hand. "I don't know, man. I told her before the police came that this did not have to happen."

Sighing, Trent replied, "We'll just have to wait and see."

There was a buzzing that went off from Cortez's shirt pocket, interrupting them. He alerted Trent that he needed to answer the call.

"Boy, what have you gotten yourself into?" The man's voice was distinctly older, rural and with a Gullah dialect. "Great day in da mornin'!"

"You too?" Cortez answered his uncle Cleo.

"All I'm hearing is that you got yourself in a mess of trouble. Had some crazy woman come up to your job wanting to kill you," his uncle said. "It's a good thing you got people prayin' for you, boy!"

"I guess so." A hint of Cortez's native dialect now crept into his conversation.

"Ain't no doubt about it! And they're saying she was a married woman. You ain't got any business messin' with a married woman! You should know from all them stories you heard back here in on the island about married people gettin' in trouble."

Cortez had heard enough. He felt as if the world was converging in on him and he had nowhere to elude it. Thinking back, there was an unspoken mantra that he went by that suggested once the two parties became silent, and there was no contact between them, simply don't look back.

That was the message that he thought he conveyed to Deloria.

"Uncle Cleo, it's not as if you're the best example," Cortez countered. "Where did you think I learned it from?"

"I ain't never had any jokers puttin' my business all up in a newspaper, on television, and on the Internet. Now think about that!"

He had a point. It was just word of mouth on Lady's Island, and for some reason it never got back to his aunt Ruthie. He reasoned that maybe it was a different time and era back in his uncle's heyday.

* * *

Cortez contemplated avoiding Alcione all together. She had called him four times already and he had yet to listen to a single voice mail message.

Finally, he rationalized that he had nothing to hide from her, and all of this should pass.

"I have to find out, Cortez, what is all this talk about you with a married woman who was shot by police?" she asked. "It's in the news, and all over the Internet. Of all places, here; Columbia, South Carolina—"

He closed his eyes and tried counting backwards from ten. After taking a deep breath, he finally responded. "For the hundredth time, I had nothing to do with a married woman." He spoke slow and deliberately to her.

"She was somebody I broke up with before meeting you. She did not like that I stopped seeing her and she came to my job. . . . A gun went off and then another gun. Next thing I know, the police was calling for an ambulance."

"I'm sorry, Cortez. Maybe it's because I'm from Brazil. I don't understand."

He tried explaining again what transpired. He was emphatic to say, "I have not been involved any other woman since we started dating."

"How am I supposed to believe that?" she responded. "Back in my country, long ago both you and her would have been killed."

"Well, this is the United States."

"Don't get funny with me!" she yelled.

"I'm not." He paused, trying to collect his thoughts. "I'm sorry. It's just been crazy lately." He began explaining to her the things that had already happened since he left home.

"Cortez, I think that what you need to do is take care of your problems," she interrupted him. "If I knew you had all these problems, I never would have had anything to do with you. Goodbye!"

She hung up on him.

Ugh!

* * *

It's been that kind of day, Cortez mused, as he stopped at a gas station on the way home. All he wanted to do now was go home and crawl under his blanket. It had to get better.

While pumping gas, a black 500 series two-door Mercedes stopped at the pump across from him. The man stepped out the car and tipped his head at Cortez, who reciprocated the same gesture.

In the time it took Cortez to turn around after placing the as nozzle back into its receptacle, the man now stood next to Cortez's car. He queried, "Haven't I seen you before?"

Cortez, who became suspicious, noticed the man was angry. "I don't think so."

Giving him a quick look up and down, Cortez figured he could handle the man if there was any altercation. After all, the man was much older. He was dressed in a dark suit and tie. He did not appear to be in the best of shape.

The man nodded. "You have."

"I . . . I don't think so. Excuse me."

The man blocked Cortez's path. "I just had to put a face with the text messages I've read from my wife's phone."

Cortez's heart began pounding. He tried keeping his poise realizing the man had to be Deloria's widow, Primas Lovett.

"She really liked doing it with you, didn't she?" Lovett continued. "Got herself killed over it, hmmm?"

He pulled out Deloria's cell phone. He scrolled to her previously sent messages. From there he read:

"I *wish you were here lying next to me instead of hubby . . . He doesn't hold a jock strap to you . . .*"

"I *get so excited thinking about you. I need you soooo much! . . .*"

"*Gotta keep it simple. I get mine. You get yours. And the world I live in is a much happier place . . .*"

Lovett snorted and spat at Cortez's shoes. He'd been fuming over such revelations since he identified Deloria's body and claimed her personal effects. Nor did it help that details of her affair with Cortez went viral over the Internet.

He'd already contemplated running Cortez over in the bank parking lot. He also mulled shooting Cortez himself or have him beaten up for the embarrassment he already experienced.

Cortez noticed Lovett had balled his fists, although they were still down at his side.

"Look, I may be wrong for having messed with your wife. But I am not the cause of her being dead. She caused that on herself. Ask the policeman who shot her."

Lovett had raised his voice to a yelling pitch. "I know my wife wasn't worth a squat. I knew she went whoring around on me. For years, in fact!"

"So, why are you confronting me? I didn't pursue her. She pursued me," Cortez snapped at him. "After a while, I felt it was time to move on because I didn't want something like this to happen."

"If you didn't want something like this to happen, you would have been smart enough to ignore her!"

There was a steady flow of traffic in and out of the gas station. One man paused and looked at them but decided to keep walking. A woman pumping gas from the other side of Cortez's pump merely ignored their confrontation.

Cortez decided he'd heard enough. "Excuse me." He brushed Lovett aside.

Enraged, Lovett pushed Cortez from behind, causing him to break his fall by bumping against his Mustang's left rear quarter panel. He immediately turned around, staring hard at Lovett; he also held his arms out as if he was ready to throw the first punch, and perhaps more.

"What's it gonna be, huh? What's it gonna be?"

He took a step toward Lovett, who did not flinch or take any steps backwards.

"There's more than one way of handling this," Lovett snarled back at him. "Remember that!"

Both stared at each other for several moments almost oblivious to everyone else at the station. Lovett ended the showdown by calling him every kind of mother imaginable.

Hardly amused, Cortez watched Lovett return to his car and drive off as nightfall was fast descending. Then he got inside his own car and was quick to lock his doors. He stared straight ahead, collecting his thoughts. There was no sighing in relief.

I brought that on myself, he said to himself. It could have been worse.

After he looked in every direction possible, Cortez drove off, hoping that there would be no further encounters of any kind.

Chapter 15

'Don't Create Any Issues…'

The urge to get up and join Lance in the fax copier room was hard to resist. Charlotte envisioned only a naked, fit athletic body walking by—much like the one that got up from her bed the night before and strode to the bathroom—rather than one wearing navy blue slacks and a light blue long-sleeved business shirt.

It was a proud, lustful moment. The most handsome man to have come through contract services at least since she'd been there was no more than ten to fifteen feet away. Only if she could now join him and share her affection toward him without any risk.

She grabbed for her cell phone.

> You look so edible when I saw you. I wanted to rip your clothes off of you and jump on your bones in the copier room.

She returned to her workload, but was eager for the imminent reply from him.

> Really? I was thinking about last night. Are you
> wearing any panties today?

She squirmed in her office chair. A familiar warm, tingling feeling came over her.

> No :)

Lance was quick to respond.

> Third floor. Today.

Since Lance and Charlotte agreed on being an item, they were careful to continue as if they never spoken to each other. That meant they drove to work in their own vehicles, parked in different sections in the parking lot, and they entered the UCP building on opposite ends. They also agreed on not being seen at lunch together. But that was where all the inconspicuous activity ended.

Lance had a morning habit of walking through the contract services workplace entryway closest to Charlotte's cubicle. He would text ahead apprising her when he was near. As he passed by, they would make eye contact.

During work hours, they figured an occasional meeting in the fax copier room—a playful touch, peck on the lips, or rubbing against each other—was fun but also risky. So they came up with something that made up for everything: the men's room up on the third floor after regular business hours.

Since the UCP building was sparsely occupied after five o'clock, nobody would imagine them having a rendezvous inside the handicapped accommodation—a separate facility with a solid door that locked for privacy. The fifteen to twenty minutes they spent in there was more than enough time for a probable quick release.

Going to the ladies room. See you in a few.

That was Lance's cue to sign out for the day around 5:45 p.m. and hurry upstairs to "reserve" the bathroom for both of them. Then he'd stand outside in the hallway and text message her.

I'm waiting . . .

Charlotte darted over to the men's bathroom giggling both out of mischief and being glad to see him. They were all over each other once he locked the door behind them, groping, fondling, kissing, rubbing and hugging—there was sufficient room inside for them to do most of what they wanted to do.

"You make me do these things," she whispered, tugging at his zipper.

He kissed her on her neck. "No, you make me do these things."

Immediately, she dropped to her knees. Lance closed his eyes, arched his neck, and placed his hands on her shoulders.

She reached around him, urging him to thrust. He sucked air through his teeth. His eyes widened at the sensation the back of her mouth brought to him.

"God, that feels so good—"

She looked up at him and teased him by the way she waggled her tongue. Not wanting to be left out, he nudged for her to stand up. She gasped once he inserted one, then two fingers inside her while they tongue kissed.

Coming up for air, she whispered into his ear: "I want you right now. I can't wait any longer—"

She turned around and leaned forward against the wall. He was quick to step out of his slacks, pull her dress up to her waist, and position himself behind her.

Both closed their eyes and moaned while they searched for the right rhythm. They were careful not to indulge into any hard, deep humping; they did not want the slapping of flesh to give them away.

"I always had a fantasy of wanting to do it at work one day," she finally whispered to him.

"This is so nasty, but so exciting!" He then suggested that she leaned over further and grasp the handrail. "Oh, yeah. Keep it right there—"

"Like that?"

"Yeah, like that!"

Minutes later, both were catching their breath and savoring the moment. Their faces were flush but also visibly relieved. She looked back and drew a kiss from him while he rubbed her exposed soft flesh.

Lance exited the handicapped accommodation first and brought back some warm, wet paper towels for both of them.

"Do you think I'm getting spoiled by all this attention?" she asked him while rearranging her clothing. "This is stuff I never imagined doing, you know?"

"If you feel you're being spoiled, so am I," he replied. "It is kind of fun."

Charlotte licked her lips after reapplying her lipstick. "You think we ought to take pictures next time?"

"Yeah, why not?" Lance laughed at the thought. "It's only something for both you and I to remember, right?"

Once they were fully dressed again, they hugged and kissed or a final time inside the handicapped accommodation. Lance then exited the bathroom first, checking the hallway. He reached back and pushed opened the door for her. She sashayed past him and continued to the nearest elevator. They left the building in their usual opposite directions.

* * *

As much as she tried convincing herself that it was just an aberration, Shonna Chandler found herself liking Lance. They met shortly after he accepted working permanently at UCP while she commandeered a WNPW promotional event outside Columbia's convention center in the downtown area.

Lance noticed she wasn't wearing a ring. And just for the fun of it, he struck up a conversation with her. He was surprised that she gave him time amid the throng of people.

"I know this may sound odd, but you remind me of someone," she told him that Saturday afternoon.

Lance led her to continue with her thought. "I hope that's not a bad thing—"

"It's not. You just happen to remind me of an ex of mine."

She shrugged her shoulders.

"Husband?"

"No, boyfriend."

Lance took that as a possible opening. After chatting further, she gave him a business card; it also had her cell phone number on it. He took her up on the gesture by calling her during his lunch break the following week. She remembered their meeting.

They agreed to meet for lunch later that week. They met again, and then a third time.

He was not sure where this was headed, but he asked her out a fourth time. They went to a movie. This time, he sensed something different about her. All her body language hinted at her being attracted to him. So he figured that he would test the waters, so to speak, and make a trial move—he initiated their first kiss.

"I like the fact you've taken things slowly with me," she told him. "But I'm warning you that you're causing a lot of things to come out in me that I've tried ignoring."

He held her tighter and kissed her again. "Hey, maybe that's not a bad thing. You haven't run away just yet."

"No, I haven't."

Shonna liked Lance's company so much that she went along with stopping by his place. She did not leave there until the next morning. They spent the next night at her place. At the time, she shared with him she had a younger sister who was married and had a teenage son. She did not divulge anything else about her.

A few days later, she surprised him by putting the brakes on their budding affair, claiming she needed time to sort through her emotions.

"Is it because of the difference in our age?" he asked her. "Or is it something else you're hiding from me?"

"I'm not hiding anything from you," she said. "This is just happening a little faster than I would have ever imagined."

Lance took Shonna's plea for space and time as justification of remaining a free agent should another woman pique his curiosity.

"All I'm going to say is you would think something was suspicious with me if I came to you asking for time allowing me to sort things out. I doubt if you would be giving me any chance to explain myself."

"You're probably right. I wouldn't," Shonna told him. "I would think that you had another woman, or even worse. You were married or gay."

She begged him to understand her rationale. "Lance, I'm forty-three years I'm past all the booty call stuff. I'm past playing games with people. I just want to make sure this is what I want to do. Maybe I'm looking for more than what you can offer at this time."

Translated, Lance took Shonna's comment as an insult and that he was immature. "Hey, maybe you're right. You do need figure yourself out. But I'll be the same person, if and when you do ever get around to contacting me again."

He also told her maybe he'll be there whenever she does come around to wanting him again, maybe he won't. "I promise you I won't be waiting nervously by a phone. That's for sure!"

There was no contact for three months. Shonna reached out to him again a little more than two weeks ago.

"Before you say anything, Lance, I want to let you know that dating someone sixteen years younger is what I want."

She sighed into the phone. Then she went off into lecturing about how she had so often voiced her lack of patience with men. There was a fine balance she had hoped to achieve.

Whenever she set extremely high expectations for herself and the men she involved herself with, she became disappointed and vented it with her impatience. Likewise, when she set lower expectations for herself and the men she then dated, her impatience always got the best of her.

This time, she hoped to have set them for herself and Lance somewhere in the middle.

"So it was about age?" he remarked.

She was quick to correct him. "No, it was about the expectations I'd set for myself."

A strange thing occurred, however. He felt a boost of pride about Shonna wanting him. He also knew that he had some leverage in this; it's not as if he was desperate.

"Are you sure that I'm what you want?' he added. "Funny how you asked me after that first night together what were my expectations if you decided to be sexual with me. I told you that I was open to a committed relationship with any woman who appealed to me not only physically but intellectually."

"I remember what you said. I also remember what I said," Shonna responded. "But a person's thoughts always seem to change once they start removing their clothes around the other person. I wanted to make sure mine were still the same."

Lance figured it wouldn't be a bad idea keeping his options open with Shonna.

"Okay, so what are your expectations, if I decide that dating you is what I want?"

She did not waste any time responding. "I want to be happy at this point in my life. Is there anything wrong with that?"

There was no wavering in her voice.

"Not at all. We all want happiness in our lives; we never know where it's going to come from, and from whom."

Shonna thought about the depth of their past dialogue. She was intrigued that he was unlike many of the young men she'd seen that comprised much of her station's listening audience.

He was like a throwback to her era being a child of the 1970s and 1980s. They also shared many things in common, including personal values. For example, Lance often quoted one of his mother's most notorious statements to him while growing up in the Washington, D.C. area: "I put you into this world, and I'll take you out of this world. Do you understand me?"

That was an all too familiar one for Shonna. "My mother's sixty-seven, and she still uses it on us. We sort of laugh because we remind her we're no longer thirteen years old."

"And I bet she still says that's all the more reason why she can say it—"

* * *

It just so happened that no sooner than Lance drove off from work, still savoring his quickie with Charlotte, his ringtone of Esperanza Spalding's "Precious" blared inside his car. He check the phone number. He rushed to answer it.

"How was your day?" Shonna asked.

He smirked. "Interesting. Really interesting."

"Why was it interesting?"

"This job is a trip, when you really think about it," he answered. "I'm paid to answer questions to people who feel like they've been cheated out of their money. But it's a job. It's something to do until I can find something I really want."

"I'll say this much, Lance. You'll find over time that there's a reason for why we're where we are. Nothing's ever wasted in the greater scheme of things."

Lance pursed his lips. He was still trying to figure that one out. He did not think it was such a fair thing that he would follow Nayla Ramsey to her home state thinking he was in love only to be stranded.

A young man's mistake, for sure. He did not fully consider everything. He ignored everyone's warnings and advice, including his family. Now his pride would not allow him to return home.

Had he stayed in Washington, D.C., where he knew people, he could have easily established himself in his chosen field of software programming with any government contractor or agency. He would not have faced any of his family's scrutiny.

"I see why so many people hate working where I'm at. The pay is below average at best, and the people we deal with can be so annoying."

He took a deep breath and paused. Thinking about work also reminded him of Charlotte, a potentially far more pressing matter. She'd already tried lavishing him with small gifts like shirts, ties, and CDs. He told her he was reluctant to accept them; however, she explained that it was just her way of expressing affection. He did not have it within him to hurt her feelings by demanding that she stopped.

Then there were the phone calls. In the morning. Once they got home from work. Before she went to sleep. Their conversations were mostly about sex and gossip from the job—

Shonna was a welcomed change of pace.

He posed, "Hey, what are you doing later this evening?"

"Well, that's the reason why I called. I know I've been busy all this week, and I'm sorry for that," Shonna answered. "I don't want you to think I've been avoiding you. I'd like for us to spend some time together."

He smirked. "Are you sure you won't have any problems being seen with me?"

"Why would you ask such a question?"

"Just checking."

"Don't create any issues when there isn't any."

The both laughed. They agreed to meet later for dinner in the Village at Sandhill shopping area along Clemson Road.

Chapter 16

'I've Finally Caught Up With You'

The bullet hole was repaired and the office was cleaned of any blood stains. Although it was both eerie and surreal, Cortez was more than glad to be back working from his office less than two weeks after Deloria's death.

"I don't know if I would ever go back in there," Paula told Cortez, standing outside his office without any intentions of stepping in there.

"They would just have to move me to another branch."

Cortez nodded. "The way I see it, things could have been much worse. That could have been a robbery. I could have been shot—"

"I understand your point," Paula interrupted. "It's just that office would be like a haunted place to me."

Cortez looked around the office space that he'd occupied since 2009. He noticed there were new customer chairs on the other side of his desk. Otherwise, at least to him, everything else seemed to be in place.

"I understand your concern, Paula. But I'm all right. Really, I am."

Paula pursed her lips. "Well, if you say so. I just know how I'd feel right now." She turned around and walked back over to the teller windows.

Reclining back in his seat, Cortez shrugged that he had not experienced a single nightmare directly related to the shooting. Perhaps it helped that he ducked as soon as the police told her to put down her gun. Just like it helped that he never saw Deloria's corpse.

What had been more traumatizing was the uncanny attention he'd received by the news media and over the Internet. He also mused he could handle Primas Lovett in a fist fight, if necessary.

"Hey, Bishop Moneymaker. Looks like they have restored your tabernacle," Trent joked with him. "I'm surprised at how fast they took care of things."

"Uh, deacon, I knew you would handle everything. That's why I never worried."

Trent apprised Cortez that he would lift the hold on personnel not responding to any inquiries pertaining to him. He was now on his own again.

"Are you sure you're okay with that?" Trent asked.

"Yeah. Now can I get back to the business of making money?"

Trent hunched his shoulders, but also warned Cortez, "It's on you, man. Be careful."

About an hour later, all five window tellers, both drive-thru tellers, and Trent were tied up with customers when a man dressed in deer hunting attire entered the bank. Cortez, being the only one free, came out into the lobby.

"Hi, how can we help you today?" He extended his hand out to the man.

The man looked at Cortez with contempt. As he bunched his lips, it was as if he summoned up all the angry energy that was within him, and he was poised to unleash it toward Cortez.

"I sure hope y'all can because y'all have messed things up," he said.

Cortez gestured with his head in the direction of his office. "Come over here with me. Let's see how we can solve this problem."

"It's definitely your problem."

Based on his experience, Cortez was more than aware that irate customers were bound to come through a branch at any time.

He introduced himself as he sat down behind his desk. "And you are?"

"Corley. Tommy Ray Corley." He tossed a couple of envelopes on the desk and pointed at them. "When I set up these here accounts, I told y'all specifically that I wanted all correspondences to go to a different post office box. All these came to my home address."

What Corley had not divulged to Cortez, the material was a secret account that he'd set up for his mistress, Michelle Rodgers; his wife, Nora, opened the information and confronted him about it.

Cortez remained stoic. "Mr. Corley, I personally apologize for our mistake."

"You got that right it was your mistake. Now I need y'all to fix this like yesterday!"

Cortez pulled up the account information. He noticed the accounts were set up at the Harbison location less than ten minutes away.

"I told that boy to make sure that it went to another post office box," he continued ranting. "That's the problem with you people."

"Excuse me?" Cortez reacted.

Unfazed by Cortez"s response, he reared back in his chair. His thin lips opened and closed as if he tried getting rid of a bad taste in his mouth.

"What's your problem, boy?" he retorted. "I asked you to take care of that address!"

The mood was extremely tense. Cortez had already ceased typing on his terminal. Tapping his desk, he mulled retorting with a diatribe against Corley that would surely attract unwanted attention.

Quietly instead, Cortez resumed correcting Corley's information on the checking account. "Okay, finished. All statements and future correspondences should go to the post office box you've given me."

"I sure hope it does, or I'll be going above your head. I have you to know that I'm good friends with Roy Lindsey himself."

The scowl still had not left Corley's face. "You do know who he is, boy?"

"Mr. Corley, I think we're finished here." Cortez got up, walked out and left Corley sitting there. He went over to Trent's office, fuming.

"What's going on?" Trent inquired.

He spoke loud enough that only Trent heard him. "Nothing that a two-by-four can't handle."

Moments later, Trent looked beyond Cortez's shoulders at the person standing behind Cortez.

"How can I help you?"

"I want you to know that your staff here is very uncooperative and unprofessional. Y'all will be hearing from me!"

Trent was stunned. It had been several years since he had a customer to voice their displeasure at an employee under his watch.

"What seems to be the problem?"

Cortez stepped aside and walked away, leaving Trent and Corley staring at each other.

"It doesn't matter. I've got connections. Y'all be hearing from me very soon." Corley walked off mumbling about Cortez and others like him.

Trent watched Corley leave the bank. Then he walked over to Cortez's office. He gestured with his head toward the front door.

"What was the problem with Mr. Deer Hunter?" he inquired.

Cortez stared off to his right and left before he responded. Stories of what he used to hear back home on Lady's Island played prominently in his mind.

He told Trent he did the best thing by ignoring Corley and disposing of him as soon as possible. Sighing, he added, "He wanted to pick a fight with someone, but I wasn't going to be the one. I've got enough problems at this time." He then shrugged his shoulders.

"He talked about having connections, and we'll be hearing from him. What was that about?"

"He claims he knows Lindsey, the man, who sits up on the eighteenth floor," Cortez answered. "He's mad that his account information and a couple of our correspondences went to the wrong address. I checked it out. The accounts were opened at another branch, not ours."

"I see."

"Hey, you know how it is. Sometimes you can't overcome bad credit, ignorance and—"

"Stupidity?" Trent chimed in to say.

"Exactly."

* * *

It was unusually slow for a Thursday toward the end of the month. Only a smattering of people had come through since lunch. Even Trent found himself bored, looking to kill some time.

Things at home with Sonia were still frosty at best. He resisted sending her a text message. So he browsed the social networks from his cell phone. Out of curiosity, he searched for Teale's name—there was an active profile and she still went by her maiden name.

In fact, she had updated her social network page just the night before, uploading a picture of her and another woman celebrating having completed a five-mile walk for charity.

Mmmph!

She still looked good, and her bright personality radiated in the picture. So many times over the years he tried convincing himself that he was better off going on with his life, accepting that maybe some things just weren't meant to be. But it was hard to accept that a relationship that he once thought was headed in the right direction suddenly ceased to exist.

Rather than sending a friend request, Trent spent several attempts drafting and redrafting a message before he finally sent one to her.

> I'm not sure if it's right by saying that I've finally caught up with you. It has been a long time. Maybe you'll get around to telling me why you left me the way you did. I wish you would. It might help bring some closure.

Within minutes, Trent got a response from Teale. He felt his heart pounding through his shirt. More than a decade had passed since they last communicated.

> Trent, is that really you? Wow. Looks like you've taken care of yourself. You're right it's been a long time. A lot of things have happened both then and now.

Trent decided work was not the place for engaging in this kind of interaction. Besides, now that he knew she remembered him, let her think about it a bit longer.

After checking in on his tellers, Trent noticed two e-mails flashing in his inbox. Both were inquiries also copied to another person at Palmetto Fidelity, and they came from different people at the corporate office in downtown Columbia.

The first one came from the customer relations department. Apparently, Tommy Ray Corley had connections and caused some downward rumblings through the hierarchy.

The other one came from the area H.R. generalist. That one was of greater intrigue. Trent was quick to dial Neal Scanlan's extension.

"Why do your people need to speak with one of my employees?"

Trent inquired.

"You know how it goes, Trent," Scanlan replied. "We can't tell you exactly the what's and why's."

Trent sighed. "I'm not going to play any guessing games here. Has somebody made a formal complaint against one of my people in this branch?" He reached for a pen and began toying with it on his desk.

"I'll level with you. All I can say is there are no complaints that we know of among your employees. Apparently, this one is a lot more formal, and we need to speak with Mr. Anderson as soon as possible." Scanlan spoke as if he had said all he would say to Trent.

"I know something must be serious if you guys are involved.

Is there any you need from me?"

"Just have him to contact me."

Scanlan hung up, leaving Trent wondering what was brewing. He knew it wasn't good.

"Hey, got a minute?" Trent said, standing outside of Cortez's office.

"What's up?"

Taking a deep breath, Trent entered Cortez's office and sat in one of the chairs across from his desk.

"I just got a couple of e-mails today from people who really must want your scalp," Trent said. "One is from a customer relations manager, Marcy Dutton. The other, I think, is more serious. That one comes from Neal Scanlan in H.R."

Cortez leaned forward upon his forearm on his desk. "Do you have any idea what's going on?"

"Nope." Trent shook his head for emphasis. He also leaned forward. "I recommend that you call Scanlan first. The other people can wait."

Trent then tapped on Cortez's desk, got up and left, leaving him shaking his head in wonderment.

"Scanlan—"

"This is Cortez Anderson. I understand you want to speak with me?"

"Yes, I do." His voice was serious and pushy. "Do you know why I've asked to speak with you?"

Cortez sighed loudly into the phone. "No, I don't. Trent Buckner told me to call you."

"I see."

There was rattling of paper in the background. Then Scanlan began pecking on his keyboard.

"The reason why I'm calling is that the powers-that-be want to find out what really happened in that incident between you and Deloria Lovett, who was shot and killed at your branch recently," Scanlan explained.

"Okay." Cortez sounded coy, bordering evasive. "Have you not seen what's been over the Internet or what was reported in the news lately?"

Scanlan glanced at a confidential memo about Palmetto Fidelity already being threatened with a lawsuit from Primas Lovett for among other things, gross professional misconduct and negligence. It also mentioned the bank wanted to prepare itself for a legal response, if necessary.

"How well did you know this lady Deloria Lovett?" Scanlan asked.

Burying his head into his hand, Cortez felt as if he'd now entered into a free fall. Nothing was going his way lately. Lifting his head, he gazed aimlessly straight ahead.

"Cortez?"

"Yeah, I'm here," he responded. "I knew her both professionally and personally."

"Can you explain that for me?"

"Professionally, I was the officer who processed a personal loan for her. Personally, I was involved with her for a while."

"How long?"

"Less than a year."

"Like six months?"

"More like between six months and a year."

"Do you realize the seriousness of what happened? The way we see it a customer was killed in your office. And from what we can understand, based on the police report, this was a personal matter that spilled over into the workplace."

Cortez spoke with resignation. "I guess so. I told her this did not have to happen."

"Well, that's obvious." Scanlan's tone seemed annoyed by the entire matter. "Let me ask you this: Was there any time in your interaction with Deloria Lovett that you threatened her or she threatened you?"

"I never threatened her. Not once. She threatened me. She pointed her gun at me."

There was a delay in the conversation. Scanlan apprised Cortez that he was catching up with his statement while typing.

"So let me get this straight. You're saying not once you threatened her, and she was the one who threatened you?"

"That's correct."

"You're also saying you did have both a personal and professional relationship with Deloria Lovett?"

"That's correct."

"And you were aware that she was married?"

"Unfortunately, yes. But that had nothing to do with why she came to the bank."

"It didn't?"

"No."

There was another lengthy pause by Scanlan. He took the time to consider what he needed to ask next. He'd already recognized that there were a couple of policy issues that were in question, and he would have to apprise upper management of it.

Meanwhile, Cortez cursed himself for all that had happened. He thought maybe he should have taken some time off work rather than returning so fast. Something else also came to mind.

"I know this has nothing to do with what you're asking me about, but did Trent ever look into whether I could be transferred to another branch?" Cortez queried.

"I can look into it, but that is not something within my scope of responsibility."

"Okay."

Scanlan had now reloaded with additional questions for Cortez.

"You do realize, as well, that the bank has certain expectations for its staff and the way it interacts with customers?"

Cortez leaned back in his chair, rolling his eyes. "I certainly do. And I've always been mindful of that in the way I conduct business on behalf of the bank. I think my record here will show that I do well with people, and I've made this bank a lot of money."

"The thing I'm bringing to your attention is we're in financial services. So that means we are here to meet our customer's financial needs, and not, shall we say, their needs involving lust. And when that confluence exists, it opens up a can of worms that nobody wants."

So much for patience, Cortez huffed.

"All right, so what are you getting at? You want to fire me because I had an affair with one of our customers?"

"We've got a few serious issues we must be prepared to deal with," Scanlan said. "It is our responsibility to be proactive in those things. I have no further questions. We'll be in contact if we need to speak with you further."

He hung up.

Cortez scoffed that Scanlan was the latest to ruin a day of his. And Trent was right. The customer service manager could wait another day for him to respond to her.

He spent the rest of the workday withdrawn from his branch colleagues, and he did not leave his office until after closing time.

"I never got around to asking you how did those phone calls go for you?" Trent inquired.

Cortez stared at Trent, but he figured he owed him some kind of response. "Man, I don't even want to talk about it." He was visibly disgusted and his voice trailed off.

"Look, I don't know why they called," Trent tried explaining to him. "But let me know if there is any way that I can help you."

"Yeah, sure." He walked off without bidding Trent or anyone else in the branch goodbye.

* * *

Before leaving, Trent decided to check his cell phone for messages. Sonia had not left him anything neither had Taylor. Next, he checked his social network. He had not responded to Teale's reply.

After reaching out to her, he had second thoughts. But then he considered the way things had been going with Sonia lately. He figured why not see what else Teale might have to say.

> Teale, if you're serious about bringing any closure to the way things ended with us, this is my social network address and here is my cell phone number: 803 . . .

Chapter 17

'Does He Really Listen to You'

Sonia noticed that Tanya had been on her best behavior lately. She'd been courteous and patient with the people whose inquires she handled. Perhaps a transformation had taken place and she didn't know about it.

Uh-oh…

Just like that, the transformation went into reverse. Tanya slapped her desk, she glared at the ceiling, and her chest heaved and fell dramatically.

"I told this dumb wench that we're not responsible for how a claim was transmitted to us from Indiana, and she's cursing me out about it," Tanya ranted. "She has just aggravated my last nerve!"

Tanya returned to the caller. "Ma'am, the patient's home plan, which is us, can only process for benefits what has been transmitted to us. The issue is with Indiana, not us."

The caller launched into a profanity-laced tirade, and she demanded to speak with a supervisor.

"I'm sick and tired of dealing with United Care Plan!" The woman's voice was of a nasally, annoying tone. "It's always trouble whenever I deal with you people. We file our claims and we don't get paid. And it takes a friggin' act of friggin' congress to get anything done!"

"Hold, hold it! From the moment I identified myself, you have unloaded on me, not giving me any chance to explain anything to you, and I have tried to be professional in spite of you," Tanya retorted, "But it's obvious you have a comprehension problem!"

She made another quick perusal of other screens that provided her a list of previous inquiries made by the caller. "Our documentation shows that each time you've called, you've asked the same question, and we've given you the same answer."

"La-la-la-la . . .!" the caller yelled. ". . . Supervisor . . . supervisor! . . . I don't want to speak to you any more!"

"And I don't wanna speak to you!" Tanya yelled back before placing her on hold. She stormed over to Sonia's cubicle pointing emphatically back at her desk.

"Ms. Sonia, if there's such a thing as snatching someone through the phone, this woman would be it!"

I should have known, Sonia mused to herself. First of all, nothing lasts forever. Secondly, days like this never seem to fail: Invariably, whenever it was overcast, dreary, and raining outside, it was the worst kind of a combination for the phone reps. Calls of the most unusual and extreme nature seem to come through.

Road rage, meet phone rage.

The woman noticed she was taken off hold. "Who is this?"

"I'm Sonia, Tanya's supervisor." She closed her eyes and shook her head. "And who am I speaking to?"

The woman huffed in disgust and proceeded to curse at Sonia. "And by the way, name is Margie. I've waited a half-hour before someone answered—you need to have more people answering the phones!"

"We apologize for your inconvenience," Sonia answered. "We do work hard to answer calls as accurately and expeditiously as possible. However, we do average more than nine hundred and fifty calls an hour each day, or nearly two calls every second."

"I don't give a flying rat's you-know-where how many calls you people get an hour or flippin' second!" Margie yelled back at Sonia. "I want this claim paid, or I'm filing a complaint with the insurance commissioner!"

Sonia glanced over at Tanya, who returned an I-told-you-so stare. Taking a deep breath, she placed Margie on hold and made a quick research of the issue. After nearly five minutes of scanning through several screens, she returned to the caller.

"It appears you'll need to contact your carrier in Indiana to resolve how the claim was first entered into the system. That seems to be where the problem is—"

"UGH!" Margie reacted. "Who is your supervisor? I want to speak to that person! Obviously, you're not capable of doing a job that any fifth grader could do!"

Clearly, you hadn't gotten past the fifth grade yourself, Sonia wanted to tell the woman. She placed her on hold and looked directly at Tanya.

"Now that, my dear, is a fool." She then stepped away from Tanya's desk and began heading back to her cubicle. "Transfer that call to my desk."

Instead of contacting Phyllis, Sonia pulled a common trick of hers when dealing with an irate caller.

She walked over to Vicki's cubicle, whispering, "Hey, I need your help." She then apprised Vicki of what had already transpired.

"And you want me to help you with that?" she responded.

"If she starts yelling and cursing at you, I'm sure you know how to resolve this."

Vicki rolled her eyes. She then sighed loudly before taking Margie off hold.

"I need to confirm with you that since the services were performed in Indiana, you went through the process of filing your claim through Indiana. Is that correct?"

"What does that have to do with the tea in China?" Margie snapped back at Vicki. "I've had it with you, too . . . If I lived where you were, I'd drive my van through your front door!"

Vicki shook her head while mouthing *I'm not feeling any of this today* to Sonia. Then she hung up on Margie—an unspoken favor returned among supervisors.

"Anything else, Sonia?" she said, while returning to her own cubicle.

"Thanks, Vicki. That should do it."

Sonia then made a notation on her screen the call was lost due to disconnection. She also informed Tanya to make the same notation.

"We've been getting crazy people like that woman all day!" Tanya's voice was at a high pitch and her rural dialect was unmistakable.

"Have you taken a look outside?" Sonia queried.

Tanya hunched her shoulders. "No, I haven't."

Sonia hoped that Tanya would eventually figure that one out for herself.

After averaging three supervisor's inquiries each hour, the best thing Sonia received all day was a text from Trent wanting to take her out to dinner. It was a pleasant surprise from someone who had been banished back to the Dog House Inn.

Hey, I've heard a lot about this place called The

> Groovy Soul. I think it might be somewhere you'd
> like trying. Taylor says he's going over to Bruce's
> home after practice.

Of all the possibilities, Sonia thought, Trent would tell her about a place where she previously visited and still held two coupons for five dollars off.

> Sounds interesting. Besides, you need to do a lot
> more than taking me out to dinner, anyway. But
> this is a start. I'll be getting off work at 5:30 on THE
> DOT today.

> Make sure that you give Taylor some money so he
> can get something to eat. And tell him that we'll
> pick him up.

Sonia went along with getting directions and the address from Trent. She agreed to meet him there between six o'clock and 6:15 p.m.

* * *

Wharton Milner cleared his throat and licked his lips once he noticed who had just entered The Groovy Soul. His instincts had not betrayed him. He coolly walked over to the restaurant's waiting area.

"And how many will be in your party this evening?" His voice had an inviting tone to it.

"Two."

"For you and that nice lady who visited us the last time?"

Sonia returned a surprised look. "My sister?"

She shook her head. "I'm waiting on my husband this time."

"I see." He looked her up and down. "Obviously, he has good taste in women."

Milner went ahead with greeting and seating the next dinner party that entered. About five minutes later, Trent entered the establishment. Sonia immediately stood up. They smiled at each other.

"How long have you been waiting?" Trent asked.

"Oh, about ten minutes."

"I would have been here sooner had you not asked me to drop off some money with Taylor."

"Hey, it's okay. It's nice that we're having some time together."

Trent and Sonia made for a handsome and complementary couple in public. After knowing each other for more than fifteen years, they appeared settled, and as if they were ordained for each other. "How did you find out about this place?" Sonia asked.

"You remember Ms. Wanda, my lead teller?" Trent answered.

"Yeah, I remember her. She's a nice lady." And somebody she would not suspect Trent delving off into any mischief with.

"She came here last weekend. She's not one for recommending places, but this was one of them. I figured there had to be something to it."

"It sure sounds like a place that we'll have to visit again, hmmm?"

"We'll see."

"Good evening. A party of two, here?" Milner approached the Buckners.

"Yes, it will be," Trent answered.

"Follow me."

Milner directed them to the same table where he seated Sonia and Shonna. Immediately, he noticed that Trent did not
pull the seat out for Sonia. Nor did he see Trent allow Sonia
to get up first and visit the buffet bar. He noticed she had a
disappointed look while waiting for Trent's return.

When he came back with their drinks, he spoke just loud
enough for her to hear: "So this is not the first time he's done
that, hmmm?"

Sonia merely looked up at Milner. He remained subtle in
the way he handled himself in clear view of everyone. He
managed not to smile back at her.

"Some men don't appreciate what they have—how long has
he been in the dog house with you?" Then he walked off to
another dinner party to his right, checking in on them. It was
tempting to consider Trent's suggestion of coming to The
Groovy Soul as a blessing in disguise since she had already
planned on returning there on her own.

Ah, but she remained hopeful that Trent would not dig
himself a deeper hole beneath the Dog House Inn. And maybe,
just maybe, he might hold his own against the competition.

That, in itself, would be a turn-on. Surely, she would let
Trent know about it in the bedroom.

"Aren't you going to get yourself something?" Trent asked
upon returning.

Duh, I've waited all this time!

"Yes, darling. Is there anything you saw up there I might
like?"

"Huh?" Trent was already into a plate covered with salad,
pork chops, and rice with gravy. It suddenly dawned upon
him that Sonia had spoken to him. "Oh, yeah. You might like
the baked fish up there; I don't know—"

As he did the last time, Milner all but stopped what he was
doing to enjoy the view from behind while Sonia visited the

buffet bar. It was quite amusing to him how men could be so clueless, considering he was once guilty of the same thing.

Now that he was divorced—since 2003, in fact—it hasn't really mattered. He could be a perpetrator and loving it all at the same time.

Wait 'till he get a load of this move, Milner whispered to himself. "Would you like another Pepsi there?"

Trent glanced upward. "Yeah, sure."

Milner had timed his visit just as Sonia returned from the buffet bar, making sure he reestablished eye contact with her.

She sucked in her lips and held it—it finally clicked with her what was going on, considering the way Milner had positioned himself behind Trent just off to his right.

"I'll be back with your drink."

The marriage resource Web site that Sonia still visited suggested that husbands needed to understand that conversation will always be important with the wife. It explained the wife needed that sense of connection—especially if he was sincere about it.

After a day like Sonia had at work, she felt it would be nice that Trent lent her a willing ear.

"How was work today?" she queried him.

He shrugged his shoulders. "Aside from corporate appearing to be going after Cortez, it was a slow day today. How was yours?" He resumed eating.

"I wish I had a day like yours."

Before she realized it, Trent had excused himself for a second trip to the buffet bar. Her annoyance had reached the danger zone even as Milner timed his return to their table.

"How often does he really listen to you?" Milner said, placing Trent's drink on the table. He was quick with the rest of his observation. "It really means something when a man sits down and listens, hmmm?"

Then he walked off.

Milner's suave and sneaky oratory had resonated with Sonia. But she was hopeful that Trent would prove him wrong even as he returned with a second plate of what he previously ate.

"I was thinking about taking some time off as soon as we get through this month," Sonia mentioned to him. "A place like that can alter someone's personality if they don't get away from there."

"I wish I could do something like that whenever I want." He took a long sip from his drink.

"This isn't about you, Trent."

"I know. It's just that they don't allow branch managers to consider taking time off like that. It's as if we're chained to that place."

Sonia stared off in space wishing that she had simply gone to The Groovy Soul by herself. At least if she wanted to be alone, it would have been her choice, and not by default. Her mood was tempered once she caught a view of Milner standing near the cashier's counter.

Tall. Still slender and well kept. Seemingly attuned to a woman's feelings. She suspected he probably knows a thing or two about patience both in and out of the bedroom. Fighting the temptation, Sonia gave Trent a third chance at redeeming himself.

"Hey, I was thinking about joining a gym so that I can work on my back and legs," Trent blurted out to her. "It seems as I get older I'm no longer motivated to use the exercise equipment in the garage."

"And if you don't use that equipment any more, you can get additional exercise by getting rid of it!" Sonia waggled her head with her response.

Trent leaned back in his chair and smirked. "Hey, I have my

stuff neatly arranged in there. So don't say that I've junked up the garage with it."

It took all of Sonia not to unload and scold Trent for having blown a great opportunity with her: the date had gone downhill ever since he opened his mouth after they were seated.

Milner's timing was uncanny once again. This time, he positioned himself standing between Trent's and Sonia's view from the side.

"How are we doing here?" he inquired. "I hope everything's met your expectations."

Trent took a sip from his drink before he answered. "I'm glad that I came here. A co-worker of mine recommended this place."

"I thought this was your first time here! I didn't recall seeing either of you before. And may I ask who the person who told you about our place was?"

"Ms. Wanda Odom."

"I'm not familiar with that name. Where do the two of you work?"

"We work at bank together."

"Be sure to drop off a business card of yours. We have a drawing every week, and we give away free lunches and dinners."

"I have one of his cards," Sonia chimed in to say. "I'll be sure to do that before we leave."

"Is there anything else we can get for you tonight?" Milner asked. "Since it's a bit slow, why don't you take home a little something extra? How 'bout that?"

"Really?" Trent reacted. "I thought you're not allowed to do that at one of these buffets?"

Milner copped one of his diplomatic poses and smiled back at him. "It can be done if I say it can be done."

"You have connections with the management?"

Sonia dipped her head. At the same time, she was impressed by the way Milner had handled not disclosing her coming there with Shonna.

"I sure do. I own this place. But I don't share that with everyone, if you know what I mean—"

Trent nodded. "I must say that I'm very impressed with your operation here." He looked over at Sonia. "Don't forget to drop off one of my cards, baby."

"I won't."

"Thank you. I'll be back with those containers."

Sonia got up and visited the ladies' room. While she was in there, she tore a sheet of paper from her notepad and wrote down her name, cell phone number, and business e-mail address.

On their way out of The Groovy Soul, she made sure to make eye contact with Milner before she placed both Trent's card and the sheet of paper inside the candy jar by the cashier's counter.

Chapter 18

❦

'You're Not Getting Smart With Me?'

All it took was a lull in their conversation, a look of wanting more in their eyes, and it was clearly understandable what Lance and Shonna wanted to do next.

Since they were closer to her place just off Hard Scrabble Road, Shonna suggested they go there, a four-bedroom home on a two-acre lot owned by her parents.

"I must be getting comfortable with you again," she told him in the parking lot of Pacquino's, an Italian restaurant in the Village at Sandhill.

Lance leaned forward and kissed Shonna, who held the back of his head and drew him closer. He slipped his hands downward and caressed her backside. She offered no resistance, but playfully wiggled it to his touch.

Coming up for air, she mentioned, "I know I feel good to you, but you should at least know by now that I'm not much of an exhibitionist."

The dinner allowed Lance to recharge his libido. Now, spending some quiet time with Shonna being nuzzled up to him on her living room sofa was like the main event of his day. It couldn't get any better.

"Why are you so attracted to me?" he asked.

"Good question. And why are you so attracted to me?" she countered. "I'm sure there are plenty of women out there that could turn you on possibly the same way—"

"Answer my question first."

Shonna turned to the side and stared at Lance. But he was eager to press his point with her.

"I'm waiting—"

"It depends on what you're looking to find out from me. I could easily say that I knew that I could have you whenever I wanted after you introduced yourself." She sat up and stretched, extending her arms.

There was no doubt that Shonna's youthful features, high cheekbones, shoulder-length hair, and piercing brown eyes caught his attention that fateful Saturday afternoon almost five months ago.

"Oh, so you think I was just that hooked on you at first sight, huh?" he remarked.

She smiled. "Lance, a woman often has a pretty good idea about a man within the first few minutes after meeting him—and we're usually right about what we've determined." Then she removed her sweater and kicked off her shoes, giving Lance reason to think that she might experience a similar sexual fate as Charlotte had with him.

"Are you saying, then, that men are just that obvious with women?" He cleared his throat, continuing, "It seems to me that's all just a mind game being played."

"No, it isn't, Lance. You may not realize this, women are naturally perceptive," she explained; her voice was rather convincing. "You men rely on instincts. And that's the nature of a man."

Lance realized he was headed for uncharted territory if he pursued that kind of a conversation. Understanding a woman's intuition was something he'd neither considered nor was knowledgeable of.

"I'll say this much. You still haven't answered my question about why were you attracted to me." He puffed out his chest, returning an in-your-face stare.

Sighing, Shonna gave in. "I think you can figure out that I knew what I wanted, because otherwise, you wouldn't be touching and fondling me right now." She tipped her head toward him; the message was unquestionable.

It was Lance's instinct to withdraw from cupping and caressing Shonna's breasts since she'd put him on the spot. But she insisted that he continued. So, he proceeded to unbutton her blouse and unhook her bra.

"What is it you want to do?" she asked in her most seductive voice.

"I thought it went without saying what I wanted to do right now." He leaned forward and kissed her on the side of her neck. She placed her hands on his while he continued kneading and fondling her exposed flesh.

"Mmmm, sounds good. But since you couldn't tell me, I've got something else in mind."

He stopped immediately. He mused aloud whether this was her definition of being spontaneous.

"Keep doing that. I like it," she said.

"What is this 'something else'? I don't think we've tried whatever approach you're suggesting—"

"Mmmm, so you've been observant. You should continue working on that. You'll learn more about me that way."

Suddenly, she stood up before him and held out her hand

toward him. He stood up and instinctively moved to embrace and kiss her.

Next, he placed his hands on her waist. She looked up at him again.

"You know what I'd like to do tonight?" she queried him.

He did not respond.

"What I'd like is for us to take off each other's clothes, snuggle up in my bed, and we just talk tonight. That's all. I just want to feel close to you, Lance."

Before he could form any words on his lips, she went on to say, "It's a woman's thing."

He was caught off guard with her request. When he finally spoke, it was slow and deliberate. "You just want to talk?"

"Yes. Talk."

"Talk?"

"Talk." She then smiled at him. "What's wrong, you can't control yourself and you just have to have it?"

He was moved to chortling. "And this is your way of also denying yourself?"

"No," she said, shaking her head. "It's just called wanting to do something sensual. And I think that is about as sensual as it gets."

"Okay. We'll do that."

This has to be some kind of a game, Lance thought. He figured he'd go along with it and find out just where her breaking point was. They still may wind up engaged in some flesh slapping against flesh.

Both helped remove the remainder of each other's clothing. Lance then followed Shonna to her bedroom. Although he was visibly turned on by viewing the firmness and shapeliness of her body, he could not resist giggling.

"What's so funny?" she asked, stopping at her queen-size bed.

She went ahead with pulling back the covers and sheets and climbing into bed first. He was quick to join her. They cuddled up together just as she had hoped to do.

"I was thinking about the first time I came in here with you. I was sort of stunned that it actually happened." He stared up toward the ceiling.

"Didn't I mention about a woman having a pretty good idea about a man not long after meeting him?" she reminded him.

"I knew when I gave you my phone number that I'd already wanted you."

Lance ventured to explain himself further. "I believe women think all men are solely on search-and-conquer missions. That's true, but only to a certain degree." He let out a soft moan—she'd just fondled and hand-stroked him.

"Then what do you call it?" she retorted, still fondling and stroking him. "It is in your nature to pursue and conquer—"

He let out a sigh. "It's like this. You want something. You're almost there. Nothing's guaranteed that you're really going to get it. You could have easily changed your mind."

"But I didn't. I told you I knew I wanted you. I knew I could have you. What's so difficult about that?" She turned onto her side, inviting him to spoon upon her.

He complied, reaching around to caress and fondle her. He also rubbed his body against hers. She felt the pounding of his heart against her flesh as well as the thickness and hardness of his flesh pressed elsewhere upon her.

"There's so much men need to learn about women," he observed, "and the same thing goes for women needing to learn about men."

She closed her eyes, allowing her mind to drift off into another realm. "That's a wise statement there, Lance. Are you willing to do that with me?"

"I—"

"You don't have to answer that right now."

Lance caught himself from breathing an audible sigh of relief. But he sensed at some point that question might surface again.

I'll be ready for it next time.

Shonna's movements in bed stunned and woke up Lance.

"Sorry about that. I just came from the bathroom."

"I know both of us just sort of fallen off to sleep. What time is it?"

She pointed at the dresser just off to her right. "It's almost midnight. What's wrong? Afraid that you'll turn into a pumpkin or a frog?"

"Uh-uh, I wasn't prepared to stay here the entire night with you." He sat up in the bed next to her.

"And just think if you'd gotten what you'd really wanted, hmmm?" she retorted. "See, I'm glad that all we did was cuddle and talk tonight."

Lance confessed, "I just didn't come prepared to spend the night. And I don't feel like rushing back home in the morning to get ready for work."

He went on to present the converse of that argument being if she had gone to his place. "First of all, I doubt if you would have talked about us cuddling up in my bed—"

"You're probably right."

"I know I'm right."

Shonna got out of bed and walked over to her closet. Another view of her body in its immediate glory was a rather convincing argument to remain with her. She returned having put on a silk kimono robe of hers. She sat on the bed Indian style.

"You know you're welcomed to stay. I love if you would, but I guess I can understand—this time."

Lance glanced down at his body, which seemed to raise a dissenting vote against his decision. Reluctantly, he got up and strode into the living room.

Shonna followed him as well, watching him put on his clothes.

"Hey, what are you doing Saturday?" she asked.

"Nothing. Why?"

"I'd like for you to meet my sister. I told her about you the last time we saw each other."

He returned a surprised look. "You never told me you had a sister?"

"You never asked," she snapped back at him. "And it's not as if you've told me anything about you having siblings, either."

"I have told you. I told you that I'm the youngest of four in my family. I have three sisters."

"Well, maybe you did and I forgot. The station has a remote broadcast at a restaurant in Cayce. She knows that I'll be there. I'm sure she'll come if I ask her."

Immediately, Lance reasoned that it was not often a woman invited a man to meet any family members unless she thought he might pass their scrutiny—or she wanted their approval. Otherwise only a fool would bring someone around family members just for showing off purposes.

"Isn't that ironic? I met you at one of those promotional things, and now you're asking me to meet you and your sister at one?"

"Why not? Then we'll do our thing afterward. You have any problem with that?"

"Actually, not at all."

Shonna handed him his jacket just before he reached the front door. Then she gave him a hug and a long, searching kiss. To make a more compelling statement, she guided his hand between her thighs, inviting him to fondle her. He was incredulous at what he felt upon his fingertips, and more.

She said, "Had you told me exactly what you wanted to do, this would have been all yours tonight."

He shook his head—although he had not yet withdrawn his hand. "Next time."

"That's right. Next time."

* * *

Lance grimaced once he checked his cell phone that he left in his car while he was with Shonna. The message light blinked faster than any strobe. There were ten text messages and sixteen missed calls. He knew exactly where they came from.

Rather than prolonging the agony, he dialed Charlotte's number. Then he inhaled deeply and let it out slowly.

"Where have you been? I was worried about you?" She did not allow him to respond. "Lance, don't do that to me again!"

He knew this was bound to happen—an intersection of him juggling multiple women. Meanwhile, he merely held his cell phone to his ear, allowing Charlotte to continue with her ranting.

"How could you do this? Ignore all my phone calls! And we just screwed earlier this evening? Something's not right, and I want to know what's going on, Lance!"

He had heard enough from her. "Can I speak now?"

"You're getting smart with me?"

"No, I'm not getting smart with you. I haven't had a chance to say anything. As soon as you picked up, you've been ranting and yelling the entire time. I figured I'd just let you talk until you got tired."

There was a brief silence.

"Lance, I'm not the person to be played with!"

"I'm not either, and I don't play games with people."

"I hope that's true. Because what you did was not right. The least you can do is let me know if you're all right!"

"Wait a minute, you don't own me. Nobody owns me, you understand?"

"This is not about being possessive, Lance. It's about common courtesy . . . Especially since I'm the one walking around with remnants of you up inside of me. Or have you forgotten so fast?"

Lance tried explaining that he went bowling and he didn't bring his phone inside. Besides, if he brought his phone, he would not have felt like going outside to answer it.

"You, bowling?" she reacted.

"Yeah, I'm a bowler." He spoke with a tinge of sarcasm. "Maybe if you took time to ask me questions other than during sex, and about who's saying anything behind your back at work, you could have found out that I do bowl."

She huffed into the phone. "All right. If you went bowling, where did you go?"

"I'm not telling you where I went bowling. You're not my mother!"

"Oh, so it's going to be like that, huh? I can find out. You're not that stupid to play games like that with me now, are you?"

Lance took a few moments to compose himself. He refused to be put on the spot under those terms.

"Charlotte, you're right. I should have called you and let you know that I was going bowling. But it was not intentional that I didn't answer the phone."

"Listen, I wasn't born yesterday. It sounds like to me that you were doing something else, like another woman. Yeah, that's right. I said it!"

"And you're wrong! Like I said, if you'd taken time to find out a few more things about me, you would have found out that I bowl, and sometimes I bowl for money."

"Okay, if you bowled for money, how did you do?"

"I broke even."

"Humph, yeah, whatever—"

She hung up on him.

Lance shrugged his shoulders and continued driving down Two Notch Road. Just his luck, he noticed a bowling alley to his left. Since he didn't put anything past Charlotte, he stopped in there and bowled three quick games. At least he could tell her with some credibility that he had gone there.

Chapter 19

'Give It to Me Straight'

Burying Deloria was something Primas Lovett felt obligated to do. But going after Cortez Anderson was a matter of principle.

While he was in Memphis handling Deloria's funeral, Lovett also consulted with his attorney A. Mitchell Duffner devising a strategy of retaliation. Any money that might come out of it would be regarded as mere spoils of victory and satisfaction exacted.

Duffner recommended that Lovett hire a private investigator and research any paper trail that might trace back to Cortez.

He also recommended using the media to his advantage. "That's where you'll enjoy your greatest leverage. These days, no respected business enterprise wants negative and sensational press hounding it."

"I'm all for anything that will help me accomplish what I'm trying to do here," Lovett told Duffner. "You should have seen the smug look on that punk's face when I confronted him at that gas station." He hissed at the thought.

"Mr. Lovett, I wouldn't recommend you doing anything like that ever again."

Duffner was known for his flair in the court room and his savvy with the media. While he attended law school in North Carolina back in the early 1980s, he interned for a U.S. Supreme Court justice, but chose early on to pursue a law career in the private sector.

It was also in Washington, D.C. where he was first inspired about the art of argument and persuasion. A traditional practice among U.S. Supreme Court interns was arguing a case based on characters from famous plays. In the rotation of plays selected by the justices, Duffner successfully argued that the parents of Romeo were entitled to suing Juliet's estate, as well holding her parents responsible for his death.

This came after Romeo's parents appealed their case up to the U.S. Supreme Court where its decision could become law.

"You know that this Cortez Anderson fella could claim that you harassed him," Duffner reminded Lovett. "And that could work against you."

"I know. I know," Lovett said. "Now what about this meeting you're pushing to have with the bank?"

"I'm still working on that. You never know when they might respond."

Duffner said the letter he sent Palmetto Fidelity informing it of their lawsuit intentions was based on previous tort precedent.

"A business like Palmetto Fidelity should have certain policies in place regarding the conduct of their employees," he explained. "It appears that there was no true enforcement of their policy.

"Hence, negligence on the bank's part—"

"Stop talking all of that legal jive with me and just give it to me straight!"

"In other words, Mr. Lovett," Duffner began to explain, "I anticipate the bank may say that it can't police its own employees to the extent that they'll argue that may be an invasion of privacy.

"But what they've got to understand is that you've suffered great emotional pain and distress because you had to learn through the media that one of their employees was engaged in improper behavior with your, uh, departed wife . . ." Duffner made sure not to utter the word "dearly" knowing what he also knew about Deloria, according to his conversations with Lovett.

"And it was their responsibility to make sure that their employees understand that they should never mix business with pleasure."

Lovett, whose own education reached no further than a high school diploma, understood that part of Duffner's tactic.

"And if we make enough noise, you're hoping they'll blink first."

"Now you're getting it!"

"But what if they decide to fight it?"

Duffner replied, "Then we'll have to fight the good fight."

"They've got hotshot lawyers, too. You know they'll try to ignore and delay forever."

Duffner thought of saying his fighting the good fight only went as far as Lovett's money. The conversation he had with Lovett was being billed at $250 per hour.

"You're going to have to trust me on this one. Remember, as stupid as it sounded, McDonald's settled with the woman who claimed she didn't know her coffee was hot."

He then corrected himself to note McDonald's was held partly negligent because the warning on the cup was not large enough, and the woman was not given sufficient warning the coffee was hot.

A jury awarded the woman $2.7 million, but it was eventually settled out of court for less than $600,000.

"That said," he continued, "you're a businessman. How would you like to be accused of condoning a culture of corruption and unbridled, ruthless behavior?"

Lovett scoffed at the image Duffner's created. But it made even better sense to him—along with hoping to get the last laugh.

Chapter 20

❧

'You Had Your Knife Aimed at Me…'

Not again.

Cortez saw a couple of television crews in the St. Andrews branch parking lot just as he reached the stop light. He suspected there was only one reason why they were there.

The last thing he wanted to do was being caught on camera brushing aside another crazy, sensational reporter asking a bunch of stupid questions.

Instead of turning, he opted to merge back into the St. Andrews Road traffic that was headed toward the I-26 freeway. He tried calling Trent, informing him of why had not yet shown up for work; there was no answer. He then suspected that Trent was chasing off the media horde.

"Deacon, this is Bishop Moneymaker. I wanted to let you know that I saw those media folks outside and decided to keep driving. I don't have anything to say to them. I'll check back with you again shortly. I hope you'll understand."

Cortez drove around in the immediate area for about twenty minutes before he made another pass by the bank. This time, there were no television crews.

Whew!

Before leaving his car, he checked his cell phone for any text messages. There were none. Since the Deloria Lovett incident, it had been a rather lonely existence for him. It seemed that all the women in his notorious harem had deserted him.

Cortez had an uncomfortable feeling when he entered the bank. A couple of the tellers went silent and stared at him. He sensed the scrutiny had reached a frenzied state. He went straight to Trent's office.

"Did you get my message?" Cortez asked.

"Yeah, I got it." Trent appeared to be annoyed. He sighed before continuing. "Maybe it was a good thing that you weren't here around the time you left that message."

"Was it that bad?"

Trent nodded. "I've kind of put one-and-one together on this. There was a reason why corporate contacted you when it did recently. And it came to me when those reporters asked me questions about a lawsuit involving that dead customer of yours."

Stunned at the news, Cortez sat down slowly in a chair across from Trent's desk. He blinked his eyes rapidly several times.

"A lawsuit?" For what?"

Trent sat back and folded his arms. "Good question. But apparently they're claiming that Palmetto Fidelity was negligent in your customer's death."

Cortez first had a surprised look on his face. "Hah! Negligent?"

Then it changed to a scowl and him breathing loudly through his nostrils.

"How can we be at fault for somebody who walks into this bank, pulls out a gun, and threatens to shoot someone?"

"Well, there's a lawyer out there who thinks that it's worth trying," Trent answered. He paused and pondered the insanity of such a ploy. "I don't know if I would have done it, but nothing really surprises me."

"Have you heard anything from corporate?"

Trent shook his head.

"Let me ask you this, and I'll let you go afterward. Did they ask any questions directly related to me?" Cortez sat back in the chair, turning slightly to the side.

"They did ask if anything related to Deloria Lovett's shooting has been a distraction. I told them not really, but it's been a challenge making sure that it hasn't become a distraction.

"Then I told them they would need to contact corporate communications for the rest of their inquiries."

"Thanks," Cortez said, sighing afterward. "I just never dreamt something like this would go on like it has. That husband needs to stop while he's ahead. Next time I see him, I'll personally stop it for him."

* * *

About 1:30 in the afternoon, Neal Scanlan answered a phone call from Louise Driscoll, senior vice president of bank operations—human resources was within her scope of authority.

"Neal, did you see the midday news today?" she asked him.

"No, I haven't."

During his six years at Palmetto Fidelity, Scanlan never thought much of Driscoll. She was dubbed by those in Scanlan's circle of banking acquaintances as "Cut Throat" for her ruthlessness.

It was widely rumored she attained her current position at

Palmetto Fidelity after she forced former CEO Albert Schloen into resignation in 2006. She threatened to report him to the bank's board of directors after he reneged on promises he made to her during an affair that went bad.

"As you know, Primas Lovett is a prominent local banking customer of ours. And he's informed us of a lawsuit he's planning to file stemming from his wife's death," she reminded Scanlan. "My only question is do we have anything in our corporate policy that protects us against negligence since you apprised us of potentially inappropriate behavior by Cortez Anderson?"

Scanlan scooted over in his office chair and pulled out volume two of the bank's tri-volume corporate policy manual. That specific section had been marked with a pink sticker note sheet.

"When Anderson told me that he had been involved both personally and professionally with Lovett's wife, immediately I thought there might be a problem—"

"Just cut through the chase, Neal," Driscoll interrupted him. "Do we have a problem there? I've got attorneys and the board of directors I've got to answer up to on this."

After inhaling through his nostrils, Scanlan answered, "No, we don't have anything specifically in place that articulates our position on bank employees and 'improper' relationships of that kind. We don't have anything that spells out any consequences for their actions."

"Thank you."

Scanlan came back to inquire, "May I ask why is this an area of concern?"

"Are you familiar with Mitch Duffner?"

"Oh yeah . . . Mitch Duffner. Talk about drama in the court room—"

"That's right. He's the type of person who exploits any

loophole in a company's policies. We don't intend on diverting any of our resources, financially or otherwise, in defending ourselves against somebody like him."

Driscoll indicated she had another call coming in, but that she would need to speak with him again—she kept her word, contacting Scanlan about twenty-five minutes later.

"About Cortez Anderson," she said, continuing their previous conversation.

"What about him?"

"We can't afford to keep someone like him who brings us unwanted media attention. That midday broadcast went into some of the details of the affair he had with Lovett's wife. Additionally, I've already spoken with our attorneys and they felt our best and quickest move would be to settle with Duffner and his client."

"Okay, what about the bank's personnel policy?" Scanlan asked.

She smirked. "Aren't you a generalist?"

"Yes, ma'am. Sixteen years as one—"

"After you've handled Cortez Anderson's separation from this company, I need for you to work with our attorneys and come up with a company policy that addresses this in the future."

Driscoll actually bristled at the thought of implementing something of its kind while Scanlan realized he had never handled disciplining of this nature. All other previous scenarios were incidents that could be backed by company policy.

"Ms. Driscoll, when you spoke to the attorneys, did they give you any guidelines on what grounds would Anderson be terminated?"

"Again, you are a generalist. Or do I need to hire a generalist who can perform their tasks as delegated?"

"I understand."

She hung up, leaving Scanlan having to find cause for immediate grounds for dismissal.

About ninety minutes later, Scanlan phoned Cortez, who had just returned from lunch.

"I need to meet you over at our insurance building in about forty-five minutes," Scanlan said. "Are you familiar with that location?"

Cortez immediately sensed his time at Palmetto Fidelity was now numbered to perhaps minutes and seconds based on the seriousness in Scanlan's voice. It was much more intense than their previous conversation.

"You mean those buildings over next to the freeway (I-26)?" he answered.

"Yes, exactly." Scanlan was in the process of printing out documents that would be included in Cortez's employee file. He also e-mailed Driscoll a copy of what he drafted.

Driscoll was quick with her response.

> *Make sure that what we do is well documented. I don't want this coming back on us. Thanks.*

Meanwhile, Cortez asked, "Do I need to bring anything?"

"That won't be necessary. I'll see you at four o'clock."

Cortez looked around in his office and reclined back in his chair. It was not as if he would leave Palmetto Fidelity without any financial preparation. He quickly surmised he'd put away enough money to withstand being out of work for up to a year.

The sobering thing about meeting with Scanlan, he thought, was that he had not entertained any ideas about leaving Palmetto Fidelity for another job.

Before leaving, Cortez stopped by Trent's office, apprising him of his meeting with Scanlan.

"Just want to let you know I think they want me out of here. Today." He stopped to glance at his watch. "In about, oh, twenty minutes."

"Cortez, what are you talking about?"

"I said it looks like the people are telling Bishop Moneymaker to step down and get out of town."

Trent seemed genuinely surprised by the news. "Nobody's called or e-mailed me about getting rid of you. The last thing I've heard from corporate was that guy Scanlan asking you last week to call him."

That did not settle well with Cortez. "Deacon, this is me. Bishop. Not somebody who just came off the street." He stepped inside Trent's office, closing the door behind him. He did not bother sitting down.

"I'm telling you, man. I don't know anything about this," Trent insisted.

"I don't believe you! That's telling me you never had my back at any time—"

Trent leaned forward upon his forearms. "Listen, man, I may not have agreed with a lot of things you've done, but I've never said anything negative about you or ever tried back stabbing you." He stared at Cortez rather intensely.

Shaking his head, Cortez said he had heard enough. "Whatever, man! Sounds like you were in on it, too. You're like any other deacon. You had your knife aimed at me waiting to jab and twist it inside of me!"

"You know what?" Trent retorted. "I never thought I would ever say this. You've always been about yourself, and yourself only. I've been the fool playing the role of a shield for you when people would complain about you and your harem parading inside the bank—in case you've forgotten so fast."

"No, the problem is that you forgot who you were the moment you became bank manager!"

Cortez then stood up and stormed out of Trent's office. He stopped by his office, took most of his most important belongings, and he walked out of the bank without speaking to anyone.

* * *

Scanlan, who was in his mid-fifties, had a hairline and wore a goatee much like actor Hector Elizondo. He was of average height. He also wore a gray suit, a matching bow tie, navy blue slacks, and a white long-sleeved shirt.

Since neither had formally met, he arrived earlier in anticipation of someone would identify himself at the security desk as Cortez Anderson.

Exactly as Scanlan had anticipated, a man came walking toward the security desk asking for him. Cortez, who stood roughly six feet tall, wore a caramel two-piece Perry Ellis suit with matching Kenneth Cole slide-ins, a white button-down shirt by Sean John, French cuffs and a matching caramel tie by Geoffrey Beene; it was a mix from one of his lunch runs at Macy's before its Columbia Mall location closed.

"Cortez?" Scanlan said, walking over to the desk.

"Yes, I'm Cortez Anderson.

"I'm Neal Scanlan."

Neither bothered to shake hands. Scanlan suggested they take the elevator up to the third floor where the bank's offices were in that building.

After explaining why they were there, Scanlan was offered an empty office space to conduct his meeting.

"You do understand why this meeting is taking place?" Scanlan asked Cortez as they sat down.

"I've got some idea, but you know better than me." Cortez still fumed over his argument with Trent.

"When I asked you to call me last week, we were conducting an internal investigation of the shooting incident involving Deloria Lovett," he explained. "We gathered as much information and facts as we could in an attempt at making sure that we'd done everything that we could when handling the incident and what we could have done to avoid it."

Cortez shifted in his seat. He was quickly annoyed by Scanlan's corporate speak.

"So you guys want to fire me?" he asked sharply. "I asked you all that last week, but you avoided me. Why wait a week?"

Scanlan, who peered over his thin wire-framed glasses, merely stared back at Cortez. The staring showdown continued for several seconds.

Finally, Scanlan ended the showdown. He reached into his satchel and placed a stack of documents on the desk.

"Mr. Anderson, we have determined that you breached Palmetto Fidelity's Code of Ethics as spelled out in this booklet," he said, pausing to hold it up for Cortez's viewing. "Uh, you do remember this booklet was explained to you when you were first hired here and most recently after your last review?"

Cortez shrugged his shoulders and scoffed at Scanlan's question. "Whatever. Just get on with what you have to say."

Scanlan went into explaining that according to the current documentation, it was expected that Palmetto Fidelity employees would abide by both the spirit and letter of the bank's code of ethics.

Any violation of the code of ethics may result in corrective action up to termination—and Cortez's perceived professional and personal conduct had a negative effect on the bank's reputation was another cause for dismissal.

"In the spirit of this document, we have reason to believe there was a major confliction of interests in the way you conducted business with Deloria Lovett," he added.

"There's also concern that private and proprietary banking information may have been disclosed to a non-Palmetto Fidelity employee—that's also grounds for immediate termination."

Cortez sat up in his seat, raising his voice to say, "You people really just wanted to get rid of me the moment that incident hit the news, didn't you?" He gestured with his hand as if he was brushing away dust. "All this other stuff is just mumbo-jumbo supporting BS!"

Scanlan proceeded to place documents in front of Cortez to sign in acknowledgement of him being fired. "I need your signature right here." He handed him a pen.

Cortez snorted then glanced over the papers. He reached into his pocket, holding up his own pen in Scanlan's face.

Unfazed by Cortez's gesture, Scanlan went on to explain that his final compensation was a month's worth of leave, his last two weeks, plus an additional month because he'd been with Palmetto Fidelity for more than ten years. His health insurance and other benefits would expire in two months.

"Please sign here that we've gone over all your options for maintaining benefits, if you choose COBRA—"

Cortez glared at Scanlan with derision and then smirked.

"Humph. You people are a mess. You all are gung-ho about hanging me out there and be eaten by the crows and vultures, but you let others off with a slap on the wrist."

Chapter 21

'A Last Hurrah, No Doubt?'

I t was a matter of formality. Trent informed the tellers during his morning updates that Cortez was no longer with Palmetto Fidelity.

Hardly an eyebrow was raised by anyone. The prevailing sentiment was goodbye and good riddance despite Cortez's contributions in the branch's success.

"I guess they had enough of him," Tondy blurted; she then curled her upper lip. "Because I knew I would have long ago."

"I know that's right," chimed in Maytreka Blanding, who had been working at the St. Andrews branch since 2008.

Trent sensed there was nothing else to say about Cortez's departure. He then announced, "I'm sure corporate will be posting an opening at some point for Cortez's position. When that happens, and if any of you are interested, make sure that you go online and apply."

Maytreka raised her hand.

"Trent, does that mean I'll be able to have all my male friends come and visit me? As you can see," she said, looking herself over, "I need all the attention I can get."

All the tellers erupted into laughter. But there was actually some truth to what Maytreka said. She had an enviable Coca-Cola bottle figure. She was known for her exquisitely kept hair and nails. And arguably, she made the day for many of the older men who came into the branch.

Once, two men got into a shoving match over who was next in line because it meant seeing Maytreka. She ended up resolving the matter by promising to wait on both of them—but not at the same time.

"Now, Maytreka," Trent said, still trying to stop laughing. "What am I going to do if you're not here when Mr. Farleigh and Mr. Tompkins show up at the same time?"

"Don't worry," she spoke in a seductive southern drawl. "They'll do whatever I tell them to do."

Trent had returned to his office and began checking the system for any unfinished business left by Cortez. He had barely spent ten minutes when Ms. Wanda knocked on his door.

"Ms. Wanda, is there anything wrong out there?"

"Oh, no. May I come in?" she asked.

"Sure." Trent gestured for her to take a seat in one of the chairs across from his desk. "Close the door if you have to—"

Ms. Wanda did just that, and she sat there quietly for a few moments.

"Are you sure there isn't anything wrong?" Trent asked again.

"There's nothing wrong. But I didn't want to say anything around everyone out in the lobby."

In all the years Trent had known Ms. Wanda, she was not one for making trips to his office. She did not hold any known grudges against him, nor did she speak negatively about him.

She was the main one in the branch who allowed him time to grow into his role as bank manager—it proved to be influential in him earning credibility and the respect of the teller staff.

Trent brought his hand up near his mouth. "What's so important that you had to tell me in private?"

"Quite honestly," she said, "I'm glad to know that Cortez is gone, because I was concerned about the way he was allowed to do certain things as he pleased."

"I don't recall allowing any special favors—"

"Oh, you allowed Cortez special favors. Did you ever allow the rest of us to have people come in and casually visit us like all those women came visiting him?" she said. "Now did you?"

"Wait a minute. You're a teller. He was a loan officer."

"Okay, would you have allowed any of us to have people visit us if we were in that same position?"

"I don't know. It all depends. Besides," he said, "I figured he was grown; he should know better."

Ms. Wanda adjusted herself in the chair. "Again, I'm glad something was done about him."

Leaning forward upon his desk, Trent immediately told Ms. Wanda that he never tolerated anything by Cortez that would have violated company policy.

"That may be true, but—"

"What are you getting at, Ms. Wanda?"

"Did you know that Cortez and I once were seeing each other on the side?" She sat back in the seat and adjusted her designer glasses.

Trent virtually froze in mid-thought. He stared at Ms. Wanda, trying his best to process her confession.

Now, there was nothing that even suggested she was Cortez's kind of woman. She was married, in her fifties. She wore a one karat diamond cluster on her wedding ring finger, and another cluster on her left ring finger. Occasionally, she wore earrings. She always arrived at work early, dressed conservatively, and she hardly wore any makeup. Maybe it was evident that she'd picked up some middle-age pounds around the hips and thighs; the paunch in the middle was something that could be hidden with the right clothing.

"You still hadn't established this thing about favors," Trent recounted to her.

"I'll explain it this way: There were about a half-dozen times you allowed Cortez and I off on the same day."

"Okay, but that was, like, three or four years ago when he first came to this branch."

"I know. And that was when he and I were sleeping together," she said. "He bragged about being able to do me on company time because he was the reason why you were keeping your job as branch manager."

Trent dropped his head and buried his forehead into his right hand pondering what Ms. Wanda said. It was true that he was struggling at the time of Cortez's arrival. He was under considerable scrutiny by Louise Driscoll and her cronies.

Once the St. Andrews branch's performance began rivaling those in the more affluent areas in the region, Driscoll pulled back and began applauding his efforts.

"Ms. Wanda, I'm still trying to figure out why you're telling me all this now?"

"I don't know. Maybe I'm concerned about company policy—I'm sure that's why he's no longer here." She then hunched her shoulders.

Trent nodded in agreement. "But that situation had nothing to do with yours."

"Perhaps it doesn't. But I told Cortez not long ago that I hoped none of what he was doing would come back and haunt him," she said, appearing void of any emotion. "I told him I hope he gets things right in his life."

And just think, he thought, *Sonia recently made that remark about her not being somebody I'd mess with. She was right.*

As Trent paid attention to Ms. Wanda's features for the first time—ever—he figured maybe there was a time she could have attracted her share of men much like Maytreka, who was in her mid-twenties.

A last hurrah, no doubt?

Trent also wondered silently whether Ms. Wanda took pictures or videos during any of her trysts with Cortez; he did not recall seeing any shown to him by Cortez that remotely reminded him of her skin tone. Even so, he still could not envision her having a thing for the freaky—apparently, her looks were deceptive.

"Well, let me ask you this. Why did you two stop?"

She cleared her throat before answering him. "He was immature, and I could not afford putting myself at risk any longer."

"Did it bother you to see all those other women come through here?"

"No," she answered. "If anything, I felt bad for them, because I think most of them have found out the same thing I've found out about him."

The mood in Trent's office suddenly lost its intensity. He sensed there was nothing more to this conversation. Her timing being almost perfect, she stood up and thanked Trent for allowing her to confide in him.

"Ms. Wanda, you do know this is as far as this conversation will ever go?"

"I know. That's why I felt comfortable sharing this with you."

She then left his office and assumed her usual place at the drive-in teller window.

Trent was beside himself. The bombshell that Ms. Wanda just dropped and detonated was too good to keep to himself. Being as inconspicuous as possible, he placed his cell phone in his shirt pocket and casually walked out to the employee's bathroom.

There in the men's room, he was more than eager to text message Sonia.

> You wouldn't believe what I was just told today!

Trent prayed that Sonia would be able to respond to him while he still was in the bathroom. He waited a couple of minutes. Nothing occurred. Reluctantly, he returned to his office.

An incoming text message finally appeared while he was closing out Cortez's unfinished work.

> Anything wrong?

> Nothing's wrong. But you wouldn't believe who was having an affair right under my nose!

> Who?

> Cortez and Ms. Wanda ! ! !

Sonia was surprised by Trent's juicy piece of gossip. After all, he was not one for bringing bank politics and gossip home.

> I would have never thought of her sleeping with other men.

> Hah! Ms. Wanda reminds me of Esther finding out that Big Money Grip had sneaked into her bedroom

Sanford and Son.

He chortled at his own response.

Meanwhile, there was a delay of several minutes before he received another text message from Sonia. She had to be mindful of Phyllis' recent crack down on cell phone use in contract services.

> Hey, Shonna invited me to an event her station is having tomorrow. Can you come with me?

> Do I really have to? You know that Taylor has a tournament.

> What time are you talking about?

Sonia did not disclose to Trent that she was to meet Shonna again at The Groovy Soul. Then again, she hoped that Trent would pass on it.

> From 3 to 5 p.m.

> Taylor's tournaments usually start around 10 and don't end until 7 in the evening.

That was more than fine with her. She told him that it was more important for him to be at Taylor's tournament. Maybe they'd try another time—an idea that she was quick to scoff.

Chapter 22

〰

'Isn't It a Small World?'

The text messages started coming at a steady rate yesterday from Charlotte. Virtually all of them were some kind of an appeal to Lance, hoping that he'd either explain himself or come to his blasted senses.

At least during work, he had a built-in excuse—almost one hundred of them, in fact; that was the number of phone inquiries he logged in for the day.

Charlotte was bold to make a couple of thinly veiled visits next to him by chatting with Tanya. He never acknowledged her at any time, although he could not avoid the fragrance she wore.

Finally, when he got around to socializing it was after he left UCP for the day. He spoke briefly with Shonna, and she confirmed with him that she expected to see him around 3:30 p.m. at The Groovy Soul for the station's promotional event.

Lance then fell asleep. It was almost 10 a.m. when he arose to his phone's ring tone. He grimaced once he focused his eyes on the number that appeared.

"What's been wrong with you lately?" Charlotte yelled; her voice was undoubtedly distressed.

He countered, "What's been wrong with you?"

"I don't know what you're talking about. All of a sudden, you're acting like you don't want to be bothered with me!"

Lance tried collecting his thoughts since he'd just awaken. "Charlotte, you were the one who freaked out because I went bowling a few days ago. Yesterday, the call volume went through the ceiling; I had no time for anyone."

"And what does that have to do with me today?"

It pained Charlotte that her emotions were getting the best of her. Lusting and loving hard were weaknesses she tried hiding from men.

"I told you, Lance. Don't try playing me. I'm not the one to be played on!"

"Nobody's playing any games with you!" He took a moment to stretch. "Charlotte, you there?"

"Yes, I'm here . . . Maybe that's the problem. I'm here, and you're there—"

He scoffed at her response. He didn't recall making that kind of commitment with her. To avoid another issue similar to a couple of evenings ago, he was quick with announcing his plans for the day.

"Charlotte, just so you know, I need to take care of something in Charleston today, and I won't be back until this evening. I'm not sure what time that will be."

"Obviously, you don't want me coming with you," she hissed. "I hope you're going there for whatever reason you say you're going there."

This is getting out of control, he fumed.

"Let's get one thing straight here, Charlotte. How long have we've been seeing each other?"

"A few months."

"And during that time, did I not tell you that I had some unfinished business in Charleston that I'd eventually need to resolve?"

"You've been acting so strange lately," she answered. "Who knows if you're telling the truth or not—"

Humph.

All night, Charlotte tried taking inventory of herself and how things had unfolded thus far with Lance. Clearly, it was not what she expected. And it had been excruciating that she could not readily confide in anyone what had been troubling her. Nor could her fear of loneliness be easily overcome by keeping busy or simply writing about the way she felt.

With Lance, she thought, the beauty of human interaction was the best medicine. She'd already convinced herself that she was surrounding herself with the right kind of person— it also helped that he'd given her the kind of attention she coveted.

"Lance—"

She was persistent, but spoke as if she was concerned for his well being. "Why don't you do us both a big favor and tell me what's really going on with you?"

Being desired and pursued by women had always been a smooth stroke to Lance's ego. But he'd never been able to handle it when things went wrong. It was his tendency to depend on silence.

You're going to have to make a decision soon, he said silently to himself.

"Charlotte, it's probably good that you called." He spoke in a calm tone, hoping that might put her at ease. "I need to be in Charleston in a couple of hours. And if I get ready right now, I'll be there on time. I'll call you when I'm finished, okay?"

"Whatever, Lance," she hissed. "Just know that you can't

keep on avoiding and trying to play me!"

* * *

From Knox Abbott Road, Lance easily spotted a Chevy Tahoe with a WNPW paint scheme on it. There was a tent set up around it, a modest stream of people entering and exiting it, and large inflatable turntable and speakers.

Lance was determined to have a good rest of his day, although he and Shonna still had not planned anything for that evening. It really didn't matter. He had already convinced himself that anything with her was better than even the steamiest and freakiest of times already spent with Charlotte.

He parked in the cluster of parking spaces adjacent to the WNPW tent—from the south end near the Citizen's South Carolina Bank building that faced Knox Abbott Road. Before leaving his car, he reminded himself that he needed to be careful. This may be a bigger deal for Shonna than for him—it may be more of a coming out moment for her. So that meant don't do anything that would embarrass Shonna especially after meeting her sister.

At least one woman paid particular attention to him as he approached the tent. She was in her mid-twenties, slender, and stood about five-nine. Neither spoke, but her eyes transmitted the message that he was more than just eye candy to her.

Lance quickly looked to his left inside the tent.

"Hey, you made it!" Shonna said.

"Yeah, I'm here."

Shonna came over and gave Lance a hug. The young admirer could barely hide her dismay and walked away looking for her friend who came there with her.

"I want you to meet our DJ and his sound man." She gestured with her head for him to follow her.

After exchanging pleasantries with them, Shonna informed Lance that her sister would be arriving shortly. "She's coming from her son's basketball tournament over at Lower Richland—are you familiar with where that's located?"

"No, I'm not."

"Well, don't worry about that," she said. "Have you thought of anything we're going to do after this?"

"I was thinking maybe we'd go to Charleston and spend some time there. What do you think?"

"Sounds good to me!"

Shonna told Lance she had to go inside The Groovy Soul and get Wharton Milner for his guest spot. The scheduled airtime was at the fifteen- and forty-five minute marks during their two-hour show.

"Now don't do anything I wouldn't do," she joked with him while batting her eyes.

He smirked at her comment.

While waiting for Shonna to return, Lance felt he was out of place standing among radio people. He knew nothing about the business, and based on first impressions, he was hardly impressed by her staff.

"How do you know Shonna?" sound man Quetari Simpson inquired.

"I actually met her at one of these a few months ago."

"For real?"

Lance nodded. "I don't think you were at that one."

"I guess not. I might have had another gig that day." He returned to monitoring his computer screen.

Suddenly, Lance's cell phone went off. He left the tent and walked at a brisk pace toward his car. *Humph, anything to get away from those guys.*

Just as Shonna returned to the tent with Milner, Sonia entered the parking lot from the north side—the opposite end of the strip mall property—and parked adjacent to WNPW's tent from that direction.

"I remember when a clothing store was there before your restaurant," Shonna said to Milner, making small talk with him before his segment began. "I shopped there a few times."

"Well, we looked at several places before we decided this was best for us," Milner answered. "Location has a lot to do with any business' success, you know—"

Sonia stood off to the right just out of Shonna and Milner's view during his three-minute guest segment. To her, being there was actually better than observing Taylor's participation in sports.

Of all things, she often mused, sports was among her least favorite activities. Yet it was ironic that she married an athlete and her son was one in the making. She'd never been one to show or voice her enthusiasm or displeasure unlike many of the parents who watched their children. And if the choice was hers, she would position herself by the exit and be the first one to leave.

"Mr. Milner, you remember my sister, don't you?" Shonna asked him after the segment.

His face became animated. "How could I ever forget?"

Sonia came over and hugged Shonna.

"Where's your boy toy friend?" Sonia whispered to her.

"He's around here."

"Have you eaten anything today, ladies?" Milner interrupted them. "You're welcomed to get something from the buffet bar—on me, of course."

"Thanks," Sonia said. "I definitely could go for something."

It took all of Milner not to make a smart comment. But he figured he'd have a chance to make his presence—and point—known to her very shortly.

He was pleasantly pleased with the increased traffic for a Saturday afternoon, which was one of the slowest periods of the week.

"I might have to speak with your station again about having one of these events later in the year," he said, before turning toward Sonia.

"If you have any problems with anyone in there, let me know."

Sonia smiled back at him. "I'm sure I won't, if you're around here."

While Sonia was eating a plate of pepper steak and steamed vegetables, Milner made his way over toward her; the look in his eyes spoke volumes.

"I knew you couldn't resist coming to see me again." He then winked at her.

"Now why would you think that?"

"Why don't you answer about writing down your name, phone number, and e-mail address on that sheet of paper, hmmm?"

She took a sip from her drink. "Because I wanted a free dinner or lunch."

"Are you sure that's all you wanted?" He looked her up and down.

She placed her left hand on the table, looking upward at him.

"Okay, I know you're married. But it's obvious things aren't going well at home. No woman who's happily married acts the way you've acted around me."

She sat back and crossed her leg. It had been years since she flirted with a man other than Trent.

A warm feeling had actually come over her. She gave him an

alluring stare.

"Mr. Milner—"

"That's Wharton."

"Wharton," she said, emphasizing his name, "I appreciate your courtesy and attentiveness. But if and when I were willing to step outside my marriage, you'd know."

"Will I be the first?" He raised his eyebrows.

"I promise. You'd be the first."

He cocked his head back, chortling. "I'd make it every bit worth your while." He tipped his head toward her. "I promise."

He then walked away toward the kitchen. But then he decided to return.

"I almost forgot something," he added. "I thought about e-mailing you the day after you left me your information. You will be hearing from me—"

When Lance returned to the tent, Shonna almost broke into a sprint to pair up with him.

"Where were you?" she asked. "You just missed my sister!"

"I had a call from my family in Washington, D.C." he answered.

"Do you know what it's like trying to get your mother off the phone?"

"Boy, do I!"

"It's not like I hadn't spoken to her in years." He shrugged his shoulders. "But I understand. I'm the youngest. I'm also the one who lives the farthest away from everyone."

She grabbed Lance by the hand, and they walked back toward the tent.

Despite their obvious difference, Lance and Shonna were not a gaudy couple, but their appearance alone certainly begged the question of whether Shonna was a cougar or was Lance looking for a sugar mama? Both had already made it a habit not to make any references to age privately and publicly.

Shonna's DJ, Preston Coffey, who manned the popular *Coffey in the Morning Show* during the week, merely shook his head in wonderment once he saw them step inside the tent.

"To each is own, you think?" he whispered over to Quetari, who returned an eye stare in acknowledgement.

Meanwhile, Lance continued his conversation with Shonna.

"Have you mentioned anything about me to your sister?" he asked. "I've wanted to ask you about that."

"Actually, not much. When we were younger, I talked more about the men I dated but not any more. Have you told your family about me?"

He chortled knowing he was just as guilty as she. "I don't tell them much of anything after what happened to me when I first moved here to South Carolina."

Suddenly, Shonna apologized for interrupting him and cracked a wide smile. She also waved in the direction of The Groovy Soul.

"She's coming over right now."

No, it can't be, he reacted; his stomach felt as if it had fallen into a sink hole and the rest of his body went weak on him.

I've really messed up now!

He looked over at Shonna, whose attention was solely on Sonia approaching the tent. What was obvious to him was their strong resemblance—although Sonia would argue she took after her mother while Shonna bore her father's features.

I pray to God that she doesn't know anything about me and Charlotte. . . . And to think all this time I tried sneaking peaks at of all things her cleavage?

"Sis, this is my friend I've been telling you about." She grasped Lance's hand tighter.

"Hey, Lance," Sonia reacted. "I never would have expected

see you here today!"

Lance was stupefied. His first instinct, however, was to disappear into thin air, if possible; it took all of him not to do anything embarrassing.

"I didn't know you knew him?" Shonna said; she then looked over at Lance.

"How do you two know each other?"

Sonia was quick to answer. "Sis, we work together, and I'm also his boss." She was rather calm with her response.

Lance merely nodded. "Yeah, that's right. We work on the same team."

"Well, isn't it a small world?" Shonna remarked. "Since you two know each other, so much for the formal introduction."

* * *

Sonia and Lance were left standing together since Shonna went back inside the restaurant to bring Milner out for his next guest spot.

Lance tried making small talk with Sonia. "She never told me anything about you." He hunched his shoulders.

"My sister tends to do that," Sonia answered. "I shouldn't be surprised."

Perhaps the joke was all on Shonna, Sonia mused to herself. It wasn't as if she tried hiding anything. But all that talk about her sister dating somebody younger didn't carry the same impact especially when the person was someone she hired less than six months ago.

And even if was true that she might not give him the time of day regardless of her marital status, there was no way that she would dare to share with Shonna they both had similar taste in men.

"Aren't you surprised at all?" he asked.

"A little. I mean, it's not every day you meet your sister's boyfriend, and he's somebody you hired. Wouldn't you be a little surprised?"

She sighed. "My sister seems to be happy. And that's the most important thing for me."

Guilt had now consumed Lance; he was not doing a good job at hiding it.

Saving face, he gestured with his head noting that Shonna and Milner were returning.

"How many more of these I have to do today?" Milner asked Shonna.

"One more."

"Okay." He cut a glance over at Sonia, hoping that she noticed.

While Milner was on air with Preston Coffey, Sonia alerted Shonna and Lance that she was leaving—this was piece of gossip that she could not keep to herself.

"Where are you parked?" Shonna asked.

"Actually, not far from here."

"I'll come with you."

Lance knew that meant a sister-to-sister moment was about to occur. Rather than waiting for the verdict, and feeling out of place among the radio station's crew, he went inside The Groovy Soul.

"All right, I know you're not so keen on me dating somebody much younger. But since you know Lance—"

Sonia looked over at Shonna. "First of all, didn't you tell me his name was Kirk something?"

"Yes, I did."

"Why would you tell me that?"

"Because I didn't want you snooping around."

Sonia stopped in mid-stride. "When have I ever gone

snooping into your business?" She shifted her purse from her left shoulder to her right.

"I knew that both of you worked at the same company, but I thought he actually worked at a different location. And since you've been there a while, you might go around asking who he was."

"You're just worried that I had something to say about you two being so far apart in age."

Shonna let out a deep sigh. "Sis, like I told you before, I never thought that I would do anything as remote as this. But I'm at a point in life where I'm going to do me, you feel me on that?"

"Oh, I do." Sonia resumed walking toward her car.

"Obviously, Lance is a sharp guy for you to have hired him. I know you're not the type who can tolerate dull blades."

"Lance handles himself well at work. But that's all I really know about him." She resisted the urge to divulge just how hot of an item he'd been among a motley crew of women.

"It took me a while to be comfortable with this." Shonna nodded as if she wanted Sonia to accept her latest choice in a man.

"You do know that over time things may change—"

"They might. But I'm willing to take that chance. Like I told him, I know that my expectations for him and me may be different. I just hope that I'm not disappointed by them."

Sonia moved to give Shonna a hug. "Take care. And if he does anything to disappoint you, I'll fire him on the spot." She grinned at her sister.

"Don't tell mom and dad just yet." Shonna hugged her tighter.

"I won't."

"Thanks!"

* * *

Sonia called Trent no sooner than she turned left onto Knox Abbott Road. Since he did not answer, she was eager to leave him a voice message.

"*Have I got news for you!*" she started. "*My sister Shonna is dating a man sixteen years younger than her. But the kicker is that the man she's dating is somebody I hired about six months ago.*

"*You should have seen the look on their faces when he realized I was Shonna's sister and I knew who she was dating. It was priceless! Talk to you later….*"

Sonia's phone went off just as she reached I-26 from Huger Street.

"What's this about Shonna dating a younger man?"

"Just what I said. Shonna's dating somebody who's twenty seven; she's forty-three."

"Sounds like something you see on television—"

"Well, it's happening right here in good ol' Columbia, South Carolina," she replied. "I thought I'd share something with you like you did telling me about that Cortez character from the bank and Ms. Wanda."

Trent asked Sonia to hold on for a moment. He ducked back inside the gym to check the score of the game being played. There were three minutes remaining. Taylor's game was next on the tournament schedule.

"Don't you even want to know how your son's been playing today?"

Sonia rolled her eyes. "Of course, I'd want to know."

"He's had an all right day today. He says he missed having his mother watch him play. Why don't you come back over here?"

"You know that's not my kind of place. Besides, I need to wash clothes for the week. Who else does that in the household?"

Trent stopped short of laughing at his sister-in-law's choice of men—they'd always been cordial at best with each other, although it was still worth cracking a joke about it.

"Hey, that is my sister," she reminded him. "At least I know who she's dating this time. I'm happy for her so long as she's happy."

"While I'm at it," Trent commented, "you're so quick to talk about who's dating who, what about us?"

"Yes, what about us?" There was sarcasm in Sonia's voice.

"I'm kinda jealous for the young dude. At least he's probably getting some action, which is more than I can say for us."

Sonia smirked at Trent's comment. "Things could be much different if only you knew how to reach me."

"I've been trying to do that. The problem is that you don't want to be reached."

"Oh, I'm reachable. You need to figure it out a little more!"

Chapter 23

'I Hope You're Sitting Down…'

C harlotte arrived at work Monday morning fuming over Lance avoiding her the entire weekend.
    She did not expect an immediate response from the text message she sent him, but she felt there was no way that he could avoid her.

> **Lance, we need to talk.**

She noticed the incoming message icon on her phone about ten minutes later.

> **You're right. We do need to talk.**

She glanced over at the time on her computer. It was 9:35. She knew he went to lunch between one o'clock and 1:15 p.m.; she normally took lunch between 12:30 p.m. and 12:45 p.m. Three rows over, Sonia could not resist sneaking looks over at

Lance. How stunning it was the man whom Shonna's bragged of having pleased her both in and out of the bedroom was sitting less than twenty feet away.

She was okay with herself knowing that she did not lie to Shonna about him having carried himself well at work—it was all that she really knew.

Yet unlike any time before, she was more than tempted to playing mind games with him. For example, while speaking with him in her cubicle, she could easily slip in a snide reminder that he should be on his best behavior no matter where he went. She leaned back in her chair and savored that thought for about as long as it took to blink her eyes.

Reality had met its opportunity.

"Son-, uh, I mean, Ms. Sonia, I've got this doctor who's calling in about . . ."

Lance was visibly uncomfortable approaching her, bordering ashamed. As soon as he made eye contact with her, it was as if she conveyed the message that he was at her mercy and there was nothing he could do about it.

"Did you say something?" she replied dryly.

He swallowed hard and repeated the scenario. "This caller says the explanation of benefits is incorrect, and we're off by about ninety-six dollars. I'm having trouble explaining to her that everything balances out.

"I don't recall being told that we're also accountants—"

"Have you printed out a copy of it?"

He shook his head.

"Go ahead and print it out. Let's see where you're missing it." She had every intention of making him feel uncomfortable.

On his way to the fax and copier room, he glanced over at Charlotte's cubicle. She appeared to be engrossed into her computer screen.

Whew!

The sixteen-page statement was already in the copier bin by the time he reached it. On his way back to Sonia's cubicle he glanced up only to recognize that Charlotte had stopped what she was doing. Her eyes were like slits and she grimaced at him with contempt, but there was no exchanging of words—for now.

Before approaching her, Sonia had Lance to apprise his caller that he would be a few more minutes researching the problem.

When he returned, she looked at him with even greater indifference.

"Here's where the problem is," she pointed out to him. "If you look at the bottom, there was an offset for that amount."

She gave him further instructions on how to handle similar inquiries in the future. He managed a wistful smile. "Thanks."

"Not a problem." Her eyes were open wider than usual, but she did not smile back at him.

He nodded again.

Yeah, don't mess up with Shonna; I get it, he mumbled to himself while walking back to his desk.

It took him more than eighteen minutes to resolve the call. Lately, all the phone reps were being pressed to maintain shorter call-time averages—a goal of five minutes or less. He could not afford having marathons like that each hour.

Two calls later, a span of about nine minutes, he saw his cell phone text message icon light up.

> **You do know I deserve better and expect better.**
> **This is not right what you've been doing to me.**

Deserve and expect better? A relationship that had been established mostly on sex, and she felt she deserved better? Lance deleted that message and concentrated on his calls.

> What's wrong with you? Are you gay and struggling
> with it? Just tell me if you're gay. I'll even help you
> find a boyfriend.

Lance was moved to laughter. Now she wanted to know if
he were gay. Humph.

> You know I have this problem about being lonely,
> and what do you do? You play me until you think
> you've got me wrapped around your finger. I'm not
> putting up with it. I deserve better!!!

Each time Lance did not respond to Charlotte, it merely
heightened her anxiety. She could go for a drink already and
it wasn't eleven o'clock.

Vicki happened to stop by her cubicle. She flinched nervously to her knocking on the Plexiglas. "Hey, don't scare me
like that!"

"What's wrong with you?" Vicki inquired. "You look like
something's troubling you."

She sighed. "Nothing. Just had a rough weekend."

Vicki returned a mischievous grin. "Still trying to recover
from your back being blown out? Does he have a brother or a
first cousin?" She giggled at her comment.

"Funny. Like I could use the exercise, hmmm?" she snapped
back at her. "Now what is it you want?"

Vicki had a legitimate matter that needed resolution from
Charlotte's team. After a quick perusal, she promised Vicki
that she would have a new batch of explanation of benefits
completed by mid-week.

Before leaving, Vicki could not resist teasing Charlotte
again. "Hey, I haven't heard you mention anything about
what's his face lately. Given up on him or have you come to

your senses?"

Charlotte turned slowly toward Vicki. "Who are you talking about?"

"You know who," Vicki answered, looking off to her right.

"I don't know who you're talking about."

Vicki teased Charlotte harder. "Girl, how many times did you say oh, my god . . . oh, my god . . . at even the thought of you know who—Lance!"

"Oh, him?" She sucked her teeth and resumed generating reports that were due to Phyllis at the end of the workday. "Just another man who works in contract services, don't you think?"

"Well, I've given you all this time to have him for yourself, and you didn't claim it. Now don't get mad the next time you see me, and I'm telling you whether he's crooked or straight."

Vicki winked at Charlotte before she walked away.

Charlotte did not know how to react. Part of her considered sucker punching Vicki from behind and cursing her out. Another part contemplated bursting into tears.

Grudgingly, she returned to her work. Her train of thought was broken the moment she noticed Lance first stop by a counter that was less than ten feet away from her. Adding insult to injury, she then saw him walking toward the fax copier room. She was quick to save the files she'd been working on. Then she got up from her desk.

"Is this the only way I can see you anymore?" she confronted him; there was nobody within an earshot of them.

Lance slowly turned and faced her. "I don't understand what you're talking about?"

"You know good and well what I'm talking about, Lance."

She took a couple of steps further inside the fax copier room. Her voice was still at their usual hushed tone whenever they stole moments like this in the past.

"Charlotte, I agree we need to talk, but this is not the place for it. Come on, let's talk about it away from here." He went ahead with making copies.

She placed one hand on her hip and she poked him repeatedly in his back. "Uh-uh. I'm not going to be played again by you. Afraid others are going to find out we've been screwing all this time, huh?" She then rolled her neck and stared at him.

Lance took a quick peak outside the fax copier room. There was still nobody within an earshot of them. He turned back around, hoping to reason with her.

"What do you want from me? An apology? Okay, here's one: I'm sorry, Charlotte, that things have not worked out like you thought they would lately?" He maintained a calm tone toward her.

"Sorry?" she shrieked. "You're right, sorry. You're just that, a sorry excuse for a man!"

Charlotte now stood face-to-face with him. She shifted her weight from her left foot to the right, folded her arms, and dared him to respond—he was visibly disgusted, shaking his head.

"Since last week, I've been begging and pleading with you to stop ignoring me . . . Then you lied to me. And one thing I can't stand is a liar!"

Lance finally spoke up. "Charlotte . . ."

"Don't Charlotte me!" she yelled.

Immediately, he grabbed her by the hand and led her outside of the work area much to the shock of at least thirty people who saw them.

She jerked her hand away once they reached the hallway.

"Don't you ever grab me by the hand like that again, or I'll call the police on you!"

"What choice did I have back in there?" He pointed back toward their workplace.

Their conversation could be heard by employees across the hallway in national accounts. Meanwhile, word was fast circulating inside contract services about their heated exchange that began in the fax copier room.

"You made your choice when you decided that I wasn't good enough for you any more!" she yelled. "Like who do you think you are?"

Lance held up his hands. "It's over, Charlotte. It's over!"

He walked off without looking back. He also knew that meant whatever lid that had been covering their office tryst was officially blown off.

She followed him, step-for-step, back into the contract services workplace screaming, cursing, and wailing her arms.

"You got that right it's over! I'm gonna make sure that everyone all over this building know how big of a punk you are!

"That's right. Lance Miles, mister so-called fine and sexy, is a punk! He can't handle his business! The only thing he knows how to do is unzip his pants, whip it out and try poking it inside me—and I still had to show him where to put it!"

She rolled her neck and waggled her head to further dramatize her point. A few phone reps who happened to look up found themselves covering their mouths while laughing.

Hazel Wise, a supervisor whom Charlotte rarely interacted with, tried quieting her. "Have you forgotten this is a work environment, and there are people on the phone?"

She glared back at Hazel, conveying a look that she needed to shut up and mind her own business. "Tell me that when the man you've been screwing for the past several months decides all of a sudden he no longer wants to be bothered with you!"

She then stormed away from her, making a sharp right-hand turn just before Sonia's cubicle; Lance had passed by there barely seconds ago. Now it made sense to Sonia who was the source of all the commotion in the fax copier room and out in the hallway.

"Why you're running away from me?" Charlotte yelled, stopping at his desk. "Are you also ashamed that we've been screwing?

"Humph, you weren't ashamed of it just last week up on the third floor, and the week before that, and the week before that—"

She placed her hands on her hips, expecting an answer from him.

To the right of them, Tanya looked up at both of them with a goofy grin and as if a cash register's ringing went off in her head. She also groped for the bag of popcorn that she had nearby. At the end of the aisle in back of them, Alvantrae had come by with his cell phone capturing whatever he could.

Slowly and deliberately, Lance said, "Charlotte, I asked you earlier, let's discuss this away from here." He looked up at her, glaring.

She looked around. "Why not now? You haven't bothered to answer any phone calls or text messages I've sent you since last week. So, why not here at work?"

Thoroughly ticked, Lance stood up, eyeballing Charlotte face-to-face.

"I don't have anything to say. I'm finished. I hope you get the medicine you need!"

Tanya, sensing the worse was about to occur, stood up and rushed Charlotte away from Lance. "Girl, you need to get a hold of yourself, or they might have to carry you out of here on a stretcher!"

"No, the only person who'd be carried out on a stretcher is him, especially if he put his hand on me!"

Sonia finally got up from her cubicle, eyeing Lance with more scrutiny than earlier. This was by far her biggest challenge ever as a team supervisor.

Once she reached his desk, she folded her arms and stared at him for several seconds. Not even a quick prayer or counting backwards from ten could help her—or him—at this moment.

"Lance, I'm not even going to ask what happened," she said. "What I do think you need to do is sign out for the day."

He took in a deep breath and exhaled slowly. The embarrassment on his face spoke even greater volumes—and he was still within his six-month probationary period.

With nowhere to hide, and not much of a chance to explain himself to the extent he needed with Sonia, Lance placed his headset on the hook, gathered a couple of note pads, and made a silent procession past her.

* * *

The details of Lance and Charlotte's skirmish still were sketchy at best. But from her vantage point, Sonia had a good idea what went wrong and she felt it was her responsibility as Shonna's sister to inform her.

> I can't really tell you what to do with your life. You might want to talk to Lance TODAY. He's got a lot of explaining to do.

Then she resumed with generating the phone reps' daily reports that she planned on e-mailing them copies after lunch. Next, after listening in on a couple of calls for evaluation purposes, she checked her e-mails.

She was hardly surprised that Phyllis wanted to know what the commotion was all about between Lance and Charlotte. That deserved a personal visit to her office.

Another e-mail intrigued her just as much. That one came from thewarden@midstate.com with SONIA, FOR YOUR EYES ONLY in the subject field.

Curious, she opened the e-mail and browsed through it.

Hello,

Just want to let you know I was thinking of you.
Have a wonderful day!

Wharton
803.83.....

Ooops!

Sonia was quick to realize she was in such a rush writing down her information in the bathroom at The Groovy Soul that she gave Milner her UCP e-mail address rather than her personal e-mail address; there was an easy solution for that. Nonetheless, she was impressed that Milner had kept his word.

It was shortly before lunch when Shonna got around to re-sponding to Sonia's earlier text message.

> I don't understand what you're saying. Did some-thing happen to Lance today? Call me when you get a chance.

Sonia responded quickly.

> If it hadn't happened by now, I'm sure Lance will be calling you. I hope you're sitting down when he's talking to you.

Chapter 24

'If It Means Spending My Last Money...'

There was an active buzz that circulated throughout contract services after lunch. Lance and Charlotte were still the talk among many of the phone reps.

Down Vicki's aisle, Alvantrae held court, served as moderator, and periodically replayed the forty-second video clip he captured of them—YouTube was a mischievous upload away.

"Quite honestly, I never thought he was all that and a bag of chips," he whispered over to Janine Townsend; he then snapped his finger in reaction to another call dropping into his queue.

After the call, Alvantrae looked over to his left, waiting for Janine's call to end.

"Why don't you put yourself in [Charlotte's] shoes," Janine suggested, making sure that she mouthed Charlotte's name.

"All we know is what she was yelling about: She says he'd been avoiding her, and he was freely accepting all the booty she'd been giving him."

Alvantrae sucked his teeth and rolled his eyes. "Humph, he can have all the booty he wants—"

Suddenly, both were being called out. "What is it with you two, Janine and Alvantrae?" Vicki yelled from her cubicle. "Both of you have been in not ready for more than five minutes, and I know both of you aren't on any calls. Come on now, get with it!"

Alvantrae waved his hand effeminately at her. "Ms. Vicki, you just make sure that you keep that candy jar on your desk well stocked, because that's all that you do around here."

He opened up his phone line for the next call to drop into his queue. "Contract services, this is Alvantrae—"

"I heard that, Alvantrae—you think you're slick!"

He stuck out his tongue at her.

Two rows over, Tanya was fully animated describing how she reacted to all the commotion that occurred next to her, as well as offering her opinion.

"Y'all know that Charlotte and I are like that," she said, holding up her middle and index fingers together. "And I'm telling you, I didn't even know that she and Lance had something going on!"

Kai, whose attention span was the length of an inch worm, found herself being mesmerized by Tanya's theatrics.

"Why didn't you stop it any earlier since you and Charlotte were so tight?" she asked.

"Because, it was too good to stop!" Tanya's eyes were widened. "All I needed was some Moscato; I'd be done for the day."

"Make sure you pour me some, too!"

Tanya continued with her narrative. "And poor Lance . . ." She shook her head. "I don't know what I would have done. But one thing I know is that I wouldn't have being doing it up on the third floor—no way, not here, no how!" She sucked her teeth for emphasis. "Thirtieth floor, out on the balcony at a hotel in Myrtle Beach, maybe. . . ."

Her comment caused Kai and two other phone reps to double over in laughter. From the corner of her eye, however, Tanya noticed Sonia walking back to her cubicle; the laughter stopped.

"It's Porky Pig time . . . That's all, folks!" Tanya told Kai.

Sonia left a meeting with Phyllis explaining what she knew about Lance and Charlotte's spat. Both agreed to wait until Lance returned the next day, if at all, before deciding on any punishment.

She managed to turn on her computer and browse through six e-mails in her inbox when she received a phone call from the security desk down on the first floor—she did not rule out any scenario just yet.

"Ms. Buckner, this is Officer Baylor. I have a package that needs your signature."

"Are you sure something needs my signature?" Sonia reacted.

"Yes, ma'am. You do work in contract services, second floor, section three?"

"That is correct. I'll be down there."

A half-dozen of red roses awaited Sonia at the security desk. She nearly blushed at the sight of them. She last received roses on the job for her birthday in January 2011, and she missed things like that from Trent—it was also when sex was last enjoyable for her.

Immediately, she read the card:

> *If it means spending my last money so that a smile appears on your face, I'll do it—*

Sonia then thought about the relationships Web site she

still frequented. It mentioned that tokens of affections like roses could go a long way toward de-thawing any marriage that had entered into a deep freeze. She even recalled the writer mentioning that he detested flowers, but he knew that his wife loved them. So he always brought her flowers whenever he returned from his business trips.

"I sure ain't mad at you," Officer Baylor said, interrupting her thoughts.

She smiled back at her. "And I'm not mad at him, either." She left without looking back at the security desk.

At her cubicle, Sonia was more than proud to display her roses. She was the only one among the seven female team supervisors who had anything like that on their desks.

Vicki could not resist paying a social visit with Sonia. In fact, she simply helped herself to sitting in the chair adjacent to hers.

"We know those flowers didn't come from Lance, don't we?" she joked.

They both laughed.

"Ain't that sweet. Hubby sends you roses just because," Vicki observed.

"Yep, they seem to be just that," Sonia answered. "My birthday isn't until January, and our wedding anniversary isn't until next March. So, yeah, they're just because."

She stopped to inhale their fragrance.

"Are you sure he's not in the dog house?"

As if Sonia would answer yes. "No, he's not in there."

Vicki sucked her teeth, commenting, "See, that's why I decided long ago that I would listen to any reasonable offer out there."

"And how many of them have come your way?" Sonia retorted.

"Hah! Now you're getting into my business." Vicki wagged

her finger at Sonia. "You need to mind your own business!"

They both laughed again at Vicki's mocking of Charlotte's outburst while Tanya tried calming her down.

Sonia felt that Trent had more than earned his get-free card out of the Dog House Inn. She entertained thoughts of preparing dinner for him, proposing to give him a neck-and-shoulder massage, them taking a shower together, and then awaiting for him to join her in bed stark naked. He would not have to initiate anything with her because he'd already won her over mentally and emotionally.

Feeling desirous for him, she text messaged Trent just to make conversation.

> How's your day going? I've been thinking a lot about you today.

Her phone buzzed before she placed it back onto her desk.

> I'm always thinking about you. How's your day going for you?

If Sonia were a unit manager, she would have had the privacy of an office, and she could envision herself with a silly grin on her face. She merely nodded to herself and reminisced about how Trent won her and her grandmother over with his letter of apology more than fifteen years ago.

Those were the good old days. They also triggered a tingling feeling in a familiar place where she had not experienced any in quite a while.

Chapter 25

'If He Only Knew…'

The playful cell phone dialogue between Trent and Sonia lasted throughout much of the afternoon, and it had him feeling good about himself. Sonia just might be coming around again.

All that was missing during their exchange were provocative pictures being sent to each other.

I can't get up from my desk now (hint, hint . . .)

Trent was eager to read Sonia's reply.

I wonder why. Did I have anything to do with it?

He chortled. Then he caught himself. It wouldn't look good if the boss was seen as being engrossed with text messaging his wife. That was something Cortez might have gotten away with.

He put away his cell phone, adjusted his posture in his office chair, and resumed reviewing the ATM reports.

Minutes later, someone whom Trent was familiar with through Cortez was standing in the bank's lobby. He got up from his desk.

"Hello, we meet again . . . How can I help you?" The pause in his voice suggested that he'd forgotten her name.

"Alcione."

"Yes, that's it! I recalled not being able to pronounce it correctly."

She smiled back at him. "I'm here to see Cortez." His name was pronounced more like Hortez, a product of her native Portuguese.

Thoughts of the nude pictures that Cortez was so enthusiastic to show Trent were vivid in his mind while he chatted with Alcione. He attempted to look her up and down and envision her just as she was in those pictures.

"I'm sorry, Cortez no longer works here."

The steady parade of women that once came to the bank for Cortez had already diminished. Alcione was the first to find out this week. She had not spoken to Cortez since she confronted him about his name being linked to Deloria Lovett's death.

Over time, though, she thought about giving him a second chance while she'd been overseeing her family's restaurant operations from Florida.

That was until she saw Trent during this unscheduled early-summer trip through Columbia.

"Do you know where he's working?" she inquired.

He shook his head. "I've not spoken to him since the day he left. Is there anything that I can help you with since you're here?"

She did not hide her willingness—her eyes lit up to his offer.

"Yes, there is something you can help me with," she answered.

He led her toward his office. He allowed her to walk past him, enabling him to sneak a look at her view from behind.

Sitting across from him, Alcione crossed her legs and folded her hands in her lap.

"Uh," she glanced down at his name plate, "Trent, my family is looking to expand by two restaurants over the next two years. The first one would be built in South Carolina, in Myrtle Beach."

"I-I'm not familiar with your family's business," he responded.

"Have you ever heard of Fogo de Janiero, the Brazilian steak house here in Columbia?"

He shook his head. Married life had severely limited his days of exploration.

"Well, before we can talk any business, we need to get you familiar with us." She shifted her sitting position to upright in the chair.

"Do you have any printed material about your family's business?" he asked. "Or is there something I can access online?"

"Sure, we have a prospectus, two videos on YouTube, a television commercial we're running in this market, and a media packet. But I think the best way you will become familiar is to visit us."

Trent seemed unsure and slightly taken aback. But he persisted with his fact finding. "How soon are you looking to expand?"

"We were looking at opening a restaurant in the Myrtle Beach location in 2014. A lot would depend on how soon we can secure the financing. We have owned the land we will be building on since 2012."

He nodded. "I see." He clasped his hands and rested his chin atop them.

"May I ask you something?" Alcione returned to crossing her legs and folding her hands in her lap; she also cast an alluring stare at him.

"Sure." He raised his eyebrows as if he'd encouraged her to continue.

"I was thinking that perhaps we can discuss this over dinner. We can meet at my family's restaurant—we have a great menu planned for tonight."

Trent sat back in his chair. Fifteen minutes ago, the only business he planned on conducting was with Sonia. Mentally, he began undressing Alcione. And the lilt in her voice had him thinking of other suggestive poses she could have made in front of his own camera.

While sitting there, she mused silently how much she was already attracted to him. She was willing to go further if it meant getting what she wanted for her family's business, and perhaps personal satisfaction. She offered a smile as an enticement.

"What time were you talking about?" he asked.

She glanced at her watch. "How about six o'clock?" She then searched her purse and handed him a business card.

Six o'clock meant that Trent would have only enough time to drive from the St. Andrews branch into downtown. "Great, I'll meet you there."

She arose from her chair, extending her hand out to him. "I look forward to it."

The same sensation that both felt the last time they shook hands happened again. This time, there was no Cortez interrupting them. Both were slow with releasing their handshake.

"Six o'clock." He spoke loud enough that only she heard him.

She licked her top lip. "Yes."

Finally, she let go of his hand and insisted on leaving the bank without him escorting her to the door.

In the time it took for Alcione's fragrance to dissipate from his office, Trent came crashing back down to reality, realizing that he'd just created a problem for himself. It had been several years since he last used the *I've-got-an-after-hours-meeting* line with Sonia, although it would be partially truthful.

He decided on waiting until after banking hours before he'd apprise her of his unexpected "appointment." He sent her a text message knowing she was still at work.

> I'm going to have to ask for a rain check on that dinner you wanted to prepare for me.

He was not surprised that Sonia would respond so quickly.

> What are you talking about? I was already making plans to stop by the store.

> A customer of ours came here talking about a business loan for expansion. They want to discuss it over dinner since they didn't have much time here at the bank.

> Why couldn't these "customers" come back tomorrow?

> You don't ask questions like that when their money is doing that kind of talking.

> Whatever, Trent ! ! !

Once again, Trent sensed he'd been remanded to the Dog House Inn—and in record time. He understood Sonia's apparent disappointment; however, he felt this meeting with Alcione was more promising.

While driving to Fogo de Janiero, he tried saving face by contacting Sonia directly. He reasoned that hearing his voice might take away a text message's edge since it could be easily misinterpreted.

"Yeah, mmm-hum?" she answered, taking the call out into the hallway. "You know you really messed up this time!"

"Sonia, I had no idea about this meeting. These people didn't come into the bank until after 4:30. It all happened so fast."

"Okay, if you knew you may have a dinner business meeting, didn't you think of asking if you could invite me?" She began pacing down the hallway, heading in the opposite direction of her workplace.

He slammed hard on his brakes, an overreaction to the car stopping ahead of him at the I-26/Bush River Road intersection. His attention was not fully on his driving.

"Sorry about that."

"Trent, this is the kind of stuff that got you in trouble before," she said. "So-called meetings that turned out to be dates with other women you had Cortez setting up for you. You must think I'm stupid?"

He took several moments to compose himself before he responded. The thought of her already hurling accusations at him merely strengthened his resolve to follow through with Alcione.

"Sonia, I'm not even going to stress myself out on this. You're going to believe what you want, anyway." He shook his head before continuing. "You know the kind of work I do."

"And you know kind of wife that you have! The least you could have done was text message me asking if I wanted to go!"

He contorted his face to her comment. "So, you're telling me that I need your permission to do my job? Because that's what it sounds like to me—"

Sonia tried tempering down the agitated tone in her voice only to emphasize her point. "Let's not be stupid here, Trent." She began walking back in the direction of her workplace.

"Who are you calling stupid?" he reacted.

"It's stupid if you do things without taking your wife into consideration," she snapped back at him.

He tried reasoning with her again. "Sonia, these are big-time people who are not from this country. I've done my research on them. They've financed cars with us. They've financed a couple of buildings with us—and they're all paid off.

"When a business like that calls, you don't ask too many questions. All you want to know is how much money will be involved."

"Whatever, Trent!" she hissed. "You better not come home at two o'clock in the morning expecting that I'm going to give you anything."

That moved him to laughter. "It's not as if I've been getting anything lately!"

"Who's fault is that?"

"It takes two, baby. Remember that."

"Humph," she retorted. "I heard if you're really in the need, there's always five sisters on Palm Street looking for business—"

Trent decided rather than spewing obscenities at Sonia that he'd simply hang up on her.

Meanwhile, Sonia shrugged her shoulders. She decided to stay later until seven o'clock rather than leave at 5:30 like she originally planned.

* * *

In all his time visiting downtown Columbia, Trent never paid any attention to Fogo de Janiero, which was located at Main and Hampton streets. It had an upscale presence. The tables were immaculately prepared for the guests and there was an extensive wine rack in plain view. It bemused him to think a place like that could thrive in South Carolina, but what did he know?

He'd waited there no more than a minute before Alcione greeted him.

"I'm so happy you came," she said. "Come, follow me."

She led him to a table toward the back of the establishment, offering a semi-private setting. There, she slid onto one side of the "L"-shaped cushioned seating. He joined her from the other end.

"This is our restaurant. We are very proud of it," she said, looking around first to the left then right.

Trent also looked around, still trying to take in its ambience. "I can see why your family is so proud. How long has your family been at this location?"

"Since 2005. We were very pleased with the reception that we received. We did not know what to think; however, we felt we did our homework before coming to Columbia."

He began thinking that maybe he was right about not asking if Sonia wanted to accompany him. Very rarely she ever did. There was also the possibility that she could be a hindrance, anyway.

Alcione waved for one of her waiters clad in a white chef's coat and black slacks to stop by her table. They engaged in a conversation in Portuguese—Trent figured that she wanted to be apprised of all final details for their dinner menu.

She snapped her finger, catching her waiter's attention. He turned around once she said the name Pauliño.

"May I get you something to drink, Trent?"

"Sure, I'll have a glass of white wine, thank you."

She then turned her attention back to Pauliño. They conversed again in Portuguese. Then he walked in the direction of the bar.

"You speak English as fluent as you do in your native language," he observed.

"You mean Portuguese?"

He nodded.

"My parents insisted that I learned English while I was a teenager. There are a lot of American visitors in Brazil, so it helped," she explained. "Now I do a lot of business on their behalf here in the States."

Pauliño was quick to return with two glasses of white wine. He nodded at Trent, presenting him his drink; he also nodded at Alcione, presenting her drink.

After taking a sip from his glass, Trent figured he would talk business. At least he would be able to give Sonia some kind of a truthful account, if interrogated.

"Will the Myrtle Beach location be similar to this location?" he asked.

She also took a sip from her glass. "That one will follow in the design of our South Florida locations."

Then she sat back against the cushion, making additional small talk with him. Within ten minutes, she informed him that her assistant will come by the bank in the morning with all of the necessary paperwork to initiate the loan process.

"Now that is over, she announced, "I was thinking of getting away from here and relax."

Trent was short of being dumbfounded. A potential million-dollar deal was decided upon just like that, and she's now talking about leaving?

"W-w-what is your idea of relaxing?" He was noticeably unsure in his voice.

She took a final sip from her glass. "Do you play billiards?"

"You mean playing pool?"

"Yes, I forget people in the States have different terms for everything."

Trent now found himself playing catch up to a woman whose moves were faster than he made as a world-class track athlete.

In the athletic arena, the reaction time to the gun and the actual start of the race meant almost everything unless the sprinter was gifted with exceptional closing ability. Trent's reaction time was pathetically slow and he was left in the starting blocks going up against Alcione.

"I love playing pool," he remarked. "I know of a couple of nice places we could go."

Alcione placed her hand near his on the table, looking directly at him. "Since you are married, I do not want you to get into any trouble. We go to my place."

He swallowed hard.

"Uh, that might get me in more trouble."

She shook her head. "If we go where you would like, someone might see us together. At my home, they can't see us."

I'm being routed here, Trent thought to himself. *I'm definitely out of my league.*

He began wondering how in the world Cortez had so much success with the same woman? When making a quick comparison of himself to Cortez, the differences were clearly evident: He had been away from the game a long time whereas Cortez had many opportunities to refine his skills.

Facing that reality, he figured the best thing he could do was go along with whatever she proposed, so long as it resulted in him getting that loan processed.

"Shall I follow you there?" he queried.

"I would like if you drive us to my house. I can have Pauliño drive my car."

Trent was curious. "Who is Pauliño to you?"

"He is my cousin—my uncle's son. We grew up together."

He did not bother asking how that might be accomplished. He figured since that was a family business matter it would be handled within the family.

They began walking in stride toward the front door. Before leaving, Alcione stopped and signaled for Pauliño. They conversed again in Portuguese. He acknowledged her with a smile before walking off.

* * *

It had been nearly five years since the last time Trent was in the company of another woman. That resulted with him being confronted by Sonia about him taking a picture with Annette Sloan.

He did not seem overly nervous with Alcione as his passenger. In fact, it gave him reason to think that he may have a second chance at making a better impression with her; he just might make up a lot of lost ground to her.

"Are you familiar with Longs Pond Road in Lexington?" she queried him.

"I know there's two ways of getting there, but the one I'm most familiar with is taking the I-20 freeway."

"Yes, that is the route I take."

Trent took what he thought was the most direct route to her place. From Main, that was taking Laurel Street back over to Huger Street, which became the I-126 spur channeling into I-26 westbound. He would not be on I-26 long because the I-20 westbound exit—No. 107A, otherwise known as Malfunction Junction—would soon come up.

Once on I-20 westbound, it should have been a straight

shot. However, he noticed that he'd forgotten something since he left the bank in a hurry.

"Excuse me," he alerted Alcione, "I need to get gas or I'll be embarrassed to explain why we're on the side of the road."

"It's all right," she assured him. "I'm fine here with you."

Without thinking, Trent turned off on the Bush River Road exit, and he safely made it into the Circle K gas station. He could have also driven farther down Bush River to a BP and be about a half-mile away from the bank.

After putting in fifty dollars' worth—about three-quarter's tank full—he darted out onto the frontage road. What he did not know was Sonia was two cars behind him—UCP's just down the frontage road from that same Circle K.

It startled her to think her husband could be in such a hurry. But what was even more stunning was the person in the passenger seat.

"What is he doing with that woman in our car?" she reacted aloud. "Uh-uh, I knew something was up. Feelings like that never fail me!"

Provoked and angered, she cut in front of a woman driving a Honda Odyssey minivan so that she could follow him on the I-20 freeway. She trailed him in the far right lane while he drove in the fast lane heading westbound toward Augusta, Georgia. Even more galling to her was how casual he was with the woman.

She thought of speeding up and driving along side of him, but the road was soon to contract from three lanes to two once they passed exit No. 61. Another tactic she considered was calling or text messaging him.

She decided, however, that she'd seen enough and turned around at the Highway 1/Augusta Road interchange, which was exit No. 58.

"He's definitely eff'd up now!" she shouted. "I've had it with his crap!"

Trent and Alcione continued with their small talk en route to her place in Lexington County. She shared with him that she was thirty-four and the second oldest of four children by her parents Nelson and Tassia Amaral de Oliveria. Her father and uncle Rolando—Pauliño's father—started their first Fogo de Janiero restaurant in São Paulo back in 1985, and they began opening restaurants in the United States in 1998.

"That was the year that I met my wife," he mentioned.

"That's fifteen years ago."

"Do you have any children?"

He shook his head. "One, a son."

"I would love to have children some day," she said, "but—"

"But what?

She went on to say she's had several boyfriends and other male acquaintances, but her traveling back and forth between the United States and Brazil doesn't bode well for relationships.

"I like American men," she was bold to say. "I also like my *Brasilieros.*"

He looked at her, visibly questioning that statement.

"That means men from Brazil, or Brazilian men."

"Oh, I see."

The thought of her mentioning her liking for American men begged the more obvious question with him.

"If you know I am married, why are you so attracted to me?" he asked. "It's not as if I hadn't noticed."

She pondered his question for several moments. Before answering, she informed him that he was close to her exit. "My neighborhood should be about three, no more than four kilometers from here."

He looked at her again with confusion.

"You are not familiar with the metric system?"

He shook his head.

"That is what everyone in the world uses."

"This is South Carolina," he retorted. "We talk in terms of feet, yards, and miles; this ain't cosmopolitan, baby!"

She chortled. "Back to your question, I know that you are also attracted to me. That is why I felt it would be easier if we discussed our plans for expansion at the restaurant."

"Really?"

"Yes."

"It still doesn't change that I'm married." He chortled at his own comment, hoping that he might convince himself otherwise that he could resist the temptation sitting to the right of him.

"No, but it makes it much easier doing business. We both want what is in each other's best interests, right?" She watched him with admiring eyes while he turned into her driveway.

Once inside her home, Alcione was quick to make a confession to Trent.

"I do not have a billiards table."

Trent was reduced to laughing. "Is there anything else you don't have that you told me you had?"

"Yes," she answered, looking upward to him. "You."

Alcione led Trent by his hand over to her sofa, inviting him to sit down. She sat across from him in a love seat; he was well within her striking distance.

This home might be considered luxurious if she were back in Curitiba, the largest city in the Brazilian state of Parana; it bordered the state of São Paulo. It had a vaulted ceiling in the living room and an unobstructed view of the golf course. The large windows made her home appear even more spacious.

"Trent, do you listen to music?" she asked.

He smirked. "Of course, I listen to music. What do you have?"

She got up and pranced over toward her entertainment center that consisted of a fifty-five inch flat screen television and a Sony sound system.

The samba and bossa nova music she played seemed different to Trent, but it quickly became rather enticing as she was to him. He was mesmerized by her fluid movements with her waist and hips.

She motioned for him to stand up. "Come, you look like you're a dancer. You'll learn that Brazilians love to dance and sing."

And just like that, she began singing to the song "*Corrente de Aço*." Her voice was impressive, although he didn't understand a single word she sang.

She reached out to guide him by the hand, encouraging him to mimic some of her dance moves. "Just move your foot like this, and your hips like that . . . And start with your other foot and move your hips like that—"

"Like this?"

"That's close. Come on, I'll play the song again."

This time, Trent proved Alcione correct. He was able to string together a couple of steps while she sang and danced before him. He was no doubt open to something different—and perhaps the next step in her thinking.

"You're a quick learner," she said, smiling.

Humph.

Trent thought of other things in life that he was quick to learn. But most of those seem to have gotten him in trouble with Sonia.

The next song she played was a modern standard titled "*Chega de Saudade*." She explained to him that song had been covered by many performers and in many different tempos, but the one she liked the most was a duet by singer Leny Andrade and renowned harmonica player Toots Thielemans in a live performance. They were accompanied by her trio of musicians.

The slower, jazzier tempo allowed her to entice him into dancing closer. That was more his liking and dancing expertise, anyway.

"I can probably get into this kind of music," he remarked to her.

Toward the end of the song, Alcione and Trent were in a tight embrace. Her body, so shapely and firm in all the right places, had him thinking along the lines of those pictures Cortez had taken of her.

"Trent, are you going to deny that you are attracted to me?" she queried him.

He stared at her. Then he breathed deeply through his nostrils. "I would be lying if I said I wasn't attracted to you. You are a very beautiful woman. I wished that I met you at a different time and place in my life."

Their eyes locked in on each other. It was as if there was a gravitational force that pulled at them to take their activity into another part of her house.

Although things moved at a slower pace, Alcione felt that Trent was a welcomed, refreshing and refined change whereas Cortez represented an unbridled, carnal side to her.

"I feel like I have known you for a long time," she said, rubbing up against him; her body emitted much warmth.

As if it were second nature, Trent leaned forward and kissed Alcione softly on her lips. The moment also seemed beyond realistic to him. Never in his wildest imagination when he woke up this morning would he find himself in the arms of another woman—and a decision away from her bedroom.

Teasingly, Alcione slid her hand down along his stomach, below his waist, and traced a trail on his pelvic region. She sucked air through her teeth once she hit the jackpot with him.

Trent moaned to her touch. He was more than tempted to reciprocate.

"I knew you would not resist me," she said softly to him. "And I will never resist you."

She looked upward and led him into another kiss.

Don't do it. Don't do it. You'll regret you ever did it! a still, small voice spoke up within Trent.

His desire was to undress Alcione in her living room and find solace in her arms and between her thighs. He was more than certain there would be nothing faked, and he would be desired and appreciated even if it were for mutual selfish gain.

The still, small voice spoke up again with him. Against all probability, he heeded it: He broke the kiss and moved to hold Alcione by her hands. Then he sighed loudly.

"What is wrong, Trent?" she asked. "Are you afraid?"

"Yes, and no," he answered. "Yes, because it's been a long time since I've been with another woman. No, because I am attracted to you and I do desire you very much."

He led her over to the sofa where they sat and faced each other.

"I don't think the timing is right to be doing this," he explained.

"The timing is never right when one person is married and the other is not," she countered. "That is why I took my chance tonight. It still will not change my family's decision to do business with your bank."

Inwardly, Trent felt relief circulate through his body. Perhaps, too, he supposed to himself this is what often went through Cortez's mind when he conducted business and pleasure with his clientele.

He glanced over at the clock on Alcione's music system. It was almost 8:40. That was early in the evening according to her Brazilian tradition, but it was becoming rather late for him being that his family awaited him.

"Maybe next time?" she asked.

He hunched his shoulders. "Maybe."

"I know it will be very beautiful."

They stood up and walked hand-in-hand to her front door. There, they gave each other a warm embrace and bade each other good night.

* * *

Trent's head literally buzzed while he drove home. Both body and soul were enlivened by Alcione. He was unsure of what other thoughts he was capable of processing. But he knew that reality awaited him in the form of the former Sonia Chandler.

There was yet another dark cloud of unresolved issues that was bound to overshadow him. He reasoned to himself that while he broached the dividing line between fidelity and infidelity, he never crossed it. His conscience was partially clear; it would be sufficient if he needed to defend himself.

* * *

Sonia had already decided on the tact she would take after witnessing Trent driving another woman around in one of their cars.

When he entered their bedroom, she was already dressed for bed wearing another of her silk kimonos along with some boy shorts.

"Hi, how did things go?" she asked.

He pursed his lips, breathing through them. He unbuttoned his shirt and stepped out of his slacks. "It went better than I thought. They will be coming by in the morning and start the paperwork on a loan."

"That's nice." Sonia sat there quietly, internalizing all that occurred.

He queried, "How was your day?"

"Long. Very, very long." She shook her head at her comment. "Are you still hungry?"

"No."

"What did they serve?"

He shook his head. "I've never seen so much food at one time in my life. They have a really good concept."

"What's the name of the place that's looking to expand?"

"It's a chain of Brazilian steak houses called Fogo de Janiero. They have one here in Columbia, but they are looking to expand in Myrtle Beach and Hilton Head."

"That's interesting. What are the owners like?" She now sat with her arms folded while watching him join her in the bed. "The husband along with his brother founded the restaurants. They are in their late sixties. The wife is a sweet lady."

He nodded while pondering the description he gave her. Then he shrugged his shoulders. "All that matters to us is them signing the papers tomorrow. Afterward, we hope they'll send us more business."

"I see."

Sonia was more than convinced that Trent spent the evening with another woman. The mere fact that he came up with the story about a family business enraged her, yet she chose not to erupt and unleash her fury upon him.

That day will come, she thought silently to herself. After Trent trailed off to sleep, Sonia got out of the bed and headed for his work office down the hallway. She had already committed to memory Wharton Milner's e-mail address. She spent little time typing a response to him.

Hi,

Thank you for your concern and thinking of me. I hope your day was wonderful as well. I look forward to hearing from you very soon.

She logged out of her personal e-mail account and returned to their bedroom. There, she slid under the covers and nuzzled up to Trent—still brooding over what she knew.

Chapter 26

'Hope It Works Out for You'

The image of another woman in the passenger's seat with Trent was seared into Sonia's memory.

There he was chatting away with a woman who seemed quite comfortable. For all Sonia knew, they've had something going on for quite a while.

She felt she should have done more than ask him a couple of cursory questions. She should have demanded answers. Facts. The truth. Anything less would be conceding that it was all right for him to do what she saw him doing.

Bored of staring at the ceiling while he snored, Sonia decided to tap Trent on his shoulder.

"We need to talk," she said; her voice was void of any seductive tone at a little after one in the morning.

"Huh?"

"Trent, I said we need to talk."

He remained on his side. He wanted to dismiss it as an unwanted interruption of a dream he was having of Alcione: She was nude like in the pictures that Cortez had shown him. Her eyes were desirous of him. And they were about to go further than what transpired in her living room. He saw her bedroom in the distance. Things were about to happen.

Thump, thump, thump!

"So, you're going to play 'possum on me?" she said, hovering over him. "I need you to get up!"

Trent did not like the sound of Sonia's voice. It was about as bad as him being awaken by his mother with a leather belt, fulfilling a promise to him that she would beat his tail when he least expected. But Trent was not nine years old.

"What is it you want, Sonia?" he grumbled. "I need to get some rest!"

Now, she sat up in bed, expecting him to do the same. Mentally, she replayed the image of him pulling out ahead of her onto the frontage road, darting onto Bush River, before he turned onto I-20 westbound.

It just didn't add up. This was the same man who sent her flowers earlier in the day.

"Maybe I didn't understand you, but I just wanted to know again how did that business dinner went?" she asked.

He yawned and stretched. "It went well. Their representative will be coming by in the morning to start the paperwork."

"I see," she said, nodding.

He sensed she was not satisfied with what he told her. Grudgingly, he sat up next to her. "Okay, what's the big deal? I told you these are top-notch customers. Their money is really good money."

"You do realize that you missed out on what could have been a very nice night for you? I was willing to be at your beckoning, but you decided that a dinner date with a customer of yours was more important."

"Yes, I explained to you why. What are you getting at?"

Although he had shaky ground that he stood on, Trent still felt it was not loose enough to crumble under her intense scrutiny and interrogation. He believed he had enough factual information to cover his tracks spending time with Alcione.

"You forget that us women internalize a lot of things."

"Boy, do I know. I've not heard the end of things that happened ten years ago—"

"Do you think I might ever meet these people?" she asked. "They sound interesting. You did mention these restaurants were started by a pair of brothers?"

He figured if he reacted angrily to her questioning that she would immediately suspect he went somewhere he should not have gone. It took all of him not to blurt out something that he would later regret.

"Yes, darling. Fogo de Janiero was started by Nelson and Ronado Olivera, or something like that; I've never pronounced their names right. But the one thing I know is there's a lot of money that should be made if this loan goes through."

Each response he gave her was like coals tossed into her fire. There was no way that she'd be able to sleep. She knew it might have been easier if she simply erupted into a rage and confront him about the woman in their car.

But Trent had his chances, she surmised. Since he could not volunteer the truth to her, there were more forceful and convincing ways of getting him to admit to his infidelity without her ever having to raise her voice.

"I hope it works out for you," she said. "I better get some rest, too. I've got a disciplinary matter to deal with as soon as I get into work."

"Really?"

She nodded. "It actually happened today, well, you know, yesterday. But Phyllis and I agreed to handle it in the morning."

"Oh, I see. Care to share anything about it?" He looked over at her.

"You just never know what someone will do once one person gets tired of the other person's games, and that's what happened."

"I see."

She then turned onto her side facing the wall. Her comment had Trent feeling uncomfortable and on edge. Somehow, though, he figured he'd survive the night.

Chapter 27

'No Questions Asked'

Lance was too ashamed to confront the mess he made with Shonna. He managed putting it off until the next morning. Then his conscience got the best of him.

Around 7:30—forty-five minutes before he usually left for work—he dialed Shonna's number. He figured by now the Chandler sisters had already discussed how his ruse had unraveled in a matter of fifteen minutes.

Humph.

Fifteen minutes of absolute shame.

Shonna didn't bother to say "hello" after picking up. *The noose is already set around your neck*, a still, small voice spoke up within him.

"I was too embarrassed to call you yesterday," he said, voicing the exact sentence had prepared himself to say.

Shonna still had not spoken.

He also expected that any conversation with Shonna, for sure, and possibly with Sonia, would not be cordial. He continued, "I'm sure Sonia told you what happened—"

Still no response from her. With each word, he was less

sure of himself; he envisioned himself on his tip-toes as the hangman's platform was giving way beneath him.

"Shonna—"

He resumed several moments later.

"I don't want her. I regret having had anything to do with her," he said. "I was thinking with the wrong head."

Meanwhile, Shonna rolled her eyes and tilted her head from side to side. One-and-done was definitely the order of her business.

"Shonna, I should have shown more patience. I didn't really trust your words when you said you needed time," he said. "If knew you actually had feelings for me, I'd never given her the time of day."

She finally spoke. "Do you expect for me to believe that?" Her voice was full of irritation. She hissed before continuing. "I don't even know why I'm listening to this!"

Out of pride, Lance wanted to remind her of all the pillow talk she made with him. He felt tempted to describe how she writhed, clawed for anything she could, and moaned out his name the night they spent in Charleston.

Yeah, there is a reason why you're listening, he wanted to say. He also thought of telling her the other reason why she hadn't hung up on him was because she was proud to have shown him off to people who were important to her—staff from the station and Sonia.

"Shonna, I know you didn't have to answer my phone call. I'm calling you because I want you to know that I want you. I don't want her."

"Humph. That's not the way it was told to me," she retorted.

"Then you've heard only one side of the story. Not mine."

Lance glanced at the clock. It was 7:45. He had thirty minutes before it was time for him to leave. He figured he'd also delayed his probable fate by fifteen minutes.

If he had any chance of extricating himself with Shonna, he figured it would take him having to win back Sonia as well; the latter was more so for his professional viability.

"If it means anything, Shonna, I feel the embarrassment for you, too. I thought I could handle this transition quietly; it never works out like that."

"My sister told me that you had been screwing her at work. Is that true?"

He swallowed hard before answering. "Yes."

"I don't like being made the butt of anyone's jokes. Especially another woman's." Her words were piercing to his conscience. "I don't like the idea of another woman thinking she'd have the pleasure of saying, 'Yeah, when she kissed him she also tasted me.'

"Do you see where I'm coming from?"

"Shonna, if it helps any, it was the other way around. She was tasting you before all that happened at work—"

"It doesn't really matter!"

Lance knew her hand was still on the lever. He sensed she was poised to pull it. Hard, in fact.

"I'm asking you, Shonna, to give me a chance to prove that I'm serious about you," he said. "I feel like before this is over, I'll be having to make it right with your entire family, and I hadn't met all of them."

"Well, that's the choice you made. And I really don't have to be a part of any of your damage and spin control."

Inwardly, Shonna knew that she would have her own damage and spin control to manage. It bothered her that others might think she was not in her right mind by involving herself with him.

This was why she struggled with setting realistic expectations for herself.

"Lance, I'll need to think about it. I don't deal well with

drama."

He sensed an opening. "Why do you need time? You had it before—"

"Hold it," she interrupted him. "This is not about me!"

"Maybe it isn't," he replied. "But last time you said you needed time; there was no guarantee of you coming back. Because if I knew you would, I never would have considered anything with her."

Shonna refused to give any ground to Lance. "Oh, really? Sonia said this other woman had been hot on your trail from the first time she laid eyes you.

"Even if I weren't in the picture before, obviously you thought she was worth checking out and pursuing—do you think that I was born yesterday?"

He looked at the clock again. It was eight o'clock. Fifteen minutes before it was time to leave for work. Thirty minutes that he'd prolonged his fate with her.

"I kind of figured that out about her. But it was only after she made the first move; I wasn't looking for anyone. I really wasn't."

"Really?" There was some relenting in her voice despite her best effort at denying her emotions. He spoke with contrition. "It's true. I wasn't."

Shonna figured there was only one way of dealing with Lance, and she was not about to let him wear her down by attrition over the phone—she had long since chalked that tactic up to experience.

While she was leaving out the front door for work, she said, "Lance, I've already said I don't deal well with drama. You've got to decide what you really want. That ball is in your court.

"Have a good day!"

She hung up.

* * *

Lance may have been too young to recognize or remember Antonio Fargas' character in Keenan Ivory Wayans' blaxploitation spoof *I'm Gonna Get You Sucka* when everyone laughed at him for wearing pimp attire that was past its era. Yet, that was the kind of mockery he anticipated once he was seen by his contract services colleagues.

True enough, he noticed a couple of phone reps whom he had never spoken to making head gestures and pointing back in his direction.

Look at him. Just look at him ... Ain't he got some nerve coming back after that?

He figured he was undoubtedly the punch line to their jokes and many others. That merely added to the anxiety he'd already felt.

Making a left-handed turn into the workplace, he bumped into of all people, Alvantrae.

Lance wore a pin-stripped business shirt, a solid-colored tie, dark slacks and loafers. He could have easily found his way onto a men's fashion magazine cover. Whereas, Alvantrae wore a white Polo shirt with a pink pull-over vest and tight-fitting lime green slacks.

"What's up?" Alvantrae greeted him.

Lance could hardly stand the thought of speaking to him. "What do you think?" He then looked down at the carpet.

Alvantrae spoke fast while passing. "You need to gird up your loins and keep it moving." He continued scooting off to the other side of the workplace for office supplies.

Neither looked back at each other and Sonia's cubicle was in plain view. Lance figured it was to his advantage to stop there since she was the one who sent him home. He didn't say anything while sitting in the chair adjacent to her. While waiting, it was as if she became Shonna in appearance. He recognized the similarity in their profiles. Her voice even sounded like Shonna's once she finally acknowledged him.

"I'm glad you came by here first so I didn't have to look for you," she said.

The words that Lance formed on his lips were of an apology; Sonia raised her hand, halting him.

"Here, I am your supervisor first. Away from here, I'm Shonna's sister, and will always be."

He responded with a head nod.

"I'll let Phyllis know you're here." She typed an e-mail and then dialed Phyllis' extension.

The work area still was relatively quiet. He overheard Phyllis' voice. "Okay, bring him in here."

Phyllis stood up from behind her desk and greeted both Sonia and Lance. She walked over to her left where she had a small round table near the corner and three chairs already situated for them to sit.

In his time at UCP, Lance associated Phyllis being in a position of authority because everyone reacted differently whenever she roamed the workplace. But he'd never spoken to her until now.

"I've heard a lot of things about you, Lance," she said as they all sat down. She also brought with her a small stack of papers.

"I hope it was good—until now."

"That might be accurate."

She then looked to her right at Sonia, who had a legal-size yellow note pad and was preparing to take notes.

"Yesterday, your immediate supervisor and I discussed briefly about what happened. We decided to wait until you came back [today] before any decision was made."

Sonia nodded in agreement while Phyllis brought her hands up to her chin and leaned on them.

Next, she glanced down at a Microsoft Excel printout before looking up at Lance, who sat across from her. Sonia followed along reading the same printed information.

"Your production has been coming along nicely. Last month, you would have met the department's goals had it not been for a couple of errors you made in your phone evaluations," Phyllis said. "The month before that, you were right at the department's goals."

Lance, who entered the meeting expecting the worst, darted his eyes downward, avoiding both Phyllis and Sonia.

"So, it appears that you want to work here," Phyllis said. "But we have a problem: You are still in your probationary period, which does not end until next month on the fifteenth. And what happened yesterday is grounds for termination without cause."

Phyllis now went through her stack of papers again. She placed multi-copy sheet atop of it.

"May I interrupt here?" Sonia said, leaning back in her chair.

"Sure, Sonia." Phyllis looked directly at her.

"If you look at Lance's time here, he has been a model employee at least if we evaluate him solely on what he's done on the phones and in his training classes—"

"Yes, Sonia. I realize that."

Lance sat back in his chair watching their exchange.

"I'm also sure that word of what happened yesterday has probably reached the fourth floor," Phyllis continued, "and I'm sure you know where they stand on things like this."

Sonia argued, "This is his first offense; he's not even missed a day of work or has been late."

"I am aware of that, too," Phyllis retorted; she began toying with the pen in her left hand.

"But such behavior will not be tolerated. What I do for one in here I also have to take into account for almost one hundred people out there!"

Lance took a deep breath while shifting his weight in the chair. "Ms. Phyllis, I don't expect much to come out of this in my favor. I know what I did with Charlotte was not acceptable. Humph, I'm quite embarrassed for myself and everyone in here."

"You don't leave me with many options here, Lance," Phyllis replied.

Sonia folded her hands and leaned forward at the table. She looked first at Lance then at Phyllis. "It may not be my place to say this, but I'll say it, anyway. I sent Lance home yesterday immediately afterward. The purpose was to let him know that what he and Charlotte did was not tolerated in the workplace."

Phyllis nodded. "I would have done the same thing in your position. The question is what do we do from here?" She took in a deep breath and leaned back in her chair. She stared at Lance for several seconds.

This time, Lance decided to cut glances at both Sonia and Phyllis. He figured it really didn't matter at this point what either of them thought.

"Lance, part of my job is to make decisions that are best for this department. I've taken into consideration your production since you've been here," Phyllis said, with an uncompromising glare at him.

"And for that reason, and that reason only, I've decided to give you a written warning; it will be your final written warning. If you're even as much as late twice within the next six months, or your overall production drops to less than three percent of the department's goals during that time, you will be terminated. No questions asked."

"Yes."

She slid the multi-copy sheet in front of Lance to read over and sign in acknowledgement.

After he signed the sheet, Phyllis was the first to stand up. What she did not tell him was that she handed out a similar punishment to Charlotte, and her decision also took into consideration her exemplary work.

"Lance, I don't want to meet with you again on these terms," she warned him again. "Do I make myself clear?"

"Yes, you do."

For a moment while walking back to her cubicle, Sonia saw herself as Shonna's sister. Watching Lance from behind also allowed her to imagine what Shonna had experienced with him—she was hardly envious of her. But she was just as quick to reassume her place as supervisor.

Lance suddenly looked back at Sonia. She held up her hand, halting him before he spoke. "Don't forget to sign in."

* * *

Later in the afternoon, Charlotte stopped by Sonia's cubicle. She placed a stack of claims, appeals, and inquiries to other departments that had been processed for documentation in UCP's system for Sonia's phone reps.

She also went out of her way not to look down the aisle to the right of Sonia—the third desk, which was where Lance sat. Her conversation with Sonia was mixed with obscenities and derisive comments about him.

After all, she spent most of the day telling her side of the story to anyone who would listen about her being the victim. She managed to find a few sympathizers in Tanya, Alvantrae, Kai, Janine, and a couple of team supervisors.

"I see that dirty mother still has a job," she hissed. "I can't believe Phyllis did that."

Sonia stared at Charlotte. It was stunning to witness the

change of attitude toward him. This was the same woman who went as far as to say she needed to spend time alone in the bathroom taking the edge off her arousal and lust for him.

Crossing her legs, Charlotte adjusted her skirt so that it covered her knees. "Humph, punk thought he could get off screwing over me like I was a toy of his." She paused and sucked her teeth. "Like I told him, I didn't care who knew.

"He should have thought about that when he decided I wasn't good enough for him."

This was the kind of conversation Sonia preferred avoiding.

"It's my understanding that you got the same written warning as him," she said. "The way I see it, you should be glad you're still here. Both of you were wrong."

Charlotte was visibly miffed. She stood up and walked off without commenting.

Chapter 28

〰

'Your Smile Makes My Day'

S onia picked up her cell phone and rushed out into the hallway to contact Harold Thompson, a Columbia-based attorney. He just might be the solution to the lies and disappointments she'd endured since being married to Trent.

"Thompson and Associates, how may I help you?" the receptionist asked.

"I'd like to schedule an appointment to see Mr. Thompson." Sonia began walking in the opposite direction of her workplace. "What's the earliest possible on his schedule?"

"What kind of representation are you seeking?"

"Divorce."

The receptionist asked Sonia to hold; she began pecking away on her keyboard. Meanwhile, Sonia began having flashbacks to what she witnessed almost twenty-four hours ago; her conversation catching Trent omitting the truth from her was now her impetus.

Although she never got a good look at her, the woman appeared to be entirely different from those she'd caught him gawking at in the past.

Then she thought about Taylor. It pained her to think the solid relationship he's had with Trent might be endangered because of his father's indiscretions. She envisioned growing old with the man who once won her heart 'till death do they part.

"Are you still there? I apologize for that delay," the receptionist said. "It's right at the end of the day—it's after five o'clock—and it seems that everyone's coming out of the woodworks for something."

"I understand."

"Now, about an appointment . . . The only one we have is a late cancellation, and it is at 9:30 tomorrow morning. Can you make that one? If not, Mr. Thompson won't have another opening until the end of the month—"

Sonia slowed down the pace of her walking. She let out a loud sigh.

"You say that's the only one?"

"Yes, ma'am."

This was something she wanted to act upon now, not later. Clearly, she reasoned to herself, that was Trent's thinking when he decided to risk it all with that woman.

"Okay. Put me down for tomorrow morning at 9:30."

"Your name is?"

"Sonia Chandler-Buckner." She felt liberated to include her maiden name. And with Thompson's help, she expected to go solely by it soon—as early as six months according to South Carolina law.

The receptionist apprised Sonia the first meeting was at no charge. And if she and Thompson agree upon representation, he charged $150 an hour, although they may be able to work out some kind of package deal since it was a divorce.

"Okay, Ms. Buckner. We'll see you in the morning."

"Thank you."

* * *

On her way back to her workplace, Sonia's emotions caught up with her. She never thought that she would ever consider divorce. At least among her colleagues, friends, and family, she considered herself among the most stable of people. She was the one people came to for inspiration and advice. It was a status she enjoyed, although she did not aspire for it.

About midway through the corridor was a women's bathroom just off to the left. She stopped in there to wipe away several tears she began shedding. While composing herself, she also offered up a short prayer:

> *When You were in the garden you said not Your will but His will be done ... I am far from perfect, but in my heart I can't take it any longer. I just can't. I ask You to put my tears in that bottle and consider my pain ...*

Sonia was quiet while returning to her cubicle. She went out of her way to avoid Vicki's cubicle by entering from the next entrance.

After settling into her chair, she made a quick check of the call monitoring screens. It was apparent that the call volume was entering into its non-peak hours. Usually, that meant all the notoriously crazy callers were already gone for the day.

She glanced at the roses that she received just the day before. Disgusted by what proved to be ulterior motives, she considered throwing them away. But before doing that, she figured that she'd checked her e-mails a final time. Then she could toss them on her way out of the building since her shift actually ended at five o'clock.

There were sixteen e-mails in her inbox. She made a quick

perusal through most of them before stopping at one that came from Milner. She was not inclined to reading it, but she reasoned why not?

Hi,

I appreciate the e-mail you sent. I hope your day has been great as the one I'm having. I also hope red was your color when it comes to roses and that smile is still on your face.

Sonia brought her hand up to her mouth, stopping herself from wanting to curse. Trent didn't send those roses after all. It was Milner who sent them. Smooth Operator himself.

And to think Trent almost had me in the mood…

So much for tossing the flowers. Sonia intended to keep them since they came from someone who at least took the time to convey that he was thinking of her. The sentiment seemed genuine, and it was well received. Knowing he sent them also anesthetized some of the hurt from her wanting to divorce Trent.

* * *

On her way home, Sonia decided to go out of her way and stop by The Groovy Soul. She did not bother questioning what her true motivation for going there was. It was simply her turn to put a smile on another person's face.

A young lady in her mid- to late twenties was at the cashier's counter. She was tall, rather svelte, and she wore a matching black blouse and slacks.

"I'll be right with you," she apprised Soina, who seemed surprised that she was not greeted by Milner as on previous visits.

The young lady was alone handling the duties of seating in-coming patrons and working the cash register. It appeared The Groovy Soul would soon need additional help.

"Thank you for visiting us," she told the last person. "Enjoy your meal."

Then she turned her attention to Sonia. "How many will be in your party?" She did not possess Milner's charisma, but she was pleasant.

"I, uh, was expecting the older gentleman would be here—"

"Oh, you're talking about my uncle?" she replied, chortling; she was not surprised by the way Sonia was fond to describe Milner. He had a knack for charming female customers who came there.

"He's in the back overseeing the dinner menu. My moth-er—his sister—was not feeling well today, and he's filling in for her."

Sonia's eyes widened. "Yes, that's right. He told me that you and your mother help run the operations here."

"How did you know that?" The young lady seemed genu-inely surprised by her knowledge of The Groovy Soul's orga-nizational structure.

"Uh, I met him while my sister's radio station was here. He gave us a little bit of a history lesson about this place."

"Oh, yes. He's been so excited about how well that promo-tion went last Saturday." She looked around the dining area, which was almost filled to capacity. "As you can see, it's al-ready had an impact."

Sonia began feeling as if she'd wasted a trip over to The Groovy Soul since there was no guarantee that she might even see Milner.

She was also aware that it was also not in her best interests to portray herself as a Milner groupie as well. So, she did the next best thing.

"I'd like to get a to-go plate," she mentioned to Milner's niece.

While preparing herself a plate, Milner came out with a cart that had several items to be included on the salad bar. He smiled and licked his lips once he recognized who it was from behind.

"Mmmm, dessert is being served!" he said, passing by Sonia.

She looked over at the other end of the buffet bar. "All I see over there is banana pudding and a couple of pies."

"That's for the customers. I'm talking about for me because you're here—"

Sonia cast an alluring stare at him and smiled. That was the kind of attention that she could get used to in due time.

"That's what I'm talking about." He made himself busy with stocking the salad bar nearby her. "Your smile makes my day. I'm glad you stopped by."

"Thank you for the roses. That's the reason why I came by here." She was nearly done with filling her Styrofoam to-go containers.

"You're welcome. I'd like to get to know you better. When can we talk?"

"I'll e-mail you first."

"Good. I'd also like to see you some time. I hope that's possible—"

"It just might be."

"Don't go just yet—meet me over by the cashier's counter."

He rushed back into the kitchen with the salad bar items. Meanwhile, she stopped by the cashier's counter and waited for him. She felt slightly out of place.

"Is there anything I can help you with?" Milner's niece asked.

"Yes, there is something. I forgot to mention that I had a couple of coupons. Are you still accepting them?" She searched her purse for them.

Milner's niece appeared to be frozen in thought. She liked the idea of a steady flow of cash filling the register rather than having to apply discounts and any refunding of money.

"Ah, here they are!" Sonia handed her a coupon.

Grudgingly, Milner's niece accepted the five-dollar coupon toward a customer's next meal. Her uncle had now joined them as well. When paired together, it was apparent to Sonia that tall people were prominent in Milner's family.

"Katrina, I see you've met Ms. Chandler. Her sister is the one who runs the radio station that was here this past Saturday," he said.

"Yes, sir, she mentioned that to me."

"So, you're taking care of her coupon?" he asked Katrina.

"Yes, sir, I am." She began counting back to Sonia $5.43 in cash; her original total was $11.92.

"Good."

Sonia thanked Milner and Katrina and left The Groovy Soul. As it had become a habit of his, Milner watched Sonia's view from behind while she walked to her car. This time, he folded his arms and sucked his teeth as if to savor the meal he just ate.

Chapter 29

❧

'The Decision Is Yours'

The law office of Harold Thompson and Associates was in an office building just off Greystone Boulevard and down the street from the South Carolina Baptist Convention's headquarters.

Before leaving her car, she thought of calling her parents, but that could wait. It just didn't seem to go well with her immediate intentions.

Thompson's office was on the third floor and right as she exited the elevator.

"Good morning, who are you here to see?" the receptionist asked; she appeared to be in her early to mid-sixties.

"I'm Sonia Chandler-Buckner, and I have an appointment with Mr. Thompson."

The receptionist offered her coffee or tea and glazed donuts.

"No thank you, I'm fine."

Then she glanced at her computer screen. "Yes, have a seat. I'll be right back."

Musing to herself, Sonia wondered where the "Associates" part to Thompson's practice was. The office suite had several rooms, but most were empty and the lights were off. The receptionist's desk appeared to be the only active area.

"Mr. Thompson will see you now," the receptionist returned to say.

Thompson met Sonia in the hallway. Compared to the portrait on his Internet site, the man had to be at least a decade older in person—more like in his early seventies. He was slightly bent over, and he had thick gray hair with dandruff flakes on his shoulders.

"Ms. Buckner?" he said, extending his hand out to her. "I'm Harold Thompson. Pleased to meet you. Come right in."

What a sight.

Thompson's office was a live re-enactment of Einstein's desk. There were a half-dozen stacks of papers and several books and envelopes scattered. A flat screen monitor was on a separate desk to his left—all in stark contrast to the way she maintained her desk and cubicle at UCP.

"Please excuse my domain, have a seat."

Surprisingly, she noticed his chairs were not old and worn; they were actually rather new and comfortable.

She also noticed on the walls several pictures of Thompson with what appeared to be notable people—there was a mixture of black and white photos as well as color photos.

"Melissa has been hounding me for years to do something with my desk. And I tell her to leave me alone and don't touch anything!" He laughed heartily at his short explanation. He then pointed at his temple. "I know where everything is on here."

Thompson adjusted his chair closer to his desk. "Melissa says you're looking to file for divorce? I'm sorry to hear that."

Sonia returned a confused expression; Thompson explained himself.

"That is one of the ugliest parts of my profession," he said.

"To me, a divorce is like cutting off an extremity. It is very disfiguring. The human body is an amazing organism. It adjusts; people don't always adjust afterward."

"I see what you're saying." Sonia sat back and crossed her legs.

Thompson then reviewed with her there were two avenues of pursuing a divorce, according to South Carolina law: filing for a divorce outright; filing for divorce and temporary separation.

"One of them is considered the express route. Can you guess which one is that?"

"Filing for divorce outright?"

He nodded.

"That's the one that I want."

He pushed a couple of books forward on his desk. He folded his hands and placed them in that spot. "Okay, and what proof do you have?"

"Early on in our marriage, he, my husband—"

"How long have you two been married?" he asked. Then he searched for a note pad under a stack of papers off to his right.

"Seven years."

"Okay." He scribbled down her name and being married seven years.

"As I was saying," she continued, "early on in our marriage he admitted to improper relationships with other women."

"Of what kind?" He never looked up at her but continued writing.

"Phone calls. E-mails. Admitting to going out on dates. Pictures."

"What about the actual act of adultery?"

She bunched her lips. "I've never proved that part." She began feeling uncomfortable especially after he looked up at her.

"Ms. Buckner, please forgive me if I sound so matter-of-fact with you. If you accept me as your attorney, my job will be to fight for you. But I have to know what I'm fighting with, okay?"

She breathed hard through her lips. "Okay."

"Now, was there any admission to adultery at any time?" he asked.

"No, sir."

Thompson explained to Sonia divorce was readily recognized on grounds of adultery, physical cruelty, desertion, and habitual drunkenness and drug abuse.

Immediately, she recognized that seeing another woman in his car would not hold much of an argument in the context of the law. She would have to prove that he had sex with that woman.

"Are you suggesting that all I'm able to do is file for a divorce, but it would have to be with that separation thing you were telling me about at first?"

"Yes, most likely."

"But doesn't that takes longer?"

"It does, but life goes on."

"Humph, I've heard that it does."

Thompson first explained to her that she would have to file for divorce, but then she would have to appear before a judge to be granted a temporary separation. Upon being granted, she and Trent would have to maintain separate living arrangements and they could not have sex at any time with each other for at least twelve months.

"If that is broken, the clock starts all over again." He hunched his shoulders. He then added alimony, support, custody, and division of property might also be decided during that hearing.

He went on to ask Sonia if there were any children involved. Her face began contorting. Immediately, Thompson left the office and returned with a stack of tissues. He also had Melissa to accompany him.

She finally composed herself. "Yes, we have a son who is thirteen."

Thompson asked Sonia a series of background questions about herself and Trent: where they were from; when they met and were married; highest level of education; current employment; property and other assets.

He then explained to her he would handle her case for $1,500.

"Ms. Buckner, the decision is yours. If you want to go ahead with this, we can start the paperwork today. We can serve papers to your husband by early next week."

He explained that Trent would have thirty days to respond to the divorce decree and be ordered to appear in court. The separation would go into effect once the case is heard. After closing her eyes in brief thought, Sonia nodded that she was willing to have papers served. She would pay half up front to Thompson; the other half would be paid in thirty days.

She said, "I get paid on Friday. I'll be back here with a check during my lunch hour."

Chapter 30

'For You ... I'll Make Time'

Friday could not have come any sooner for Sonia. Each night she went to bed during the week was like a trial. Turning down Trent's begging her for sex on Monday. Wondering how her family might react to her divorcing him on Tuesday. Thinking about what adjustments she'd have to make without him on Wednesday. On Thursday, it was worrying about how he might react to the divorce papers being served—she couldn't imagine him taking it calmly.

Despite her sleep-deprived state, she felt embolden driving over to Thompson's office with the check. She also kept telling herself it was an investment into her future and Taylor's.

"Are you sure you're all right with your decision?" Melissa asked her while she printed out a receipt.

Sonia sighed. "It's not every day that I spend $750 on myself. Maybe I should have done it more often so I could be used to it by now."

"You'll be all right," Melissa assured her. "Mr. Thompson always says the biggest challenge is people adjusting after life events like this."

"I hope I can say that eventually."

Melissa's maternal instincts took over—and her experience as Thompson's receptionist for the past twenty-five years.

"You still love him, don't you?" she inquired.

"It's not something that I can shut off just like that!" Sonia snapped her finger along with her reply.

"I'm sure Mr. Thompson gave you the illustration about losing an arm or a leg. You never grow one back, but eventually you learn how to adjust your life without it.

"Right now, you love him because he's been a part of your life for how long?"

"All together, fifteen years," Sonia answered. "Going on almost half my life."

"Eventually, you'll learn how to still love him, if things are amicably reached, but that void will be filled by other things. Hopefully, they'll be for the good."

"I guess so."

Melissa apprised Sonia that papers will be served on Trent no later than Friday of the following week. She suggested that she work now on creating a support system for Taylor because he would need one once he learn that his parents may be splitting up.

"Be sure you let him know that it's not his fault. Also let him know that his parents still share the same values about his upbringing and their desire to see him succeed in life."

Although Melissa's words seemed not to resonate with her, Sonia acted as if she was open to constructive advice.

"Thanks. I appreciate your talking to me."

When she returned to work, Sonia went ahead with printing out reports that Phyllis had requested earlier that morning. One of them was an update on unresolved inquiries. Sonia's team and Vicki's team were headed for Saturday over-

time if they still were above seven hundred unresolved inquiries by five o'clock. As of two in the afternoon, they were at
nine hundred and eighty.

Around 3:30 p.m., Sonia asked Tanya if she would help Kai
and Hannah Freeman with their respective backlog. She took
it upon herself to work with Lance since he had the most individually with more than ninety unresolved inquiries.

"Log off after that call," she alerted him.

He looked up at her, wondering whether he'd done something that cost him his job. But Sonia placed a printout in
front of him, pointing at it.

"We need to work on your backlog," she mouthed to him.

He nodded and continued with his call. Once he finished,
he stopped by Sonia's cubicle. It was the first time they'd spoken since his disciplinary meeting in Phyllis' office.

"Do you have your inquiry log with you?" she asked.

He shook his head. He went back to his desk and returned
with it.

"I want to make sure that you're being efficient with resolving your inquiries," she said. "When I was a phone rep, we
used to call this being taken to the woodshed because our
supervisor would pull us off to the side like this."

"So I'm being taken again to one?" he responded.

The quip almost went past Sonia, but then she caught onto
it. "I think I would leave that alone, if I were you—"

Without divulging her own personal issues, Sonia had only
text message correspondences with Shonna during the week,
of which Shonna confided in Sonia she thought Lance had
proven to be less of a man lately by his silence.

> I told him the ball was in his court. He must de-
> cide what he really wants. I guess either he doesn't
> know or he doesn't want to deal with it.

Sonia tried encouraging Shonna to keep her options open; there's lots of men out there. She also reminded Shonna:

It speaks of the man who finds himself a woman finds a good thing . . . It's up to the man being able to identify that good thing.

Meanwhile, Sonia went into Lance's main directory and pulled up a couple of screens with his unresolved inquiries. She pointed out nearly a third of them were unnecessary because he still had not fully grasped researching claims. Others could have been avoided if he had handled his phone calls more effectively.

"Everyone goes through the same learning curve," she assured him. "I had as many as one hundred and twenty-five during my first six months. Once it clicked with me, I consistently managed a backlog of less than fifty; that should be your goal."

He queried, "How long did it take you to get there?"

"About eight to nine months. Tanya would tell you the same thing with her."

Sonia then turned to him with a more serious look. She spoke loud enough that only he heard her. "How have you really been?"

He hunched his shoulders. "I've been doing a lot of thinking lately."

"I hope that it's been productive."

She did not bother to ask him anything concerning Charlotte. She figured that was already a hard lesson learned—both at work and away. Besides, things had been quiet three rows over to their right because she had been off since Wednesday. She was not expected to return until the following Wednesday.

Lance figured this was as good a time as any to speak up. "I do want to thank you for what you did in there with Phyllis. You didn't have to do that."

"In there, I spoke as your supervisor," she reminded him. "You've been a good worker. Don't mess it up." She then tipped her head at him as if to emphasize her point.

He nodded in acknowledgment He also thanked her for helping him whittle down his backlog.

* * *

Before leaving work, Sonia noticed from her cell phone that Milner had sent her an e-mail.

Let's talk. I really want to know more about you.

Milner's timing was uncanny. With her having started the process for divorce, she was coy to find out what he was all about. She decided to send him a text message reply than e-mailing him.

What is it you want to know?

She was surprised at how fast he responded knowing that he was manning The Groovy Soul's dinner shift.

I want to know more about you. I want to see and feel your emotions while we converse. I want you to know more about me.

Now those were lines she'd never neither read nor heard before, but it didn't really matter. It was soothing to her that another man found her desirable.

In her text reply, she mentioned to him if he wanted to meet with her, his best chance would be after Saturday's overtime shift. They usually wrapped things up by noon.

> If I agree to meeting with you, have you considered where?

He asked if a hotel would be more her liking.

> We'll just talk, nothing else.

> NO, NO, NO !!!

So, he suggested that they meet somewhere in the greater Columbia area like in Blythewood, which was the next town northward on Highway 321 and the I-77 freeway.

> Too close. I have to be very careful.

> What about in the other direction, Augusta?

> Maybe.

> I know of a bar and grill in a nice location. I think you'll be comfortable with it.

Sonia figured traveling forty-five minutes away from where she worked might be a safe distance. She could justify her trip by browsing the city's department store mall before leaving.

Time should not be an issue, either. Trent and Taylor were traveling to Greenville for another basketball tournament. They would already be more than an hour away from their home in Chapin, and a trip to Augusta would place them away by nearly two hours.

> I will call you before I leave work. You won't have a problem getting free, yourself?
>
> HA, HA, HA !!! For you, my dear, I'll make time!

Chapter 31

'*You Still Promise…*'

At ten minutes after twelve, Sonia marched out of the UCP building. This was the first time she ever had ulterior motives in her marriage.

Her conscience reminded her that anything could happen while meeting Milner. She could be involved in an accident. He could be involved in an accident. Even worse, she could be spotted by a mutual acquaintance of hers and Trent while she was with Milner.

With her mind, she wondered whether she brought the right dress, a twilight-colored ruched stretch satin sheath dress; it was mid-August but unseasonably mild. She also wondered whether she could handle the one-on-one attention by someone other than Trent.

She was undoubtedly out of her comfort zone, but she was determined to pursue it.

"Hi, it's Sonia," she called Milner at The Groovy Soul once she turned onto I-20 westbound.

There was noise in the background. He was slow to respond.

"Wharton?"

"Oh, yes. Sonia. . . ." His voice changed from cautious to being debonair. "So, uh, you're on your way to Augusta?"

"Yes, I'm just leaving."

"I'm on my way."

"Where should I meet you?" Sonia asked.

Milner instructed her to meet him in the parking lot of Lucky's Hideaway, an oyster restaurant about two blocks west on Washington Road after she exited the freeway. It would be across the street from the Mercedes-Benz dealership.

"How will I know you're there?" she asked.

"You'll know because I'll be wearing the biggest smile in Georgia."

"I trust you that I won't get lost since you're not giving me directions I can put into my GPS."

"Don't worry. And if you're not sure, call me."

Sonia turned into the parking lot of Lucky's Hideaway an hour after hanging up. About fifteen minutes of her travel time was spent inside the ladies' room at a Courtyard Marriott changing into her dress, brushing her hair with frenetic strokes, and reapplying her makeup.

"How close are you?" Milner called her from his cell phone.

"I'm already here." She noticed her heart pounded harder and faster. This was actually happening—the very behavior she despised of Trent after all these years.

"I'm no more than five minutes away. You'll know I'm there because I'll be the one in a silver E-Class sedan driving slowly in the parking lot looking to find a space next to your car."

She reacted, "You don't know what I drive—"

"Excuse me, ma'am. You drive an M35, and you look good in it. That's all I need to know. I'll see you shortly."

Well…

While she awaited Milner's arrival, Sonia noticed Trent calling.

This would happen the one time I decide on stepping outside of my marriage, she grimaced.

Chalking it up to karma, she realized that she'd probably done the same thing to him several times in the past; it still didn't change her sentiment about him being served divorce papers.

"Hi, Trent."

"Hey. I missed talking to you this morning."

Whatever!

She was more than convinced that he should have thought about missing her the day she saw him with another woman in the Taurus.

"I told you last night that we had Saturday overtime, and I would be going in a little early to get a jump on closing out some of our backlog."

"Yeah, you did mention something like that."

She rolled her eyes, mocking him silently. "How many times I've complained about you not listening to me?"

"Can we not go there?" he pleaded with her.

"Okay, I won't. How is Taylor's team doing today?"

"They lost their first game, and they have to play out of the loser's bracket. They still have a chance to win it, but it will be much tougher this weekend."

So much for the small talk, she thought to herself; it was tempting to rush him off the phone.

"What are you going to be doing today?" he asked her.

She was surprised that he broached such a question. The roles should be reversed, she thought. He should be the one scrambling to conjure up a believable alibi.

"I'm going to get some shopping done for myself. Summer's

still here, and I think I need something new and different."

"Yeah, right . . . I hope our accounts won't be spinning on a new and different axis once you're finished."

"Humph, don't worry about me."

Trent mentioned that he expected to be back home around 8 p.m. It was about 1:15. She figured she had at least four good hours exploring an entirely different world than she'd been accustomed to since the year Taylor was born.

Just as he described to her, Milner turned into Lucky's Hideaway parking lot creeping along at a pedestrian's pace. Once he spotted her, he positioned his car so that their driver's doors were facing each other. He also greeted her with a wide grin.

"This is definitely a day the Lord has made, and I'm so glad I'm in it!"

Sonia found herself blushing. "You need to stop while you're ahead."

"I'll stop for now. But I feel so privileged to see that smile of yours."

"Well, it's nice seeing you finally."

Sonia found herself letting out a small grunt in admiration once Milner stepped out of his car. He wore a light blue Polo shirt, beige slacks and black loafers.

If she were going to step outside her marriage, she thought, at least it appeared that she had done it right. This wasn't scrap heap material. Milner appeared as if he was a man of authority and prestige.

While walking inside the establishment, their contrasts in appearance were more than complementary. Much it had to do with how well-maintained he was for his age.

"I've got a small confession to make," he whispered to Sonia.

She braced herself for something shocking.

"I was so nervous coming here to meet you," he said. "And I'm still nervous."

"So am I. Maybe it's more about us being excited to see each other?"

Milner puffed out his chest and chortled. In his next move, he told the server they would sit at the bar. Looking Sonia over from her legs up to her face and back down, Milner recounted to himself how he had pursued other men's wives with moderate success. Timing had a lot to do with it. And those whom he went all the way with were still casual contacts of his.

"I'm surprised you didn't know that I was the one who sent you those roses," he said. "A woman like you is quite perceptive."

"I had my suspicions. I figured somebody would eventually take the credit."

The bartender stopped by where they sat. Milner ordered himself a margarita, heavy on the salt; Sonia ordered a peach daiquiri.

While they conversed, Milner studied her poise and mannerisms. He noticed she was not consumed with who might be coming in and out of the establishment. That would have been a sign of nervousness or lack of interest.

"I forgot to ask you about your sister when you came by the restaurant the other evening. Please pardon my oversight."

Sonia, although careful with her response, was impressed. "She and I haven't talked at all this week. We've only exchanged a few text messages about much of nothing."

He nodded, taking in her response. The bartender returned with their drinks. He placed a twenty-dollar bill on the counter and held up his hand, thanking the bartender.

"Now, where were we?" he continued. "Oh, yeah. You said you and your sister had only exchanged a few text messages.

Are the two of you very close? Who is the oldest?"

Sonia mentioned Shonna was the oldest without divulging her age.

"As we've gotten older," she added, "we don't have as many sister-to-sister moments like when we were younger. She's well established in her career, and I've got a career, husband, and child that take up most of my time."

"Do you have any other siblings?"

"No." She then took a sip from her drink. "And you?"

He seemed quite eager to share information about himself. "There are four of us. I'm the youngest. My sister, Willette, is older than me by three years. I have another sister, Constance, who is older by five years; a brother, MacArthur, is the oldest.

"That's one of the reasons why running this restaurant means so much to me. This is really a family venture with Willette and my niece."

"You sound like a loyal brother and uncle."

He was quick to return the conversation back to the roses. "I'm glad that you responded to my e-mail. At least I know now you were interested."

"I'm sure you know a woman always lets a man know if she's interested or not." She sat straight on the bar stool, crossing her legs.

"Why are you, I might ask?"

She smiled. "Good question. I liked your attentiveness whenever I came by the restaurant. You're quite handsome. And I—"

"You don't have to get into that."

"Thank you. I didn't plan on mentioning anything about my husband, anyway." She was more than aware of women who readily divulged their marital problems to other men often find themselves exploited. At least that was what she'd witnessed with Vicki whenever she needed a sympathetic ear.

Their conversation turned from his intended fact finding about her to him sharing more information about himself. He volunteered to her that he was originally from Rogers, Arkansas; a town neighboring the center of Walmart's universe, Bentonville, and about twenty-five minutes from Fayetteville.

His family moved to Los Angeles when he was nine. He lived in South Central—Compton—throughout the 1970s to the mid-1980s. Then he enlisted in the Army where he served for eight years, attaining the rank of staff sergeant.

"Were you ever married?" she asked.

His lips tightened while he nodded. "When I was first stationed at Fort Lee, Virginia; we stayed married for almost ten years before we separated. I've been divorced for another ten years."

"Children?"

He breathed loudly through his nostrils before he replied. "I have a son, who should be twenty-five."

"You don't sound so certain."

He leaned back on his bar stool and contemplated how he would frame what had been an acrimonious relationship with Delano and his mother Kivette.

Baby mama drama to the extreme. This was someone whom he often proclaimed if she were in a burning car he would run to the nearest gas station with his last two dollars, ensuring that she would not escape.

"Let's see, I was stationed at Fort Hood, Texas when I happened upon her. I was still an E-2 (corporal) at the time, so that means probably late 1980s." He nodded his head with certainty; he clenched his teeth and his jaws tightened.

Sonia was quick to recognize the animosity in his body language.

"May I ask you this question?" she queried.

"Absolutely."

"You've been married, divorced, and from what I can tell you had a son before you were married. The relationship with his mother is something you care not to talk about at this time, which I understand and respect." Her face showed an expression of wanting a clearer understanding while pausing.

"What is it you want from me? And what is it do you expect of me?"

There was no searching for words or Milner scratching his head or chin, hinting his discomfort with her question.

"I'll answer it this way: Obviously, I want something I should not be having." He took a sip from his drink and toyed with the sweat streaming from the glass.

"I'm glad you recognize that," she commented. "But if I were to hold that against you then I'm a hypocrite."

It was nearly three o'clock. Milner suggested they catch a movie. However, they went back and forth for several minutes over whose car they should drive to the Regal Exchange Stadium 20 theater.

"I'll drive us over there," he proposed.

"Uh-uh. I'm not comfortable with that."

He proposed next: "Okay, we drive there in my car. But you drive—"

She shook her head emphatically. "I've never driven a Mercedes, and it won't be today!"

"All right, we drive over in your car—"

Immediately, she thought of Trent's transgression. That surely would make her a hypocrite. "We can't do that!"

"Then what can we do?"

Suddenly, they realized they were getting nowhere and burst into laughter.

"Sanity does prevail, huh?" he joked.

"Yes, it does. I'll just follow you over there."

The moment was spontaneous and somewhat comical, yet

it was something that gave Sonia reason to think Milner was not a bad option at all.

They could talk. They could disagree. They could be perplexed, yet able to laugh it off. It reminded her of her parents who had been married for nearly forty-five years.

Sonia fell asleep about halfway during the showing of *Oz the Great and Powerful*. The movie was not boring, but the lack of sleep during the week and Saturday overtime finally caught up with her.

She leaned solidly on Milner's shoulder. He was reduced to reclining back in his seat and with his hands clasped behind his head—it was more than tempting to make better use of his hands on her body.

"I fell asleep, didn't I?" she said, looking up at him after the lights came on. "I'm so sorry."

He chortled at her. "You talk about expectations? I would have expected something like that from my nieces or nephews when they were younger." Now it had become a deep laugh, and it left her scrambling for an excuse.

"Please forgive me. It's been a very long week. I hope you won't hold this against me. This has never happened before—"

She was so vulnerable before him. At least to him, it had the makings of a romantic moment. He stood up and offered his hand. She felt obligated to accept it. They walked out of the theater holding hands.

It was fast closing in on six o'clock in the evening. She began entertaining another array of thoughts.

First, at least to her knowledge, she survived not running into anybody who knew both her and Trent. She also needed to stop somewhere along the way home and change back into the clothes she wore to work.

Finally, as much as she felt attracted to Milner and desired to spend more time with him, she could not shake the embarrassment.

"I never thought I would fall asleep during a movie and on the first date, if you want to call that one, with somebody. I'm so sorry—"

Milner held up his hand, signaling to her that all was well. Following his instincts, he gazed into her eyes and pulled her closer. But he felt resistance from her. The moment was not right, so he backed away.

"I don't want to do something yet that I might regret," she said. "I think you're an awesome man, Wharton; I feel so comfortable around you. That's a scary thing."

"Sonia, I enjoyed seeing you today. I'm glad we got a chance to find out more about each other." He was tactful not to bring up her sleeping during the movie. "Let me know that you've made it home safely, okay?'

"Thank you, I'll do that." She eased inside her car, starting the motor.

Milner motioned for her to let her window down before she drove off.

"You still promise that I'll be the first to know when you're ready?"

She smiled back at him. "Yes, you'll be the first." *And quite likely the only one*, she said to herself.

Chapter 32

'Why Didn't You Tell Me???'

Trent had just finished helping a recent college graduate with opening a checking account and a second account that also served as overdraft protection, as well as applying for a bank card.

He recounted to himself what it was like at his new customer's age—twenty-three. Nobody helped him with setting up any checking accounts or managing his finances, nor was there anyone he trusted.

Days like these were most satisfying to him because he was able to steer the young man, who was to begin work as a radiology technician with Palmetto Healthcare System, in the right direction.

He took a moment to text message Sonia:

> I missed talking to you this morning before you left.
> Look forward to seeing you later . . .

Expecting a reply from Sonia at any moment, Trent went out into the bank lobby and checked on his tellers. All five windows and both drive-thru tellers were occupied—always a nice thing seeing transactions taking place.

A Lexington County sheriff walked into the bank as Trent returned to his office. He stopped to greet him.

"I'm looking for Trent Buckner," the officer said.

"I'm Trent Buckner."

The officer handed Trent an envelope. "This is for you, sir." He turned around and headed back out the door.

Trent did a double-take once he read the letterhead. *Lexington County Family Court?* It took all of him not to shriek out the name of the place.

Slowly, he walked back to his office; and quickly, he thought back to his past. He had not committed adultery with any woman in more than five years. And he figured there should be some kind of statute of limitations by default for the other women he was involved with prior to marrying Sonia.

Nah, can't be any phantom child support order . . .

Trent was careful to open the envelope. Suddenly, he jerked his head back and his eyes were bugged.

PETITION FOR DIVORCE!!!

He looked at the paperwork again. Sonia Delaine Chandler-Bucker was the petitioner and Trent Lawrence Buckner was the respondent. Both were ordered to appear before the Honorable Sabine H. Bly on the thirteenth of August.

All feelings left Trent. He could not believe Sonia wanted to ditch him. It just didn't make any sense. He buried his forehead into his hands and closed his eyes. However, he knew that he could not fully act out the way he felt because of where he was.

He was quick to grab his cell phone. There was not enough profanity known to man that could adequately support the string of words that filled his mind.

With bunched lips and clenched teeth, he angrily punched

each letter that comprised his message to her:

> WHY DIDN'T YOU TELL ME ! ! ! WHAT REASON DID
> I GIVE YOU???

And to think, he grumbled to himself, she had gone the entire week as if nothing was wrong. She cooked for him. She washed clothes for him. She even ironed one of his business shirts. They shared a couple of laughs when they mused about their neighbor, Mr. Rembert, who was a cantankerous geezer.

Humph.

They even made yet another futile attempt at sex—although he was reduced to another perfunctory get-me-off session just to say he'd kept his sanity.

> DON'T PLAY DUMB WITH ME. ANSWER MY TEXT!
> WHY ARE YOU DIVORCING ME?

* * *

All week long Sonia was eager for the moment Trent would read the divorce papers. Despite meeting Milner in Augusta, she still felt her actions were justified. It was time to do something for herself. Trent had his time.

Anticipating what might ensue, she debated whether she should have moved out the house. She decided Trent should be that person, and she'd simply call the police if things got out of hand.

Other things she considered was whether they should have gone to counseling with one of the church ministers. But that had always been an exercise in futility. Trent always refused whenever she broached it earlier in their marriage.

"*I don't want any of those hen-pecked hypocrites telling me what to do!*" he once yelled at her. "*I've never heard any of them side with a man on anything … They'll go as far as to say he's wrong for going to the bathroom … The man is always at fault in those counseling sessions!*"

She once suggested that he find a counselor that he was comfortable with visiting. He never got around to it. He promised that he'd change.

Perhaps he did. It appeared, however, that his infidelity was dormant for only a few years, she surmised.

When she saw the first text from Trent, she breathed a sigh in relief. She also knew that she'd just fired the first shot in this marital war.

> Trent, I've been telling you for some time that things could be better in this marriage. It's too late now.

Maybe there was no true way of preparing for this moment, she realized. Trent called her cell phone two dozen times within a forty-minute span. He also sent a dozen more text messages before she responded a second time.

> Trent, please be moved out of the house by the time I get home tonight.

That message merely incensed Trent even more.

> HELL NO! That's my house. You wouldn't be in that house if it weren't for me! If you're going to divorce me, I want you to tell me in my face why you're divorcing me. I deserve at least that much!!!

> Okay, I'll tell you in person. Meet me in the parking

lot of Five Guys in Harbison at 6 p.m.

* * *

Trent stood outside his car looking for Sonia to turn into the parking lot on Columbiana Drive. It was already 6:05 p.m. She had yet to show up.

Annoyed and wiping sweat from his brow, he called her cell phone.

"What's taking you so long? You're the one who set the time. Now you need to be here!" he demanded of her.

"I'm just now leaving work," she replied. "Trent, I don't want any trouble with you—"

He yelled, "Just what do you mean by that? You can't even give me the common decency of telling me why you want a divorce . . . You've not even tried working on this marriage!"

"Trent, I'll be there as soon as I can."

She then hung up.

All things considered, Sonia was surprised at herself that she maintained her composure during Trent's outburst. But she wasn't sure how long it would last.

On her way over to Five Guys, she noticed a black Taurus just like Trent's driving past her on St. Andrews Road. There was a man about the same age as Trent as the driver; a woman was in the passenger's seat. They appeared to be laughing it up, a reminder of what she saw Trent doing.

The anger that she'd suppressed for nearly two weeks took over. Forget about the love of God shining abroad in her heart. Forget about casting down arguments that might exalt itself. This was one time she felt no shame if she was cheered on by the devil and his imps to raise all kinds of hell.

Turning into the lot, Sonia didn't bother to offer up a quick prayer for guidance. She expected to unleash an opening flurry on Trent that might score a first-round knockout.

"About time you made it!" she heard him say just as she parked her car next to his.

He didn't wait for Sonia to turn off the engine before he went into his tirade. He waved the envelope at the driver's side window.

"You couldn't even tell me, huh?" He then held out his hands in protest.

She let down her window and leaned against her center console, looking directly at him.

"Trent, I've been telling you for a long time how I've been feeling about things in our marriage, but you never listened."

"Hah! I've never heard of someone being divorced over orgasms!"

"This isn't about orgasms, Trent. This is about being tired of being disappointed. It's about tired of being tired."

"About what?"

When she did not immediately respond, he took the opportunity to fire another question at her.

"Does Taylor know anything about this yet?" he inquired.

"No, but I plan on sitting him down this weekend and talk to him about it."

"What am I going to do about tomorrow? He has another tournament—"

"I can take him, and I'll tell him you had a banking function to attend."

He bunched his lips and shook his head. "That's only a small Band-Aid to a bigger problem that *you* created, Sonia. I don't know if you really thought this thing through."

"Trent, when someone decides to do something like this there's never a right time. It will always be wrong." There was a much sharper edge to her words.

"Why, Sonia? Why are you doing this?" He shifted the

weight from his right foot to his left and folded his arms.

She looked straight ahead, yelling, "I'm doing it because I'm not going to put my life in danger any more because you can't keep that crooked thing between your legs in your friggin' pants!"

"What are you talking about?"

She turned slowly and faced him, unleashing a stream of obscenities. "Who was that hussy I saw in that car last week Monday?" She also pointed at the Taurus for emphasis. "You were driving around like you were Stanley D. Stud, and you didn't even notice that I was following you, hmmm?"

Both scowled at each other.

Initially, Trent thought of denying Alcione was in the car with him, but then he caught himself. Sonia jumped at the opportunity.

Wagging her finger at him, she said, "I asked you twice that same night how did things go—"

"I told you how things went!"

"Humph, I just sat there watching you make a complete fool out of yourself like you always do. That's when I decided to file for divorce." She returned to looking straight ahead.

"Sonia, that was my customer. She's Nelson Oliveria's daughter."

"Do you think I'm that god blasted dumb?" she retorted. "It doesn't matter who she was. You had another woman in that car with you. All that talk about it being a 'business dinner' was too suspicious to believe, and I was right. And the bad thing about it is you've never been a good liar!"

Trent was incensed. He walked in a small, tight circle next to her car trying to restrain himself from acting upon the impulse of using a tire iron and smash dents into her car.

He stopped after one circuit. With each word spoken, he accompanied it by punching the air with his index finger.

"You've got some nerve calling me a liar. How many times you lied to me in the bedroom? Let me help you out there: Each time you faked an orgasm!

"There's no telling what else have you've lied to me about all these years—"

Sonia shook her head and sighed loudly. "I told you, Trent. I'm not doing this because you can't satisfy me in bed. It's obvious you're making up for it elsewhere!"

Trent waved her off in disgust.

"Whatever, Sonia. I wish you well trying to prove it in court that I've been cheating on you."

"Humph, don't worry. Once I tell them about your past they'll forget about the present and future."

As much as it pained Trent that he did not indulge himself to the fullest extent with Alcione, he felt the best thing he had going for him was being able to rebut with conviction.

"Sonia, I'm only going to say this once. I'm telling you. I was not messing around last Monday. It was all business. No sex. Nothing!" he said forcefully. "And to be honest with you, I don't need your permission or approval on how I conduct my business especially when we're talking about millions of dollars involved.

"I promised you after all that other stuff that happened I would be faithful to you, and I would never disappoint you again being unfaithful . . . So if you want to divorce me, fine. Maybe it might be a good for both of us. But it will be all in your mind why it happened!"

He threw up his hands in disgust. Then he put them on his waist.

"Trent, I expect you to have your stuff out before I get back from Taylor's tournament tomorrow." She looked into the rear-view mirror and shifted her M35 into reverse.

"Is that's what you want?" he reacted, keeping up with her

while she backed out of the parking space.

"Trent, I've told you why I'm divorcing you. Have a nice life!"

She snapped her finger, gave him the back of her hand, and she drove off.

He flipped his middle finger at her. "Fine! I'll be out tomorrow. Yeah, that's right. I'll leave . . . Go ahead and find yourself someone who'll put up with what I've put up with you. He'll find out you're a head case who has problems coping when you can't have it your way!"

Chapter 33

❧

'What's Your Point?'

Within days after Shonna placed the onus on Lance about his choice of women, she looked to the Internet with expectations of making a new connection of her own.

The Internet was familiar territory. Starting back in the mid-1990s, she was a frequenter of America Online's chat rooms and personals, and she met a handful of men as a result of using a keyboard. Those were the pioneering days of online dating. Meeting someone via the computer was new and exciting experience, and it was done in the privacy of one's own surroundings.

At the turn of the century, she happened upon the adult online dating Web sites. Those intrigued her more because there was no pretense about everyone's intentions. The risks were the same as AOL, if not greater. But she swore off that kind of activity the day she turned forty.

Although tempted to venture back to the adult dating sites, she resisted and tried the mainstream sites. So much had changed. The first thing she noticed it actually cost to find somebody that might pique her curiosity: She could post a profile and hope that someone would contact her. But the only way she could initiate any contact with anyone was paying a monthly membership fee.

I'm not going to sit around here and not get my groove back on . . . Humph!

A week of regular perusals transpired before Shonna felt she had a prospective connection with Turner Cottrell, forty-four, who lived on the other side of the state in Spartanburg. According to his profile, he was divorced, a non-smoker, and a light drinker. He liked movies, dancing, and he had a knack for singing.

Surprisingly to her, three days of exchanging e-mails and additional pictures passed before Turner made the first move asking for her phone number.

"I'm impressed that you weren't like some of these other clowns who bombard you with their phone numbers and wanting to meet you at a hotel two hours later," Shonna mentioned to him.

His voice was a smooth tenor. "You'd be surprised how some of the women act on these sites, too. I kind of question my sanity why I come on here. But it's much easier meeting someone online than walking up to them trying to start a conversation."

"I guess you have a point there. I've not tried this in a while. Three years, in fact."

"Well, I'll be honest with you. I went out on a date with someone two weeks ago."

"Really? What happened?"

He was diplomatic with his response. "It turned out she wasn't my type."

Sonia knew there were several possible reasons for the missed connection. She mused aloud to him it meant she refused to have sex with him on their first date, and he didn't like that. Neither of them were attracted to each other, but they had sex anyway. She was hardly what she described herself to be. Or, the date was an absolute disaster.

"Which one was it?" she quizzed him.

He chortled. "I'm sticking to my story that she wasn't my type."

"Well, what guarantee there is I'm your type?" she retorted.

"I guess that's the insanity about dating online. If it doesn't work with one, it might work the next time around with another. And I'm still looking for that person."

"Same here. The last person I dated—I didn't meet him online—turned out to be a disappointment. But the impact was lessened because I didn't expect much from the beginning."

Shonna and Turner agreed to meet in Greenville for dinner. At first glance, he was everything that he'd described of himself. He stood six-three and was athletic in build. He had keen features, a megawatt smile, and an engaging personality.

There was one problem, however.

He reminded her of Lance; she was careful not to tell him. During dinner, she found herself being disinterested and wandering in thought. All she saw was Turner's lips moving; his words were insignificant.

"The last concert I went to see was Sade in Charlotte in 2011. Man, she was out of sight! That was worth every dollar I spent listening to her for two hours!" he said. "I'm thinking about going to concerts again on a regular basis. What was the last concert you saw?"

"I go to concerts all the time. It's a part of what I do."

"Really?" He seemed genuinely intrigued.

She shrugged her shoulders. Her mind went adrift thinking of Lance again.

"Is there anything wrong?"

"Oh, nothing. I was thinking about some of the performers at these concerts aren't even worth mentioning. The talent just isn't there. It's like working around money. When you're exposed to the real thing, you can spot a counterfeit just like that." She snapped her finger.

"I know what you mean."

Turner and Shonna agreed that they would meet again. But when he called her back a few days later, she was evasive.

"There's a Will Downing concert coming up in Columbia next week. I'm thinking of going. Would you be interested in being my date?"

"I'm not sure if I'll be available," she said. "I'll need to check my schedule and get back with you."

She never called him, nor did he attempt contacting her.

* * *

Shonna was on her way to Publix at Two Notch Road and Sparkleberry Lane when she recognized the phone number calling. She grumbled about the caller having some nerve. She disconnected the call before answering.

The number appeared on her phone again. Sighing, she relented and answered.

"So, you're still alive, huh?" she answered.

It took Lance two weeks to work up the nerve to call Shonna, but more than a month had passed since he last contacted her.

"You know what?" he responded. "You've got some nerve making a comment like that. I didn't say a single negative word once you decided that you could handle dating someone younger than you."

Shonna knew Lance was not exaggerating the facts. Their

making up became one of the most passionate nights she'd spent with a man in recent memory.

"Lance, the biggest complaint I had with you was your inability to appreciate the amount of thought that went into my decision to date you," she said. "So, why are you calling me now? What is it you want?"

"I want to see you."

"I'm sure you still have a picture or two of me still on your [cell] phone. Isn't that enough?"

"No, I want you; I want to see you again; and don't tell me that you have to think about it, either!"

Shonna remained silent. She went ahead with turning into the Publix parking lot.

"I'm still here, Lance. But apparently you have other ideas on the kind of woman you want to involve yourself with. I told you then, and I'll tell you now, I don't deal well with drama."

"I don't, either."

"Humph, it was obvious you had plenty on your hand and you were thriving in it."

"No, I wasn't. Once you said you were willing to give us a try, I had already knew who I wanted," he said. "Now, are you going to find it within yourself to give me a second chance?"

She pursed her lips and stared aimlessly. There was something about him that simply turned her on. The look. The touch. The smile. The long, deep strokes inside her. He was the one who tickled her fancy—and more. It didn't matter what others thought.

"Shonna, if it helps any, I've not spoken to another woman under any circumstance other than at work since we last talked. Nobody."

"I find that hard to believe."

"Has Sonia told you anything about me?"

"Sonia doesn't waste her time giving me updates on how you go about your business at work. She's not that type of person. And before you even ask it, no, I've not asked her anything about you!"

"All right, all right. I shouldn't have gone there, but I wanted to stress the point I've been taking care of my own business. And I want you to be included in it. Can I see you tonight?"

He mentioned as a side point to her that he recently celebrated his twenty-eighth birthday alone, and he was okay with it.

"I see, so you've done a little growing up there?" she teased him.

"Ha, ha . . . I'm holding my belly laughing. Now, umm, what time will you be expecting me?" His voice was calm and convincing.

Mmmph!

Now this was the kind of man that she was proud of showing off to Sonia and her colleagues at the station. Part of what intrigued her about him was him being so definitive in his decision making and actions. She liked a man who took charge in and out of the bedroom.

For the first time in years, Shonna felt complete being with a man. She had a true emotional stake in Lance, and she sensed him having invested the same kind of resources into her. She felt secure in his arms while they were spooned together in her bed. She joked to herself that she might have to take vitamins to match his stamina, or that she might have to work at it more with him and get into that kind of shape.

"So, where do we go from here?" she asked him.

"We go as far as we want to make it go. Are you comfortable with that?"

She turned around and kissed his chest. "Yes, I'm comfortable with it."

He sat up in the bed. "There was something else I wanted to share with you." He reached out for her hand. "I'm giving Sonia my one week's notice on Monday."

"Why?" She also sat up in the bed. But he nudged her to lean on his chest while he caressed and fondled her.

"I found a job in my field of expertise, electrical engineering," he said. "Humph, it pays a heck of a lot more than what I've existed on at UCP."

Shonna closed her eyes and smiled. Yes, maybe things had their own way of working out for the good—and in their own timing.

* * *

Sonia showed little reaction when she opened Lance's e-mail indicating that he would be leaving UCP. Even the good ones tend to come and go through contract services rather quickly. Most phone reps last less than eighteen months before moving on.

Given the nature of what she knew about him, she was even more careful to treat his pending departure as merely another personnel outcome. She sent a copy of his e-mail to Phyllis' attention before leaving for the day.

> Ms. Sonia,
>
> This e-mail is to inform you that I will no longer be an employee at UCP effective Friday evening. I appreciate your willingness to help at all times and your professionalism. I don't think I could have otherwise made it.
>
> Sincerely,

Lance Miles

If circumstances were different, Sonia figured she would have at least made an effort to speak with him about his decision.

Now it didn't matter. But she figured it was worth mentioning to Shonna in passing since they had not spoken in a little more than two weeks.

"Hey, I have you to know that Lance is leaving contract services at the end of the week. He told me—"

Shonna didn't allow Sonia to finish her sentence. "Yes, I already know." She grinned with great satisfaction. In fact, she was en route to his place with an extra day's clothing to spend the night with him.

"Since when?" she shrieked into the phone.

"Saturday night . . . No, make that yesterday morning."

"You are kidding me, right?"

"Why would I joke with you about that?"

Sonia did not expect this conversation to take on this kind of twist. She was so stunned that she exited the freeway in Harbison and found a place to park so that she could continue their conversation.

"Humph, you couldn't stay away from him?"

"Maybe it was mutual. Maybe we couldn't stay away from each other—"

None of what Shonna said made sense to Sonia. Before Lance's incident with Charlotte, she confided in Shonna that she was inclined to go along with her decision about dating a much younger man. It was all about her sister's perceived happiness.

Now she'd become the critic and cynic. She peppered Shonna about the notion there's likely to be more issues of insecurity acted out by the woman when there's a great age disparity. And it's likely the younger man may eventually find sexual compatibility and happiness with a woman closer to his age.

"You have access to the news every day. If the source is correct, there's an Internet article about your favorite gospel singer Candi Staton divorcing her husband after two years; she's nineteen years older than him.

"Look at what's happening with Ashton Kutcher and Demi Moore. He's leaving her—we really don't know why, but it's easy to suspect that he became bored with being around somebody fifteen, almost sixteen years older than him."

Shonna merely rolled her eyes, pointing out to Sonia she and Lance weren't married. "So, what's your point?"

"My point? What about Susan Sarandon and her actor husband from the *Shawshank Redemption*?"

"You're talking about Timothy Robbins?"

"Yeah, him—"

Shonna told Sonia she actually went out on a couple of dates while they were separated. What she learned, however, she genuinely liked Lance; it worked out that he reached out to her again.

More than likely, she was quick to suspect, Sonia heard only what she wanted to hear. The rest, well . . .

"Don't you think two people should like each other first so they might forge some kind of friendship and relationship? Now, what is wrong with that?" she posed to Sonia. "I think he's sincere, and he has a clue about what he wants in life."

"I don't disagree that Lance has drive and ambition. Humph, I was his boss for the past six months. I saw it every day.—"

"And that's all you saw," Shonna reminded her. "You're talking as a boss. I'm talking as somebody who has shared my body and emotions with him, and I want to see how far this relationship might go."

Sonia felt there was only so much she could say about relationships before her credibility be questioned. In recent weeks, she had not shared any details about her pending divorce with anyone other than Taylor—and she'd been full of anxiety wondering if and when he might tell others about it. And God forbid if she were to divulge anything about her and Milner's growing relationship, although it had yet to become sexual.

"All I'll say is I'm really surprised you and Lance are back together again. I hope you're strapped tightly into your roller coaster ride."

She could not stop snickering about them. "You really must have put something on his mind?"

Shonna retorted, "Maybe it was more like him putting something on my mind—"

"That might be the truest thing you've said in this conversation. Humph, I still think it's dumb of you to be getting back into the same ditch with him."

"Wait a minute," Shonna interrupted Sonia. "I don't have to take any of this!"

Their relationship had been strong in recent years; however, Sonia knew that Shonna was the type of person who held grudges. The last time they had an argument Shonna didn't speak to her for more than a year. She hoped to steer away from that kind of an outcome.

She asked, "Give me one good reason why dating Lance again will be worth your while, and I'll leave it alone—"

Shonna had already reached a breaking point, and she was determined to get in the last word. Emphatically. Forcefully. Unrelentingly.

"You know what your problem is? You think you're always right," she snapped back at her. "Since you always like quoting scripture, remember it talks about the person who thinks they're something when they're not . . . They're delusional!"

She hung up and deleted Sonia's number and recent text messages out of her cell phone.

Chapter 34

'Mind, Body, and Soul'

This was sheer insanity, Trent fumed.
Kicked out of his own home that he'd been paying the mortgage and insurance over a knee-jerk reaction. Living in an apartment that was nearly as expensive as his home. Reduced to visiting Taylor on the weekends and having to dodge his questions over why his parents were not living in the same place? Walking around hiding the stigma of a failed marriage looming.

With the court date being five days away, he cringed at the thought of appearing before a judge. Who wants to be on the other side of any so-called fair and impartial application of the law that often leaves a defendant wanting to do more than just curse the whole human race?

Humph, and they say it's cheaper to keep her?

Enraged over its likelihood, Trent resolved to himself that if Sonia wanted a divorce she'd better have all the facts and not something circumstantial.

Somebody has given you bad information. I hope

you're smart enough to figure that out.

Trent felt better sending that text message to Sonia even
if it was all about venting his rage. He didn't expect any response from her, and he didn't get any. But there had to be a
better way of getting his point across to her.

The plan he came up with involved going back to the other
principal involved in his predicament: Alcione. They had not
seen each other since the day Sonia spotted them.

I've got nothing else to lose...

Trent was calm when he contacted Alcione. Very rarely as
a track athlete did he ever approach the starting blocks, no
matter how prestigious the race was, and he wasn't a nervous
wreck.

This was different. Because this was for his marital survival,
he willed himself into thinking he needed to be focused until his plan reached its logical conclusion. There would be no
time for flirtations with lust, which got him in trouble with
Sonia.

"Trent, how are you?" Alcione greeted him.

Her voice was soothing and intriguing as ever. If perhaps
in a different life, he might have been more than game to try
balancing relationships with Sonia and her. Cortez "Bishop
Moneymaker" Anderson would have nothing on him.

Realistically, however, she was the first person whom he
interacted with since Sonia kicked him out of their home.

"I'm not doing well."

"I'm sorry to hear that."

Alcione had mixed feelings about chatting with Trent since
he backed away from what she thought was a near-certain
rendezvous in her home. No man had ever denied her sexually. But the sting from Trent's rejection did not last long. She

more than made up for it during her current business swing in South Florida.

"Listen, I need your help." He sighed into the phone.

"I am leaving for Brazil this week," she answered. "Is this something that can wait?"

She went on to explain that she was almost behind schedule returning to Brazil this year. However, with expansion in South Carolina, and business being its best in South Florida since 2007, it's required more of her time staying in the United States.

"Alcione, this can't wait. I need your help like it was last week."

"I don't understand—"

"Remember our dinner date?" he queried her.

"How can I forget?" she answered. "You said you could not have me."

"I like you, Alcione. But I just couldn't do it."

A warm, sensual feeling came over her. "You could have, if you wanted, Trent. Is this the reason why you're calling?"

"No, it isn't."

This is a crying shame what I'm having to put myself through, he mumbled silently to himself.

"Alcione, listen. My wife says she saw us together in my car. She says you and I, uh, had sex that night. I'm in a lot of trouble right now."

"But Trent, you came over to my house. We did not have sex—" She closed her eyes and shook her head, bemoaning the missed opportunity.

"I know, and you know. But my wife doesn't know. That's the problem."

Although she was well aware of the risk of being with a married man, controversy had never found its way to her until now. Even so, she also had a convenient escape: Reservations for Delta flight no. 2160 was scheduled to leave Miami on Saturday, the first leg in her return trip to Brazil.

"Okay, Trent. How do you think I can help you?"

"Simple. You tell my wife, in her face, nothing happened," he answered. "Then it's on her to decide whether I was lying to her or I was telling her the truth."

"*Você é louco?*"

"I don't speak Portuguese."

"Trent, are you crazy?" She made sure to enunciate her words as clearly as possible in her broken English.

"No, I'm not crazy. But my wife is crazy. And this is a crazy situation. If I can't get her to see that I only met you for dinner to discuss Fogo de Janiero's plans, she is going to divorce me, and a judge who doesn't give a flying—however you want to say it in Portuguese—is going to make me pay a lot of money."

Alcione stared at the ceiling. "Trent, I'm sorry to hear that. But when I go to Brazil, I will not return until March or April. I do not see how I can help—"

Balling his fist, Trent pounded the carpet from where he sat in his apartment. "All right, what is it going to take for you to help me out?"

She grinned at the possibility. "You, of course."

"But you can't have me."

"Excuse me, please—"

Trent heard in the background Alcione conversing with somebody in Portuguese. She was quick to return.

"Trent, if I help you . . . Business is always about a give and take—you will have to give me something in return. You know what I would like to have."

He swallowed hard, almost choking on himself. "Can it wait? I need help now!"

"We will talk about that." Her voice had turned seductive on him. "See, that was not hard?"

Over the next five minutes, Trent and Alcione discussed the logistics of her making a special trip from South Florida to Columbia before leaving for Brazil. She gave him a only small window of opportunity.

"I will get back with you no later than tomorrow," he told her.

* * *

Sonia didn't realize how tough it was raising a child alone until a few weeks ago. Now, she was faced with making herself available for all of Taylor's activities, as well as taking him to them, in addition to the maternal things she did when Trent was in the house. She had no choice especially after those oft-times long, wild, and outrageous days in contract services.

If she left UCP fuming, she could no longer ask Trent to fill in for her while she calmed herself. She now had to be mindful around Taylor that nothing should be mistaken as his fault.

Ah, but she did have Milner.

She was careful to purchase a Tracfone so that any interaction she had with him could not be traced directly to her. That meant she freely sent him text messages during her lunch break and as she left UCP in the evening. Then she would call him at home late at night when she thought he was back from The Groovy Soul.

Milner still sent her e-mails on a daily basis for her to read while at work. But he still was unaware of Sonia's pending divorce from Trent.

"Don't you ever think of us lying together one night talking, hugging, cuddling, and pleasing each other?" he asked.

"Of course, I do," she answered. "But you know that I can't do that when you think it should happen, or even when I think it should happen."

"I understand. I also understand that you can't exist being unhappy forever. It isn't good for you. Sometimes, you have to seek different avenues to make life worth your own while."

Sonia's convictions told her she was wrong for contacting Milner, and she should allow God to work things out with her and Trent. But her mind and flesh kept urging her to do what she need to do for a change.

"Wharton, you're really trying to break a woman down, aren't you?" she joked.

"I wouldn't say breaking you down. I'd say it's getting you to see the bigger picture."

The bigger picture to Sonia was not the same as what Milner described to her; however, she still wanted him in the picture that she still was crafting for herself.

"Hold on, I've got another call coming in," she alerted Milner.

She almost made the mistake of talking into her Tracfone rather than picking up her actual cell phone.

"We need to talk."

She grimaced upon recognizing Trent's voice. "Hold on, Trent—I'm talking with Shonna. I need to get her off the other line."

"Wharton, can I call you back? I didn't know hubby was still awake. He's on the warpath around here."

"Hey, do what you have to do. I know my place. I know how to stay in my lane."

"Thank you."

She switched back to Trent.

"What is it you want?" she asked, hissing.

"I've been thinking about this divorce that you want."

"You should have thought about it before you chose to drive women around in our vehicles," she snapped back at him.

"Now, if that's all you're calling me about, you can discuss it with the judge next week!"

Trent began rocking back and forth trying his best to suppress his mounting anger. "Sonia, I want to sit down and talk with you. I think there are some things you need to know before you go through with your decision."

"Like what?"

"I want you to hear from the woman whom you claim that I was sleeping with."

Sonia did a double-take. Surely, Trent must be drinking, or he's been pummeled by guilt that it's caused him to crack.

"Did you hear me?" he asked.

She rolled her eyes. "Yeah, I heard you."

"I've told you several times now that what you're accusing me of is false. You've called me a whore. You've called her a whore. You've called me every mother, sons of, and whatever else you can come up with—"

"I call them as I see them. And you've proven you've been just that for as long as I've known you. This is your last warning, Trent—"

Trent was unfazed by her threat. "Sonia, if you think you're woman enough to assume that I cheated on you, be woman enough to at least meet the woman you claim I was sleeping with. Then you'll have all the information you need for the divorce that you want."

He has lost his natural mind, she thought to herself. *He really has!*

She retorted, "I already have seven years' worth of information."

"Like what?"

"It doesn't matter what I have!"

"Hey, I'm helping you out. Meet the woman for yourself. I've asked her to meet you, and she's willing to do it."

"So, you've already thought about running off with her,

huh?"

"Does it really matter?" he countered.

He went on to rattle off some of the likely scenarios why divorces were filed: the scorned wife confronts the cheating woman after catching her in the act; she's made a surprise confrontation of the cheating woman after discovering her identity through stealth means or investigation; or after the wife's confronting the husband by interrogation had produced the information.

"But this is not the case," he insisted. "You've already convinced yourself into what you want to believe, so why not meet her?"

Before responding, she mulled several potential motives why Trent proposed the meeting. None of them still made any sense to her. But the more she thought about the image of a woman with long, thick hair as a passenger in the Taurus, the possibility of exacting some kind of revenge—even if it was verbal—might quench her anger.

"Why are you so willing to do that now?"

"Just answer the question: Are you willing to meet her?"

Now Sonia was suspicious. This could be a trap, and she could be ambushed.

"No, Trent, we'll just let the judge decide things."

"Wait, Sonia," he persisted, "I'm asking you to do this one thing. I have nothing else to lose, anyway. You've already kicked me out of my home. I'm living in this joke of a place. Taylor's all confused and he's not the same around me. You're going to take everything I've worked to build up in my life—I just want to make things easier."

Why would a cheating woman be willing to meet the scorned wife? Sonia asked herself.

Maybe the woman's just as dumb as him, she's just that arrogant to do it, or the woman simply doesn't care; she must know plenty of sap husbands to exploit after him. All those scenarios still didn't make sense.

"Tell me this, Trent: Was it really worth it?" she questioned him. "Was it really worth losing your family over a decision like that?"

It depends, Trent thought to himself jokingly; he also berated himself again for not going all the way with Alcione, considering all the trouble it's caused him.

He willed himself into speaking with contrition. "No, Sonia. It never was."

"All right, Trent. Where do you want this meeting to take place?"

"Thursday evening. At Fogo de Janiero."

"Why there?"

"Because I want you to see it all. I want you to see their place of business. I'm not withholding anything from you."

"Suit yourself. I'm sure Taylor can hang out with one of his friends until I pick him up," she said. "As for this bodacious slut who wrecked your marriage, I'll say this much: She'll know next time not to mess with another married man!"

Trent mouthed as if he breathed a sigh in relief. He went ahead with thanking her for her agreeing to the meeting.

* * *

Trent was full of anxiety throughout the day Sonia was to meet Alcione. If it weren't for the bank being short staffed, and him also having to conduct the first of four interviews scheduled for Cortez's old position, he would have left early.

The risk that he took—however recklessly calculating it was—meant everything to him. Anything short of convincing Sonia not to pursue divorcing him would be a failure.

Around 4 p.m., Trent received a call from Alcione indicating that she just landed in Columbia. He felt as if he dodged a major obstacle by the slimmest of margins. Collecting himself, he thanked Alcione profusely for going out of her way in his moment of need.

"You don't know how much this means to me," he told her. "How are you getting to the—" He checked his comment. Offering to pick her up, if needed, or even asking her about it would not be the wisest thing to do.

"I owe you big time for this."

"Yes, Trent, you do owe me." Her voice was rather serious and businesslike.

He suspected the thought of making this special trip to Columbia on top of the thirteen hours it would take flying into Rio de Janiero in two days suddenly seemed insane to her— but she still had not backed out of it.

"I'll be at the restaurant right at six o'clock," he said.

"I will be there waiting for you."

To kill time, Alcione worked the greeter's stand while she waited for Trent. Fogo de Janiero was already besieged by an early dinner crowd. Waiters and servers briskly crisscrossed throughout the dining area. The bartender covered the bar area with fast, lateral movements as if he were a soccer goalie while attending to his patrons.

An evening like this was commonplace at the restaurant chain's South Florida locations. This was an encouraging sign for the Fogo de Janiero brain trust that expansion in South Carolina was the right decision.

When Trent entered the restaurant, Alcione motioned for another server to take over at the greeter's stand. She caught his attention with what she wore: a beige Garbardine jacket, a white short-sleeve shirt beneath it, and matching beige boot-cut slacks.

The wrong kinds of thoughts flooded Trent's mind, and the bond of attraction that enticed him into trouble had him feeling captive.

Alcione looked at him as if she solicited his approval. "Trent, you and I would make a great couple—"

They would indeed. If in a different life or a different situation, Trent would have moved to give her a hug and a soft peck on her cheek.

"Sonia, my wife, said she would be here in a few minutes."

Alcione, before walking off to the kitchen, indicated she'd return momentarily.

Sonia had to stop and regain her orientation once she entered Fogo de Janiero. This was far more elegant than the homespun setting Milner created for The Groovy Soul, which reminded her of a country dive in the middle of nowhere.

She was more than glad to have worn something that was fitting for the setting—a watermelon colored shawl collar jacket and belted sheath dress—rather than what she felt like wearing, which might have been an ordinary pair of jeans, a blouse, and a bad attitude.

Actually, Sonia still had the bad attitude. She experienced both nostalgia and disgust once she noticed Trent walking toward her.

"You look nice, Sonia."

"Humph."

Trent did not bother to make any other small talk with her. He turned around and looked for Alcione while shifting his feet from side to side.

Meanwhile, Sonia found herself not taking any liking to the restaurant's ambience. This had to be a place for the eccentric and phonies. She made no immediate connection with the samba and bossa nova being played over the sound system, nor did she really care.

"Here she comes," Trent announced suddenly.

Sonia reacted with a loud hiss while trying to figure out who the woman was. Then she noticed a woman with long, thick hair walking in their direction. It triggered a flashback that set her on alert.

That's the hussy! Sonia mumbled to herself.

Even worse, the woman was not what Sonia expected. Rather than an immature, uncouth tramp without any tact, it was apparent this woman was refined—and she had the look of money.

Trent had actually one-upped her. The fool really lucked out. She never thought she would be envious of another woman who might have held or was holding her husband's interest.

Trent cleared his throat. "Sonia, this is Alcione de Oliveria. Her father is Nelson Amaral de Oliveria, co-founder of the Fogo de Janiero restaurant chain that I've been telling you about."

The nerve of Trent trying to be proper with her, she fumed; she also waved off Alcione, who had not yet spoken.

"I'm Mrs. Sonia Chandler-Buckner."

Alcione suppressed her pride for Trent's sake. She asked the Buckners if they would follow her to a table near the back of the restaurant. There, Sonia made sure that she sat across from Trent, but with Alcione sitting to her left. She was also the first to speak. "My husband says the two of you discussed a business loan and he drove you to your home only because you asked him to drive you there."

"Mrs. Buckner, yes, that is true. I put him in an awkward situation."

"Uh, Alice," Sonia interrupted her, "that awkward situation is going to cost him his marriage—" She then cut a mean glare at Trent.

Alcione, who remained tactful, did not correct Sonia's mispronunciation.

"Mrs. Buckner, I had asked my cousin who works at this location and lives in my home to take my car to Myrtle Beach. We had meetings scheduled with architects and builders; I could not be at two places."

Sitting up in her chair, Sonia glared to her left and hurled obscenities at Alcione. "Alice, or whatever your name is, I don't care what business you had to take care of in Myrtle Beach! Your business was finished after you agreed on taking out a loan with Palmetto Fidelity!"

She then looked over at Trent angrily. Trent first placed his face in his hands. He then shifted in his chair.

"Mrs. Buckner," Alcione continued, "I have met businessmen from around the world. Many seek sexual favors or look to having affairs. But your husband was an honorable man with me."

Sonia rolled her eyes and snorted. But Alcione persisted.

"Mrs. Buckner, you should be very proud to have a husband like Trent. My father is a very honorable man. Trent reminds me of him."

"That doesn't mean anything with me!" Sonia lashed out, aiming her index finger directly in Alcione's face. "Your father could be the apostle Paul, for all I care! I can't believe you could be that audacious asking my husband to do something that's so compromising."

Inwardly, Alcione fumed at Sonia. She was in her domain, the restaurant, and she could have easily had Sonia escorted out of it—without any shame on her part.

Sonia turned her rant toward Trent, looking across at him with narrowed eyes. "And you're so stupid that you've forgotten how to say the word 'no'? Don't you know how to act like a god blasted man and do what is honorable and with integrity?

"If you knew what that meant, you would realize what's right no matter what situation it is. You're a stone fool for having another woman in our car!"

She glared back over at Alcione, who tried looking away from her. "No, Alice, you need to look at me . . . I should beat your tail until you cry 'mama'!" She went on to mumble disparaging comments about Alcione's exotic look and broken English, suggesting she needed to know the phone number to Blue Cab the next time she needed a ride somewhere.

Then after hissing, she gathered her purse and was poised to stand up and storm out of the restaurant; Trent finally spoke up.

"Sonia, I've had it with you! I've listened to you rant, yell, curse me out and curse out a customer of mine!" he said forcefully.

"You need to listen and listen good . . . I will not let you go through with this divorce. I may not have used the right judgment, but I did nothing wrong. You need to look beyond the trees and see that I'm telling you the truth. I've put it all out there on the line with you today—"

"Mrs. Bucker, I have a plane to catch. I am sorry for the trouble I have caused you," Alcione intervened. "I hope you will find it in your heart to forgive your husband and forgive me."

She stood up and walked off.

Trent slid over to the chair adjacent to her right. He wiped the beads of sweat that had formed on his brow. Then he placed a hand on her forearm. It was the first time he touched her since the morning he was served papers, a span of nearly two months.

"That woman went out of her way coming here to tell you

in person that nothing happened." He spoke sincerely, yet it was with much urgency.

"She's supposed to be flying back to Brazil the day after tomorrow," he added. "She's not supposed to be back in Columbia until next March—she didn't have to come here at all.

"Now you're a woman. What woman would do that?"

The truth had a way of penetrating. Sonia recognized that while she may have been entitled to her righteous cause and indignation, Trent appeared to have been telling her the truth. And as a woman, she suspected Alcione may have also told the truth. There was no logical reason for her flying up from Miami just to withstand being cursed out and insulted. But she was unsure if she would have done the same thing had Milner faced a similar situation.

"Sonia, I've made a lot of mistakes. But I know I didn't make any mistake when I wrote you that apology letter and asked you out on a date fifteen years ago. And I know I didn't make any mistake the day I asked you to marry me that we might spend the rest of our lives together."

He looked at Sonia again expecting a response from her. "I love you. Will you give me another chance?"

She closed her eyes in thought. When she opened them, she answered, "You have only one chance with me, Trent. One. Do I make myself clear?"

Trent brought his hand up to his chin and stroked it. He nodded slowly.

"I understand," he answered. "I miss you, Sonia."

"I miss you, too."

They stood up and left Fogo de Janiero together with him walking her to her car.

Suddenly, Trent stopped shy of where she was parked near the corners of Main and Richland streets. She returned a confused look.

"Sonia, I used very poor judgment. I'm sorry. I should not have disappointed you like that. Will you forgive me?" He then held out his hands. She accepted his invitation to hug her.

After they separated, Sonia looked up at him. "Yes, Trent, you can come back to your home." She did not smile, but there was a warm feeling in her heart.

* * *

Taylor was more than glad to learn that his father was returning home. He demanded that Trent come and pick him up from his friend's house just so that he could see him.

When Trent arrived, Taylor did his best to walk in his coolest of walks and hide his true emotions. Once inside Sonia's M35, he immediately turned to Trent.

"Mom would only tell me that you and her had to work something out, and she hoped that maybe you would be coming back."

"Well, I am back, son." He smiled at Taylor, recounting to himself how thirteen, nearly fourteen years had passed by so swiftly. Before long, he mused, Taylor would be going to high school. And dare he not think about him driving?

"Dad, can you promise me something?"

"What is it you're asking me to promise you?"

"Don't ever leave like that," Taylor said. "That was really tough. I didn't know what to think. It's a good thing it's still early in the school year or I might have flunked all my classes."

Trent could only fathom what Taylor went through despite having grown up in a broken home. "I promise." He paused and collected himself. "I never wanted to leave, but I had to. Your mother and I didn't want to be fighting in front of you. I'm sorry I disappointed you and I've told your mother I was sorry for disappointing her."

He put his fist out for a bump.

* * *

Later that evening, Sonia and Trent adjourned to their bedroom. Trent first informed her that he would bring the rest of his clothes and other items over the weekend. Then he mentioned that he was thinking of trading in the Taurus just so that she would not have any reminders of what happened.

He shrugged his shoulders at the thought. "It's not something I'd like to do, but it might help with the healing."

"You've already done a lot by mentioning it," Sonia responded.

Without saying much, they went into the bathroom, helped removed each other's clothing, and took a shower together. That was something they once did regularly before they were married. It had become somewhat of a distant memory in recent years.

Initially, Sonia stood under the stream of warm water with her back turned toward him.

"Trent, I'm willing to start again with you. But I can't take being disappointed like that any more."

He nestled up against her, rubbing his body against hers; he also reached around and caressed her. She did not offer any resistance.

"I know what you're saying is really important to you, and it's important to me as well."

She turned around slowly and faced him. She was partly surprised and happy that Trent spoke in those terms. It evoked memories of the marriage enhancement Web site she often browsed before their separation.

"Is it really that important to you?"

"Yes. You are the most important person to me on earth."

"What about your son?"

He chortled. "Second to you."

"Do you really miss me?" Then she looked downward. "Because it seems that you do."

She reached down and stroked him, causing him to gasp, close his eyes, and suck air through his teeth. She also moaned along with him.

"Do you miss me?" he asked her.

She smiled, looked upward at him, and continued hand stroking him. Her expression spoke volumes to him. He made the next move by kissing her fully on her lips. They then hugged each other tightly and entered into a long tongue kissing exchange while the water still cascaded on them.

Moments later, Trent slid his hands between them and began caressing and fondling her breasts. She did not bother silencing her moan once his lips touched her nipples.

"Trent, baby. Let's finish up in here—"

After drying off, Trent led Sonia by the hand back into the bedroom. He then guided her over to the bed and laid her down. She was more than willing to accommodate by parting her legs for him; he was quick to find his place there.

Sonia had long since voiced to Trent that she had needs. But this was the first time that he'd truly addressed them. It helped that he was vigorous in defending his marriage and with declaring his true intentions with her—it was soothing to her conscience.

Trent had only indulged between her thighs for barely a couple of minutes before Sonia tapped him on the shoulder. She presented him an aroused and steamy reception, to which he grunted and moaned into her ear upon entering. It did not take long for the Buckners to achieve a rhythm.

She matched him stroke-for-stroke while they kissed passionately in motion.

Suddenly, Sonia felt something welling up deep from within her. "Trent, baby—" she moaned.

Unlike in times past, he was attuned to her. He slowed his pace, allowing her to fully commit herself. He whispered, "Baby, you're turning me on. Keep talking to me."

Then she placed her hands on his shoulders—she still was matching him stroke-for-stroke. "Oh, Trent . . . This is feeling soooo good . . . God, I miss this!"

Trent reared up and was more forceful in his action. Sonia closed her eyes and bit her bottom lip. Then she dug her nails first into his chest and later his back. She also held her legs apart for him before clasping them around his waist.

Soon, her breathing changed, and she gasped and moaned. Her body stiffened and jerked beneath him before going limp. There was no faking this time.

"That was intense," she whispered to him, while catching her breath. "Baby, now that's what I call love making!"

Sonia then nudged Trent to stop. He was more than incredulous that she was willing to accommodate him in other positions. She, too, was attuned to his body and his facial expressions.

"You know where I want it," she spoke to him in a sultry voice. "Don't tell me. Just give it to me—"

In the quietness of their afterglow, Trent was sound asleep. He was more mentally drained than he realized having staved off divorce. He slept comfortably knowing, too, that he was back in his own house and in his own bed—he'd been sleeping on the floor of the apartment that he'd been renting during their separation.

Sonia, however, still had not gone to sleep. So much was on her mind. Trent had helped her reach fulfillment. But look what it took for him to get there? He had no choice if he expected to get a reprieve.

In what had become a habit of hers, she read Milner's daily e-mail from her Tracfone before she went to sleep. This night was no different:

> *I have never wanted a woman as much as I've wanted you ... I want to taste every inch and contour of you ... I want to feel your flesh against mine ... Let's make it happen ... I want to make love to your mind, body, and soul.*

The Bed I Made
by N. Wood Lane

T his was the kind of message that Wharton Milner wanted to receive from Sonia Buckner. He had to read it a second time ensuring that his eyes had not failed him:

> Wharton, I've been thinking about us a lot lately. I want to take our friendship to another level. Can we talk about it?

It was a good thing he was consumed with working the lunch rush at The Groovy Soul, or he might have taken a moment to let out a loud whoop and possibly cut a jig.

All the time spent being attentive and lending a willing and sympathetic ear had paid off. All the patience he'd shown Sonia knowing she was a married woman and mother of a teenage son also appeared to have been rewarded.

N.Wood Lane

All this time knowing Sonia, he never bothered to remember that Trent was her husband's name. It didn't really matter. He'd seen him once, and that was all that he needed to remember.

> You've just made my day, Sonia. Mind, body, and soul . . . That's the way it's going to be!

Sonia showed no emotion when she sent Milner the text message from her Tracfone while on break from her job at United Care Plan in Columbia, South Carolina. She took a moment to reflect on the magnitude of her decision.

It came at a time after she'd recently turned forty. She felt that her marriage, although it was still in repair over the many disappointments that she blamed Trent for causing, would never get any better than its current state.

Trent had finally reached her sexually, but the enjoyment she desired was inconsistent. She felt she deserved better than what she'd been receiving at home having now entered her peak years.

Her desire for Milner merely intensified over the past six months. Perhaps it was the anticipation of consummating something, which she strongly believed was justified, that made her even more confident about her decision.

Better yet, she may have convinced herself once and for all after he bought her a pair of diamond-studded earrings on her birthday while Trent forgotten about it all together. A couple of weeks later, they shared their first kiss while they were on another Saturday afternoon rendezvous in Augusta—a moment that Milner thought should have happened much sooner. Yet it worked out in its own time.

> When do you want to meet? I'll even make the time

for it (wink!)

When can we talk about it?

I'll figure something out and get back with you. :)

The idea came to her rather quickly.

"Palmetto Fidelity, this is Trent Buckner—"

"Are you always this friendly when people call you?" Sonia joked with him. "Wow, I could use someone like you on my team at work."

"Uh, noooo!"

"What's wrong? You wouldn't want me to be your supervisor?" Sonia reacted. "I've seen them pull strings allowing nepotism in contract services. Maybe I can get you to work on another team? Then it wouldn't be such a problem."

"Baby, I like what I'm doing, thank you very much," Trent said. "Well, isn't this a surprise. What did I do to deserve this personal call from you?" He checked the time on his computer and mentioned it was about 1:45 in the afternoon.

"I thought I'd do something different." Sonia rolled her eyes at her own comment. "Look here, I was thinking about stopping by that restaurant we went to in Cayce a few months ago. Do you remember it?"

"I can't say that I do. Give me a clue—"

Sonia was nearly moved to laughter; it was precisely her point. She could not believe how fast her husband was falling into this ditch—face first—that she was preparing for him.

"The restaurant that served that nice buffet home-cooked style—I think it's called The Groovy something. . . ."

"Oh yeah, that place! We talked about going back there. Were you thinking of us eating there tonight?"

"No, I was thinking about grabbing to-go plates for all three of us. I don't feel like cooking tonight, and I wanted something different."

"Sure. That will work. Just make sure it's something that I'll eat."

"And if it isn't," Sonia replied, leading him on in a seductive voice, "I'll make sure you'll have something that's always served at the right temperature, and no oven or microwave is ever needed—"

Trent was incredulous at his wife's boldness, which could be quite arousing whenever his mindset was full of mischief and raunch. "You know, I do have a taste for some of that." He went as far as sucking his teeth and grinning.

"Baby, I've known you for sixteen years. I think I've got that one under control. See you later. Time for me to go back into the asylum."

* * *

Sonia noticed a few changes inside The Groovy Soul since the last time she visited. The first thing was a new paint scheme—predominantly white but with peach colored trimming. There were several live plants brought in for aesthetics, and there were various pictures representing a southern lifestyle.

She also noticed there was new help working the dining area and the cashier's counter to keep pace with the burgeoning crowd that appeared to be frequenting the place.

Although she did not immediately see Milner, she figured he was no doubt around somewhere.

"I see you didn't get any dessert containers," Sonia heard a familiar voice from behind. She turned slowly and acknowledged Milner by making eye contact with him. They had not seen each other in a little more than a week.

She replied, "You must have told the new help that you were taking care of me personally, hmmm?"

He walked to the other side of the buffet bar as if he made a casual inspection. "I don't miss a single thing whenever you walk in here. When did you get the new outfit?"

"You have been paying attention." She looked herself over, admiring the navy skirt suit she recently purchased.

"I'll be back with your dessert containers."

Sonia was finished with filling her main course containers just as Wharton returned. "Excuse me, sir. Are you going to take care of my order for me?"

He did not immediately respond. But then it dawned upon him what she meant. "Don't worry. That won't happen again. I'll be right back." He went back to his office and stuffed two twenty-dollar bills in an envelope.

When Milner returned into the dining area, Sonia had a small mountain of Styrofoam containers that she'd carried over to cashier's counter. He was there to offer his help.

"I figured a plastic bag would not work well for you, so I brought this box. Would you need help carrying this out?" He gave her a knowing stare.

"I really appreciate your service here, sir. Thank you."

"It's my pleasure. Thank you for visiting us!"

Milner was more than eager to escort Sonia out to her Infiniti M35, which was parked directly across the driveway. He walked with great pride knowing that he and Sonia were soon to consummate their growing acquaintance.

"I've placed an envelope in this box addressing your order. Is there anything else I can do for you?" He looked over to his right at her.

"You can tell me what you have in mind for us—"

"I was thinking about us going in Charlotte next week, say, Tuesday. Would that work for you?"

"As long as I can plan three days ahead of time, that shouldn't be a problem. I'll text message you from work tomorrow confirming it."

They stopped at her car.

"Sonia, you look nice in your new outfit." He looked her up and down before licking his lips and nodding slowly for added effect. "A woman should have a nice set of legs like yours if she's going to wear business skirts."

She smiled back at him. "Thank you. I had you in mind when I picked it out."

"Did you really?" He gave her a side-eyed stare.

"I sure did. And I bet you'd like to see more than just my legs right now—"

He was moved to chortling. A few days' wait was not going to ruin it for him. "I better not make a scene. You know I would love to kiss you right here." He also entertained the thought of groping and fondling beneath her skirt.

"I don't know what I'm going to do with you, Wharton."

She thought back to how soft his lips felt against hers, the way she felt light headed once their tongues entwined, and the way her body reacted to him pulling her body toward his—this visit was fast becoming more than what she'd anticipated.

"Just don't hold back on once you start with me," he answered. "That's all I ask."

Late that night, Sonia felt unusually mischievous and she could not suppress it. And what she had in mind did not involve Trent.

She first stopped by the other closet in their bedroom and retrieved the Tracfone she used to contact Milner. Then she tipped into the bathroom.

Peering into the mirror, Sonia inspected her face. It was still free of wrinkles and crow's feet. Next, she inspected her hair. Surprisingly, there was only a stray strand or two of graying amid her naturally auburn color; she dared not to look elsewhere on her body. She'd been considering of late to keep it bald rather than neatly cropped close so she wouldn't have to worry about it.

Next, she took a couple of steps back from the mirror, removed her silk kimono and the boy shorts that she wore to bed, and she inspected the rest of her body. She made a slow one-eighty in one direction and a slow one-eighty in the other, and she was quick to determine she was still firm in all the right places.

"I don't feel old," she whispered to herself. "I actually don't know how I am supposed to feel or act now that I'm forty. . . ."

She ran her hand over various areas of her body. It felt as if it was a fun and sensual thing to do. She reasoned the worldly view of what she was doing would applaud her for simply getting to know her body and loving herself. But this was something that was never taught or encouraged by anyone she knew of in the church.

Then she reached for the Tracfone. She began taking pictures of herself. Frontal view. Side view. Back view. She even went as far as sitting on the bathroom floor, spreading her legs far apart, and adding a couple of pictures from that view.

Feeling aroused, she went as far as rubbing and stroking herself while fantasizing about Milner—it was a matter of moments before her body tensed and she struggled to remain silent while the pleasure produced a rippling effect throughout her body.

Afterward, she reviewed the photos that she'd taken of herself. She decided on sending Milner a photo that offered him a rear view of her along with the caption:

N.Wood Lane

I was thinking of you tonight. Wouldn't you like to
know my thoughts?

About the Author

Since the age of 13, N. Wood Lane has dabbled in and out of writing.

Lane once aspired to live in Brazil and start a newspaper in Rio de Janiero. The closest Lane has ever visited the Southern Hemisphere destination point was by renting videos from Blockbuster featuring actress Sonia Braga. Lane's affinity for Brazil also includes rooting for the country during soccer's World Cup and its music—but to this day still does not know Portuguese.

Back in the mid-1990s, Lane's curiosity for writing a novel was piqued after reading Connie Briscoe's *Sisters and Lovers* and Terry McMillan's *Waiting to Exhale*. That aspiration never became a reality until Lane was well past age 40.

These days, Lane considers writing a way of remaining mentally engaged since attaining AARP membership eligibility.

Lane currently resides in South Carolina and has been in the insurance industry since 2001.

Suggested Reading Group Guide Questions

1. Trent and Sonia had difficulties in their marriage stemming from past issues. How important it is to you to resolve past differences?

2. How important it is for your spouse/significant other to regard your opinion(s) or input into your relationship?

3. Communication is an important element in relationships. Are you able to communicate with your spouse/significant other?

4. Is it fair, then, for the woman to fake orgasms? Should she tell the man?

5. Did you feel like cheering for or jeering at Sonia by the end of the book? Did your opinion change of her, if any?

6. Did you feel like cheering for or jeering at Trent by the end of the book? Did your opinion change of him, if any?

7. There were several subplots in Do It to My Mind. One of them involved a May-December relationship between Shonna Chandler and Lance Miles. What was your opinion about their relationship?

8. What is an acceptable difference in age? Five years? Seven years? Ten years?

9. What is your opinion about workplace romance?

10. Have you ever experienced romance in the workplace? Would you do it again?

Suggested Reading Group Guide Questions (cont.)

11. Do you agree with Trent's gamble of having Alcione explain to Sonia nothing occurred between them during their dinner date? Would you go that far to prove your innocence?

12. Were the characters believable?

13. Was there a character who reminded you of somebody you already know?

14. Was the plot and subplots believable? Were they predictable?

15. What is your feeling about the ending to *Do It to My Mind*?

16. Who was your favorite or least favorite character in *Do It to My Mind*?

17. What was your favorite or least favorite scene in *Do It to My Mind*?

Other Books from MavLit Publishing

Warped Intentions
by S.B. Redd
9781937705121
$14.95

Love, Song & Dance
by Jevon L. Mack
9780983115205
$14.95

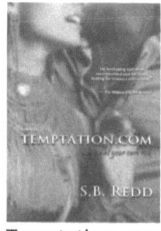

Temptation.com
by S.B. Redd
9781937705145
$14.95

The Shades of Passion
by S.B. Redd
9781937705152
$14.95

Thoughts of Life:
360 E. May St.
B.H., Michigan
by Birdman '313'
9781937705046
$14.95

Presumption of Paternity
by S.B. Redd
9780983115281
$14.95

𝜇

MavLit Publishing
www.maverick-books.com

www.ingramcontent.com/pod-product-compliance
Lightning Source LLC
Chambersburg PA
CBHW021526250626
47154CB00006BA/1991